THE MAN WHO WATCHED THE WORLD END

This is a work of fiction. Names, characters, places, and incidents are the products of the author's imagination or are used fictitiously. Any resemblance to actual events, locales, or persons, living or dead, is coincidence.

Published in the United States by CreateSpace Independent Publishing.

ISBN-13: 978-1484080511

ISBN-10: 1484080513

Cover Design: Truenotdreams Design

Author Photo: Jodie McFadden

THE MAN WHO WATCHED THE WORLD END

Chris Dietzel

December 1

It's obvious now that the end of man won't be signaled with mushroom clouds, an alien invasion, or a meteor, but with silence. Only silence, long and unceasing. We've always known this would be the case, however, it never seemed like the final day would really arrive.

My mother was fond of the saying, "All good things must come to an end," a cliché that now makes me cringe. Yet, what was there to do about any of it? Nothing except to wake up each morning, go through the normal routines, and then go to sleep. Each day we were all a little older, a little closer to the end. And each day fewer people were alive than the previous day. That's how it's been for eighty years; it's the way it will be at least a little while longer. I see now that from the very start, my life has been leading to this: my brother and I alone, witnessing the end of man's 200,000-year reign.

I watched more movies as a kid than any other boy in the neighborhood. They fascinated me. While the adults were worried about grown-up problems, I could go to my bedroom, close the door, and put on a movie that let me go anywhere I pleased. The possibilities were only as limited as the imaginations that created each story. One day, *The Godfather* trilogy allowed me to live the life of mobsters. Another day, the *Star Wars* trilogy took me to a galaxy far, far away. Occasionally, Andrew stayed in his own room, but most of the time he was right there with me. All the while my parents and the rest of the neighborhood worried about what they were going to do—if they would move or not move, if they would be able to take care of their loved ones or if they would need caring for themselves. The adults' worries, my parents' worries, didn't bother me back then because I had my movies. No matter how awful the scenario was in each film—a nuclear holocaust, aliens enslaving us, a race to save the Earth from a meteorite—the stories made me smile and gasp and giggle the way little boys do.

The actors from those movies have been dead for years. So have the writers and directors. The last movie ever made was produced fifty years ago. Not many people went to see it, but it was actually pretty good. It was billed as a culmination of everything 'Hollywood', and promised big explosions, incredible special effects, and a startling final scene. For the most part it delivered on its promises. Not many people were in the mood to go to the movies at that point, though. It didn't help things that the infamous ending was its own kryptonite. The protagonist, a handsome and charismatic man, the envy of every man and the fantasy of every woman, proclaims that life is just a huge joke. Instead of pushing a red button and launching a rocket to save Earth's population—still billions of people back then—from the dreaded invasion, he takes his lover in his arms, begins crying, then shoots himself in the face. Dramatic music kicks in. The screen fades to black.

Audiences hated it. Everyone involved with the film was lucky there were bigger problems in the world than an ending equivalent to being given the middle finger; if mankind hadn't been dwindling away, the producer and director might have been charged with some sort of indecency crime, or, more ironic yet, simply shot dead. I still watch that movie every once in a while. From a technical perspective, the film is a masterpiece—excellent character development, cinematography, editing—although I only watch the ending when Andrew isn't in the room with me. He shouldn't have to see that kind of hopelessness. He stayed one time when I was tired and I didn't feel like wheeling him out of the room just for the final two minutes of the movie. I had his wheelchair turned away, though, so he wasn't looking at the screen and couldn't see what was happening. When the final gunshot sounded, I looked over at him to make sure he didn't give a reaction. If anything could make him groan with discouragement, it might very well be the desperation in that anti-climactic scene. But of course he didn't complain: he has never had a voluntary movement or spoken a single word. No, Andrew didn't get upset about the ending. He didn't even blink. When the credits started rolling, I got up and turned the DVD player off, then the lights, and moved Andrew to the sofa so he could sleep there while I slept in my bed.

Every other time the movie's ending is near, or if I watch a similarly upsetting movie, I wheel him out of the room. Even without the ability to offer a response, he shouldn't have to see the worst that people are capable of. He's 79, only a couple years my junior, but in my head he is still my baby brother. Nothing can ever happen to make me think of him any other way. The day he can speak for himself, say, "Hey, I'll wipe my own ass from now on!" is the day he can start being thought of as a grown adult.

With the lights off, the sun having set for the night, I find myself sitting here thinking again about the end of that movie. Why not press the red button and save everyone? Why not give the people an ending that would allow a little bit of hope instead of a critical commentary on the state of mankind? Did the writer or director lose faith in people because of what had started happening in the world, or did the movie end that way because he had already become indifferent, prior to the Great De-evolution, and thought mankind deserved nothing better?

December 2

If my house is a prison, the animals are my jailers.

I was at the incinerator today, only fifteen feet from my patio door, when a bear spotted me. It was eyeing me from the edge of the woods, its claws digging into the ground with anticipation for when it had a hold of me. It was forty, maybe fifty, feet away.

Forty feet is no concern for a bear hunting an old man. Instead of turning and running, I took a single step backward. Then another. If I tried to dash for safety, it would close the distance before I could get indoors. The bear growled, then lumbered forward. An old man's heart should not have to beat as fast as mine did when that beast came toward me. My eyes stayed down at my feet. Looking at the predator would only make it angry. I took another step backward, and it took two more paces forward. Even without trying, it had cut the distance between us by half. Sweat ran down my face. My hands were shaking.

The thought struck me then that I could use the incinerator for protection. Each time the bear would circle the large metal bin, I would do the same. But just as quickly, reality sunk in: I would get tired after two minutes and, anyway, the bear can run laps around me. My only hope was to get back inside my house.

I prayed for another animal, maybe a dog, to catch the bear's attention, but for once it seemed the only animal in the open was this giant thing in front of me. Where were the other animals when you needed them! It became difficult to breathe slowly, to keep from screaming. My stomach kept shifting, offering growls of its own. The bear took another step forward.

And then, as the bear yet again closed the distance between us, this time to perhaps twelve feet, my hand grabbed hold of the doorknob, turned it, and I was back inside my home. Safe for one more day. The bear stayed there, staring at me through the glass. Although I was safe, my hands would not stop trembling.

Nature returned with a vengeance as soon as the Blocks initiated man's decline. I'm pretty sure a family of deer lives in the empty Donaldson house next door. I looked through the window of the old McGee house the other day, and instead of seeing Jimmy McGee waving at me with a cup of coffee in his hand, the way he used to, a giant brown bear lumbered through the living room looking for something to eat. Foxes, wolves, and bears have all re-established themselves as the proper owners of the forest. Their new rivals are the cats and dogs that used to be pets. Every day a different pack of animals walks down the street in my neighborhood as if the roads were made especially for them.

Gone are the days when deer have to be concerned about cars. The days of foxes sitting by the roadside, afraid to cross the street, are long forgotten. Sometimes the bears get a sniff of food and pace up and down the neighborhood. I used to be able to bang pots and pans to startle the wildlife into returning to the woods, but now they look at me with amusement, their mouths slightly open like content farm animals.

It's not just the bears that aren't afraid of me, it's all of them, every creature. The foxes, the raccoons, the wild dogs, the cats. They all laugh at my feeble attempts to reclaim my lawn. I'm constantly on alert when I go outside. A pack of wild dogs or a bear could catch my scent and see me as nothing more than simple prey. Maybe that's all I am anymore.

The vast population of cute little kitties and puppies, the same ones that relied on people for food and water, slowly filtered out into the wild when their masters moved away. Labradors and golden retrievers were left to fend for themselves. At first, these animals were easy food for the foxes and wolves, but it didn't take long for their domestication to wear off. Dalmatians and Rottweiler's united in an attempt to have power in numbers. Tabbies and Maine Coons teamed up to take over the Phei's old backyard. Some of these animals couldn't acclimate to the new anarchy. Poodles and wiener dogs weren't suited for finding food on their own. Both are probably extinct by now. But other pets were able to adjust and created a new home in the woods as though they had been waiting patiently for man to leave. I laughed the first time I saw a pack of wild chow-chows until I saw them race down a new born fox and tear it to shreds. The baby fox cried until it was finally dead. Its mother howled from the edge of the woods, helpless.

The animals, like the weeds and crab grass, have spread to every part of the once groomed community. A feral cat can have kittens up to four times a year. Beginning at three months of age, each of those kittens can start reproducing. The offspring of a single abandoned house cat could produce hundreds of cats in a single year. And none of these new cats knows what it's like to rely on humans for food or to understand that humans aren't to be attacked. Same with the dogs.

There may have been a single bear in the woods near our community back when people still played golf on the course. Now, there are probably a hundred bears surrounding the neighborhood. Hundreds of wolves have invaded the 18-hole community. And now, only Andrew and I remain to represent the old guard.

Every evening, the packs of wild dogs fight with the wolves as soon as the sun goes down. I hear free-for-alls that sound unnatural, like the type of fireworks that make screaming noises. The dogs howl and screech and bark. The foxhound, treasured for its beautiful fur, now displays stripes of scarred flesh mixed in with grimy hair. Even the bears, the kings of the forest, are never free of battle wounds.

The animals aren't to blame for this. In the three generations it has taken man to go from the planet's dominant species to sparse packs of feeble senior citizens, there have been a hundred generations of former house pets and forest animals, plenty of time for all of them to forget we were once their hunters and masters. They spy us from the edge of the woods, waiting for chances to sneak up and repay us for centuries of servitude and fear. There was one time, I laughed until I pissed myself, when the Johnsons were chased back inside their house by a pack of feral tabby cats. The same kind of cute little kitten that would lap up milk and play with balls of string was throwing itself against the Johnsons' screen door.

The smaller critters have also faired better without man. There were so many birds in the sky the other day that the sun was almost blotted out. The trees look like zoo exhibits, filled with cardinals, blue jays, little yellow birds that I'm not familiar with, robins, and crows. Vultures are everywhere, laying claim to the remains of animals left by the dogs and wolves.

The only animal that hasn't fared well is the deer. They are vastly outnumbered by the carnivores and have gone into hiding. I see a family of deer every once in a while, but every time I do I find my jaw clenched because I expect a pack of dogs to come out of nowhere and slaughter them.

Back in middle school, I learned that nature regulates itself. The eco-system is supposed to ensure there are enough insects to feed the raccoons, enough raccoons to feed the foxes, and so on, but ever since man's decline it's almost as if nature doesn't know how to control itself anymore. The herbivores are almost gone and yet the predators still grow in number. It defies everything I've been taught, but I'm seeing it with my own eyes so I know it's really happening. It's almost as if all the animals are in shock and don't know what to do except overrun everything, even each other.

No topic was discussed more during my dinners with the Johnsons than the animals lurking all around us. The three of us would sip glasses of wine, look out at the lines of abandoned houses, and discuss our plans as though all of our options still existed in the world. Sometimes, when we had too much to drink, we would joke about who would last the longest in the neighborhood and be the final person left in Camelot. We wouldn't dare vocalize such things if we were sober because the implications were that two of the three of us would be dead and our siblings were either being neglected or had also died. Sober, we would have chosen instead to talk about the falling leaves or how the golf course had gone unattended for so long it looked like a pasture instead of eighteen holes of sport.

Years ago, I would take Andrew with me when I went down to the Johnsons' house. More recently, I was leaving him on the sofa with music playing. When the Johnsons came down to my house, they would also leave their younger sisters at home, a warm fire in the fireplace replacing the soft music I offered to Andrew. Everyone has their own ways of trying to make loved ones feel more comfortable. I praised the Johnsons as the only family that was happy to stay in their own home when every one else was leaving. That, combined with our intimate conversations all those nights, is why I was so shocked when they left a week ago. It's why I'm still shocked.

There was no reason to get out of bed that night, no reason to go to my bedroom window; it was almost as if treachery could be sensed in the air because I stayed at the window, not knowing what I was looking for or expecting to see. There was nothing to signify a momentous event was getting ready to unfold. As I watched the neighborhood, the night went from the sounds of animals to their actual presence. A pack of wolves made their way down the middle of the road, a group of varsity football players, letting everyone else know they weren't to be messed with. Upon seeing them, a couple of house cats hid under the porch at the Wilkensons' former home. A pair of golden retrievers appeared a minute later, a dead rabbit dangling from one's mouth.

And then it happened: the Johnsons' garage door opened, their SUV backed out, the garage door lowered again, and the over-sized vehicle pulled onto the street. It turned toward my house. Instead of stopping, though, it continued past my driveway and left the neighborhood. There were two figures in the front and two in the back. None of them turned and waved at me as they passed. The break lights didn't even flicker. And just like that they were gone.

I was left as the final resident of Camelot.

December 3

Ideas about family, about the importance of always being there for loved ones, changed when the Blocks started outnumbering the rest of us. My parents and the rest of the community were still adjusting, back when Andrew was born, to the concept that a living person could be exactly like you or me, except they didn't move, didn't talk, didn't do anything. Being that Andrew was one of the first Blocks, it took everyone in our neighborhood some getting used to. The day before my parents brought him home from the hospital, my father sat me down and talked about how Andrew should be treated. "You know how much you love Bumper?" he asked, referring to the stuffed rabbit I carried everywhere. "Your brother also can't move or talk, but I want you to love him even more than Bumper. But be careful. You can't drag your brother around the house by his arm the way you do your stuffed animals. He won't cry out, but you can still hurt him."

It was an odd concept until you saw a Block and realized they really did look just like everyone else, they just didn't smile or sigh or do anything at all. A month later, another family on the street had a baby and that child was also a Block. The Stevenson's new daughter was a Block too. I don't remember another regular baby being born after that.

It would have been nice to be a little older when my brother was born so I could remember the details more clearly. I'm left with vague impressions, the accuracy of which I can't verify. I remember having a babysitter for a couple of days while my parents were at the hospital. The girl, barely qualified to be a temporary custodian of anything, popped her bubble gum as she asked, "So, is your brother going to be a Block? That's gotta be weird." There's no telling what my answer had been. Shortly after that I remember my parents coming home with my new baby brother. They put him down on the sofa with all the normal love and care given to a baby, but I also remember, even at that age, thinking it strange that Andrew was completely silent and still, never cried, never tried to do anything. If they left him lying on his back with his arms by his side, he would be in the exact same position when they checked on him an hour later.

I asked my mother why she and my dad were always putting needles in Andrew's arm—it was something they never had to do to me—and she explained that Andrew couldn't eat food the same way I could, that he needed an IV to get food and water. So in the oversimplified view of my childhood mind, I remember feeling like I had a brother who was sort of like me, he just didn't move or make noise and he needed to have a tube coming out of his forearm.

The first cases of this new syndrome had only started emerging a few months before my brother was born. Doctors in Chicago claimed to have found the first case, however, doctors in the Ukraine and Belgium reported identical findings at the same time, of newborn babies without any significant brain activity. Doctors weren't sure at first if it was a new form of autism or something else completely. It was as if babies were being born comatose. They also weren't sure what triggered it or why it started happening all across the globe simultaneously. It ended up being classified as a new disorder, something that was wholly and unquestionably its own state of being. Parents of those first children wanted to know if there would ever be a cure. Soon-to-be parents wondered if there might be a vaccine. They also wondered if there was something they could do—certain brands of food to buy, certain types of formula—that might keep their child from being born that way.

Everyone wondered exactly what the prognosis meant. What did no significant brain activity mean for these children? The best answer doctors were able to provide was that these newborns had healthy bodies, and their brains were functioning, they just weren't developing the way normal brains should. The results were bodies that still developed enough to regulate breathing, go through puberty, and eventually have grey hair, but that didn't develop motor neurons or sensory neurons. People began referring to these afflicted children as Blocks because it was as if their condition obstructed them from the world. More and more newborns began showing signs of this complete lack of acknowledgement of their surroundings.

Doctors were able to pinpoint the cause of the condition shortly after it appeared. A certain amino acid wasn't forming; the brain wasn't developing the way it was supposed to. But while they knew the cause, they were unable to find a cure. They replicated the amino acid, they manipulated every aspect of the birth process, but they couldn't force the human brain to develop the way it once had. Every step of the baby's development could be controlled, the correct amino acid introduced, but still the unborn child would reject the treatment and develop the same way as all the other Blocks. Doctors began creating new babies from test tubes. These infants also displayed stunted brains. No matter how human life was created in those years, it wasn't life that could sustain itself. The entire human race had evolved, or mis-evolved as it were, and refused to go back to what it had been previously.

A generation of people, the final generation of people, grew up just like the rest of us—healthy hearts, perfect circulatory systems, strong bones—they just couldn't talk or move or do anything else that the previous generations could. So we, the fathers, mothers, brothers, and sisters of the afflicted, took care of them and raised them as the otherwise normal people they were, all the while realizing this new generation we were taking care of wouldn't be able to produce offspring. And even if they could, they wouldn't be able to raise them.

As a little boy I didn't understand why someone who couldn't talk or move should be loved as much as someone who could do those things. It certainly wasn't fun trying to play G.I. Joe with a little brother who couldn't make exploding noises or act like our soldiers were killing each other. My parents did not share my reservations. When I was seven and Andrew was three, our parents took us to the beach. My mom and dad spent a week making sure they had thought of everything necessary for a long road trip involving Andrew. My mom checked his supply of child-sized nutrient bags in the kitchen while my dad made sure the child safety seat still fit.

I saw the amount of preparation involved and couldn't help but ask my mom, "Why do you even bother taking Andrew?"

Thinking back to it, she could have crossed the short distance of the kitchen and smacked me across the face, but she was my mother and she gave a gentle laugh, as though my question was silly.

"Because he's my son. Because he's your brother."

"But he doesn't know he's going to the beach. He doesn't even know what a beach is. He doesn't even know we're here."

My mom paused as she looked for the right words. "I can't argue with any of that," she said.

"So why are you making him go, then?" I said it as though Andrew were being forced against his will, even though nothing could have been further from the truth. In the years since, I realized I said it that way because I wanted to get all of the attention. It wasn't fair that someone who didn't talk or do chores or hit the game-winning homerun could still get as much attention as I did. At the time, I had wanted to ask what the point was of me doing the dishes after dinner or making my bed in the morning if Andrew never did any of those things but was loved as though he did do them. Luckily, for once in my childhood, I didn't say the stupid thing I could have said and instead remained silent.

My mom said again, "Because he's my son. Because he's your brother." This time when she said it, she put her hand on my cheek and smiled.

Then, as if her answer should satisfy a seven year-old, she stood up and began preparing for the vacation again. But of course what she had said didn't make sense to me. I tugged on her sleeve as she tried to walk away to pack more luggage.

"Are you going to put him in the ocean?"

"I don't know. I guess maybe if your father wants to."

"But why?"

She paused for a moment, frowned, then started again. "Because he's—"

"Mom."

She knelt down in front of me so we were the same height. I remember being only inches apart from her, her sweet breath on my face. She took my cheeks in her hands the way she would if I had scraped my knee and needed to be soothed.

"Because I love him. It doesn't matter if he won't understand that we're going on a vacation or that he won't know he's at the ocean instead of his bed. I love him so much I want him with me wherever I am. That's the way mothers are." She smiled and hugged me. "And don't you forget, buster, that your father and I took you on vacations before you were old enough to understand where you were. You were just a little baby when we went to the beach with you for the first time. How would you have felt if we left you at home?"

I didn't say anything else. She knew me well enough to know I would stay quiet.

Still eye to eye, her hands on my shoulders, she said, "He's the only brother you have. He can't play catch with you or play hide-and-go-seek but he's…" She paused, tried to smile, but even as a seven year-old I knew she was faking her happiness. She cleared her throat. "One day your father and I will get older and we might not be around anymore. If that happens, Andrew will be the last family you have. That's why you should want him with us on our vacations. He's your family, and family is the most important thing."

The words didn't really make sense to me at the time. I knew what each word meant, but not the significance they held when strung together. But even without understanding them, they somehow convinced me.

On our second day at the beach I took a picture of my dad holding Andrew in his arms as a wave crashed over them. He was laughing enough for himself and for Andrew. I continue looking at that photograph even to this day. It sits on our mantle in a frame lined with little seashells. A funny thing happened as I got older: I began to appreciate what my mom had been trying to say about the importance of having Andrew with me, even if he couldn't tell me to shut up when my stories were stupid or when my jokes weren't funny.

We were taught that evolution was a step forward, a step to further the ability of a species. This was said about the Blocks so they would be looked at as something unique and special, something greater than what we had been before. But if this really was an evolution, something positive, and not a case of a disease that was afflicting everyone we knew, then it was doing the exact opposite of what it had done the previous million years. No one could understand how a species could change itself in a way that prevented its own survival. It defied nature.

By the end of that first year, fifteen percent of babies were Blocks. Within two years, the syndrome was affecting forty percent of all babies. After five years, it was up to ninety percent. A year later, a hundred percent of babies were born healthy in every way except they couldn't do anything for themselves. This new generation was the end of our civilization.

That's how the world (at least as man sees it) will end. Not with armies conquering other nations, not with race wars or religious wars, but with people who can't love or wish, people who can't give you a hug when you need it, can't offer advice when called upon. These silent masses will continue to age until the last generation of regular adults gets too old to take care of them, and then everyone will just fade away.

There have been other times when people were afraid for their futures. My parents told me what it was like to grow up during the Cold War, never knowing if a mushroom cloud would blossom on the horizon and blot out the sun. Their grandparents lived through World War II and talked about what is was like to see the entire world fighting itself as though life wasn't the most valuable thing, but the most expendable. They agreed with me, though, that the signs of extinction have never been this concrete.

As I type this Andrew is sitting by himself on the sofa. I check him periodically to see if he needs anything. I refill his nutrient bag. I turn on a movie or some music. I talk to him so he can hear my voice. He never acknowledges any of this.

It would be funny to see his reaction if he woke up one day as a normal adult. What would he do if he woke up on the sofa with a weird old man sitting a couple of feet away from him? Would he believe me if I said I was his brother, that I had taken care of him his entire life, or would he think I was the crazy one and wonder what had happened to his memory?

His blinking eyes don't signal a need or a desire. They signal nothing. They signal that he can't take care of himself, that he is living in a healthy body but is otherwise dead to the world.

I go and check on him anyway. I always do.

December 4

I keep waiting for the Johnsons to reappear, to knock on my door like old times. In a neighborhood built to hold a hundred families, there's a surprising difference between ninety-eight houses being vacant and ninety-nine. Without them here, a collection of movies, books, and music keeps Andrew and I occupied. I love Andrew dearly, but he never tells me which movies he likes, which actors could never play a believable character no matter how hard they try, which books he wouldn't waste his time with, which authors were telling great truths. Water, food, and electricity are, thankfully, provided for me, but the one thing I treasured—people—has been taken away. My parents are long gone. The neighborhood slowly trickled away. The Johnsons are gone.

For the previous two years, the Johnsons' house has been the only other occupied home on my street, the other people all either having died of old age (slang for cancer, heart attacks, the usual causes) or leaving to join the group communities. Every person I've known, from the time I was born to today, is gone. My brother is the only exception.

How did it happen that I'm left here with the things I need to survive, but without the one thing that actually keeps me going? Sure, I thought about the end while the Johnsons were still here, but it never seemed imminent because I was talking about the end with the Johnsons. Now, I can't help but feel like it's only a matter of time until the last light on the street goes out and the animals forget what it was like having an old man for a neighbor. Like a widower losing a spouse, I could have gone on indefinitely as long as I had someone to go on with. My grandmother passed away three months after my grandfather; what's the average lifespan of a widower? I'll need to look that up.

By writing about a golf community surrounded with forest, you would think I live in a nice, quiet neighborhood, but that's not true. I live in the remnants of what used to be a nice, quiet neighborhood.

Weeds cover everything, spread everywhere. I used to have a nice cherry blossom on the side of my house. Its withered limbs are still there, but it's been years since they bloomed pretty buds. The weeds blot everything out. If I kill one, a new breed will take its spot a week later. Nature, it seems, is very serious about reclaiming everything man took from it.

The last time I ventured to the end of the street, where the community ends and the rest of the world begins, the brick sign welcoming everyone to Camelot was hidden behind thick weeds. At one time it served as a marker that people from this area used after long days at work to know they were finally home, could finally relax. Each metal letter was bolted into the brick wall in the fashionable style from decades ago. Over the years, the letters became hidden in the brush so that only the tops could be seen over the uncut grass. When I pulled back the weeds, the letters, once shiny metal, had become orange with rust. Each letter was caked with layer upon layer of dirt that told how many seasons had passed since someone cared enough to greet visitors. There was a time when people would see that sign and smile because they knew a fabulous round of golf awaited. The course was hidden amongst the trees in a way that let you feel like you were always near people, but without always having to see them.

The earth shows hints of grey where the road used to be. Underneath thriving weeds now, it used to be kept in pristine condition; anything on the street besides the two speed bumps caused uproars at community meetings. That was when I first moved here with Andrew. The speed bumps are gone now, I assume, just because the rest of the pavement has deteriorated so much. It resembles a gravel road now, full of over-sized rocks, more than it does the main path to a golf community.

Even when three or four other families were here, I could have driven my car through all of the lawns, done donuts to my heart's content, and no one would have cared. With the shutters on each house having fallen years ago, the gutters clogged and overflowing, there is no longer any pride in property. There is no one to look outside and feel jealous of how nice their neighbor's shrubbery looks compared to their own, no one to wish they had as nice a privacy fence as the family down the street.

The curtains are pulled aside in each house, not a single ray of sunlight prevented from entering the abandoned homes. The final owners probably liked feeling as though there was nothing to be gloomy about, even though the rest of the neighborhood was slowly becoming vacant. And why not leave the blinds open? There was barely anyone left to see a man walk around in his house naked, and the few who did remain were all old enough that their eyesight was hazy. With the Johnsons gone, I could play eighteen holes naked, go for a walk naked, take a stroll through the community center naked, and not a single person would know. I say these things as though there are advantages to my situation, which is not the case.

December 5

When I walked into the living room today and saw Andrew there, motionless, I was sure he was dead. His head had fallen to the side. His mouth was open. His eyes, vacant as always, stared up at the ceiling the way I see in horror movies. This is nothing new, but a sureness came over me that today would be different, that his end might finally have come.

I rushed over to him. "Andrew, are you okay?" My ear went to his mouth. There could have been feint breaths, but I couldn't be sure.

Lord, please don't let him be gone. I don't want to be alone.

"Andrew?"

His eyes didn't offer random blinks. His chest may have expanded slightly, but the movement was so miniscule I couldn't tell.

"Andrew, please."

My hand went to his chest. A heartbeat gave gentle patters against my palm. He was still with me.

"Jesus Christ, you scared me."

I put in a movie and tried to forget the momentary scare, but it took a while to get over the fright of thinking he might have been gone. The rest of the day passed without incident. I did, though, find myself checking his pulse every ten minutes just to be safe.

By the time Andrew would have been starting little league, if little league was still around then with children able to swing bats and throw balls, the things that had previously been important—getting the most for your money, electing public officials who weren't corrupt—took a backseat to more simplistic needs. During the same dinner conversation in which my parents discussed the availability of food, water, and electricity as a growing number of businesses shut their doors, they looked over at me and saw a young face that didn't understand why these things preoccupied them. They took time away from worrying about the future to tell me what it was like to grow up back when they were ten-year olds. My dad spoke about cartoons on Saturday mornings and about putting baseball cards in the spokes of his bike. My mom talked about trying on makeup with her older sister and selling cookies to raise money for school trips. A year later, in the same breath they used to talk about the government's plan to build a food processor and generator for every house, my mom and dad talked about what it was like to walk through the aisles of toy stores that were so big parents had to be paged over the intercom to find their children. It sounded like an amazing place to get lost. There were never times when I was growing up that my mom and dad discussed a rise in interest rates or how road construction was causing traffic jams on the way to work. They spoke instead about their neighbors starting to move south, and about the things they would need in order to take care of themselves and to take care of Andrew and me.

My father asked what else we needed besides food, water, and electricity. We had a house and clothes and a car. My mother frowned. "I don't know," she said.

When it came down to it, people really didn't need that much to survive in the world. It was the world my parents grew up in that had taught them to feel like they needed more. Bank accounts no longer mattered. Fancy cars didn't count for anything. I guess if you were a good enough fisherman to catch your dinner, having a nice boat was a bonus, but nobody needed a luxurious yacht when a little kayak did the trick. There weren't many things that were truly important when you counted down to man no longer inheriting the earth, which I guess is what the Great De-evolution was. Diamonds didn't do anything for you. Gold became just another metal.

Growing up in a time when the importance of these things was fading away, a time in which no new cars were designed, in which fancy movie theaters sat empty without new movies to show, in which fashion designers didn't have anyone who felt like they needed an expensive evening gown, I was given a new set of ideas to store away. Every time my parents mentioned another neighbor heading south, it reinforced the feeling that I needed other people around me. Throughout the years, as generations raced to get better promotions, more riches, nicer homes, people had become a forgotten commodity. I had a lot of friends growing up, but slowly, one by one, they started moving south, and I was left to spend more time each day with Andrew as my only companion. Every time my parents spoke about the things they did as little kids, things that were no longer available to me, I clung to my movies and my books, to the few things I had to keep me occupied throughout the day.

The priority of continuing bloodlines also trickled away once Blocks made up a hundred percent of the newborns. Baby stores went out of business before any other companies realized what was happening. Expensive fertility clinics became a punch line. Most people around the world willingly stopped having babies once it was confirmed the infant boy or girl would be a Block, but some people insisted on bringing new kids into the world even though they knew this child would have a lifeless existence. It was primarily the irresponsible segment of society, the people who couldn't support themselves, let alone a baby, the people for whom birth control was a hassle or too expensive, who were still having babies.

These people, some addicted to drugs, some too immature to take care of themselves, others just too careless to use condoms, kept bringing countless Blocks into the world. Public outrage sparked new laws to charge these inconsiderate assholes with punishments to fit the crime. Mothers who were already on welfare and had already been charged with neglect of their Blocks, continued getting pregnant every year because they didn't know how to do anything else. These Blocks were eventually taken into state custody where they made up a large percentage of the population at group homes.

My parents had Andrew a couple of months after the first Blocks were identified, when well under five percent of babies were Blocks. They loved him as though he were the same as me, but they also got disgusted with one of our neighbors for having a baby after a hundred percent of the newborns were Blocks. Even as a young boy I picked up on my parents suddenly not talking to this one pair of neighbors.

"It's just irresponsible," my father said.

My mother shook her head in agreement and said to me, "We love your brother and we never regretted having him, but we'll never try to have another baby until they find a cure for this."

Being a kid, not completely understanding the situation, I asked how they made babies. My father ignored my question and chose instead to answer the question I should have asked. "It's not fair for the people who will have to take care of that baby when it grows up and its parents have passed away, but it's also not fair for the baby. That kid will never know what it's like to have friends or have its own children."

I wanted to ask more questions, but we had to go

inside and check on Andrew. Another time, I asked my dad how long he would have gone before he didn't try to have my brother. The rate of regular babies versus Blocks changed completely within a matter of years, so I wanted to know if they would have tried if the rate was twenty-five percent or fifty percent.

He put his hand on my shoulder and ushered me out of the room; he didn't want to have to answer in front of Andrew. "I'm not sure," he said. "We wanted a duplicate of you. We wanted you to have a brother to play baseball with." He cleared his throat, then excused himself to my parents' bedroom and closed the door.

December 7

It rained all day—a massive hurricane-type rain. For the first three hours, I was able to keep watching movies with Andrew, an occasional break taken to empty the buckets scattered throughout our home. Each one had a steady pitter-patter of water dripping into it. Anytime a major scene ended, I would pause the movie, go around the house to empty buckets, then return to watch more of the DVD with Andrew.

But as the rain continued in a steady downpour, I found myself unable to keep up with the barrage of buckets strewn throughout the house. By the time I had emptied the first ten buckets, with still another ten to go, the first one would be reaching capacity again. In my younger years I could have kept up the shuttle drills all day. Today, though, with my knees the way they are, with a back that screams after bending over more than two or three times, I quickly became overwhelmed. The bucket in the bathroom was overflowing. I ignored it and focused on the ones in the living room. The bucket in the kitchen was overflowing. I ignored it to focus on the ones in my bedroom.

One drop at a time, my home was becoming lost to me. I have never wished that my brother could come alive more than I did today during those moments of helplessness as water filled various rooms around our house. His help emptying buckets would have made up for a lifetime of stillness.

Just when I was done praying that he could help lend a hand, the rain let up. Water continued to make its way through the holes in the roof, but the stream slowed to a trickle. By that time, I was too tired to move, could do nothing but watch helplessly from the sofa as drops of water plopped down all around me. Only hours later did I have the strength to get off the cushions and empty the remaining water from each bucket. When that was done, I began mopping the floors.

I can already guarantee I'm not going to be able to move tomorrow. My back is going to be angry with me for weeks.

And this was just because of some rain. Where would any of the last remaining few be if man actually had to hunt and gather food? I've never shot an animal, either with a bow and arrow or a gun. I've never planted seeds and watched them grow into corn stalks or carrot patches. Without food processors none of us would have made it a week after the grocery stores closed. The Johnsons and I used to talk about our processors as though they were our most prized possessions. It didn't matter to us that identical units were sitting in every other house up and down the street. Its creators, if they're still out there somewhere, deserve every award ever handed out for science and technology. It was a shame that most of those award-giving foundations had closed shop by the time the food processor was created.

Hell, if I had to choose between a food processor and my music collection, I would gladly sit in silence with Andrew while we ate. If I had to choose between my processor and my computer, I wouldn't think twice about selecting the food machine. Besides writing this journal, the computer is only useful for checking to see how the final colonies across the southern states are doing. I used to enjoy emailing some of my old classmates to see where they were living and what life is like there, but in the past couple of years it has become too discouraging. The amount of responses diminished every year, and I kept adding more checkmarks to the list of kids I graduated high school with who had grown old and died. Yes, I can do without the computer. All it does is remind me of my daily concerns, whereas the ice cream I get from the food processor takes my mind off any worry. The dogs can howl as much as they want, the bears can growl until they're purple, they can even lumber up to my patio door and snort in frustration—as long as I have my bowl of mint chocolate chip I don't mind a single bit.

The food processor's only rival is our television. If Andrew and I didn't have it to watch old movies every day, I don't know what we would do with our time. Sometimes I read books out loud. At least that way Andrew benefits from them too. I often feel silly, though, reading stories to him as if he's a little child needing to hear fantastic tales before bed, rather than a grown adult the same age my parents were when they passed away.

Tonight I programmed the processor to make lasagna. Ten minutes later I had a white and red dish that smelled and tasted exactly like it came from Italy. The hardest part of making the meal was going back through the processor's user guide to find which setting would produce the meal I wanted. I've memorized the settings for seasoned steak, crab cakes, and orange chicken, but lasagna hadn't been selected in a long time. The Johnsons used to come over and recommend new settings I would never think of trying. "#6731 makes a sausage casserole that's incredible!" or, "We finally tried #2601 last night. Did you know it makes ahi tuna?"

The only difference between the lasagna I had last night and the real thing, which, by the way, my mom made perfectly when I was a boy, was that it didn't come out of the machine in layers of pasta, cheese, and sauce. The food processor can recreate tastes and smells, but was never advanced enough to mimic each delicacy's presentation. It comes out as a bowl of lasagna with the meat interspersed with the cheese and pasta, rather than a square with alternating levels of ingredients. Brownie sundaes come out with the hot brownie mixed in directly with the ice cream rather than having the chocolate treat on the edge to mix in as you like. I'm not complaining though.

It tasted so good I went back through the user guide to find other food settings I'd forgotten. The variety it offers amazed everyone the first time they saw it. It can make ten different kinds of macaroni and cheese, but each of those recipes can also be modified to be extra cheesy, extra moist, and so on. The settings can also be altered to contain extra calcium, fiber, anything you can think of. Chicken stir-fry will be tomorrow. Halfway through the user guide, I remembered walnut crusted salmon was at #1016. I got so happy that I gave Andrew a low-five (he can't hold his hand up for a high-five). I forgot all of the other things I was missing out on—evening walks, vacations, neighborhood cookouts—and for one evening was content.

It makes me wonder how many other things I used to enjoy that I not only no longer do, but that I don't even remember enjoying in the first place. And once I start doing that for food, it's inevitable that my mind wanders and I find myself thinking of watching football on Sunday with my dad, playing neighborhood games of two-hand touch, trying capture the other team's flag in the forest behind our house, even something as simple as running to the grocery store to get milk for dinner. As soon as I think of one thing I used to miss, the dam breaks and I'm flooded with eighty years, a lifetime, of things I've enjoyed that are no longer possible.

During these times, I try to think of the positive things that came to fruition during the Great De-evolution. Every day I find a different reason to be thankful for the Survival Bill. Our presidents and congressmen got a lot of things wrong over the years, but they may never have gotten anything as right as the supplies that provided the last generation of functioning adults with resources to take care of themselves and their Block relatives. The Bill was our government trying to protect its citizens one final time, ensuring people like me would be taken care of when there was no more government, locally or nationally, no grocery stores or farms, no trash trucks or power companies. It gave me the resources I needed to grow old by myself. It also allowed for the population of aging adults to take care of an entire society of people who couldn't take care of themselves.

I remember watching the news as a teenager. The naysayers always asked the same question into the camera: "Well, who's going to pay for all of this?" It showed they still didn't understand the magnitude of the situation: there weren't going to be future generations to be stuck with the bill; the people being provisioned for were all that was left.

There aren't any grocery stores anymore. Remnants of some farms still exist, but they have long since been abandoned, have become weed-filled fields that haven't grown healthy crops in twenty years. There's no need for money at this point, so also no reason for people to have stores or to sell goods. If I had to work the earth for my own food, or carry a rifle into the woods for hunting, I wouldn't have lasted a single month. I would have died forty years ago. If there is anyone still alive in New England or Canada they have to be a resourceful hunter-gatherer capable of killing animals every time they need something to eat. Only that kind of self-sufficiency, the kind we've all forgotten about, could allow a man to live in the abandoned northern regions. Instead of that fate, I have a food generator that produces my meals each day. The same generator allows me to refill Andrew's nutrient bags.

The Survival Bill didn't produce thousands of each machine, but millions. And not just food processors. The incinerator in my backyard ensures I don't drown in my own trash. A power generator produces all the electricity I'll ever need. Each house is a self-sustainable unit of civilization; no one has to rely on anyone else. Luckily for me and for Andrew, if any of these items ever breaks, I can go next door, or to any of the other millions of abandoned houses, and begin using their Survival Bill units as if they were my own.

The Survival Bill's single-minded success became one of the most impressive feats in American history. The last generation of regular adults were already in their teens when the bill was passed into law, so all of the empty schools were turned into factories. Elementary schools were re-conditioned into incinerator factories. Middle schools were modified to become power generator plants. A couple of years later, all of the high schools were gutted and made into food processor factories. Teachers, no longer required to pass information to America's youth, were retrained to create the very resources everyone would need once the population got too old and sparse to support itself.

Someone told me one time that the cost of the Survival Bill, if money was still of consequence at the time the legislation was passed, would have totaled the cost of both World Wars, the Korean War, the Vietnam War, and the war in Iraq if they were combined and then multiplied by a hundred. The amount was supposed to put me in awe of how much money and how many lives were spent for killing when they could have been ensuring our future, but the numbers were vague to me, so astronomical, beyond anything I had experience with, that the impact was lost. To me, a hundred million is the same as a billion and the same as a trillion. You get to a point where it goes beyond what you know and its importance no longer matters.

Wave after wave of incinerators was distributed. Trash collectors weren't needed anymore, so they were trained to work along side the teachers in other Survival Bill factories. A hundred more outdated occupations trickled in as well. As millions of electrical generators were shipped around the country, electricians weren't needed. These people went to work in factories too. Entire sections of our culture became extinct. Farmer, professor, mathematician—these were all professions that were talked about as though they were fictional jobs made up for Hollywood.

Scientists were some of the only professionals who continued to the end, mainly because they continued searching for a cure for the Blocks. They kept conducting their tests and research even while the Survival Bill was in full swing, their hope being that the provisions would become unnecessary because humans would once again be able to give birth to fully functioning people able to support themselves.

A cure was never found, though.

December 8

Every time the furnace kicks on, I think I might hear the Johnsons' SUV returning to the neighborhood. Each time the refrigerator rumbles awake, I think I hear a truck approaching our community on its way south. My ears perk up. I shuffle toward the front door with the hope of seeing a new neighbor or a familiar face. Unlike me, Andrew never gets excited by the false alarms. It will take a day or two, but I know I will learn to tune out the noises as well. Oh, how I would welcome someone new to the neighborhood, even if they were like Andrew, unable to speak or move.

As the Great De-evolution progressed, some families began to worry about their daily existence and what was best for the remaining regular members in their household. Most of these people reasoned that the health and wellbeing of their Block loved ones couldn't endure an extended road trip to the South. This excuse didn't make sense; I can't think of someone better suited for a road trip than a brother or sister who doesn't get bored or irritated and isn't picky about what they eat.

These inconvenient Blocks, along with the ones who were orphaned by irresponsible parents, combined to form a quiet community at Block group homes. Lines of Blocks stretched to every corner of the transitioned buildings. Once they were taken to the group care centers, you couldn't tell one Block from another. The neglected Blocks and the bastard Blocks mixed together as a single, unified, quiet society.

No matter how great their numbers, they would always be a pitiful and defenseless army. It reminded me of a sci-fi movie where a battalion of androids was being created in a factory, their sole purpose to unleash terror on the masses. All they needed was the command to wake up so they could begin their war. Except the activation code for the Blocks had been permanently lost. They would never lift an arm against another being. You could dress them in military uniforms, you could put rifles in their hands. They would gladly sit through all of the indoctrination videos you could think of. But they would never pull a trigger or obey an order.

This was one of the reasons the Great De-evolution signaled an end to war. None of the newborn babies would be able to fill the empty ranks or take orders when they grew up. As the last regular adults in the military got to be in their thirties and forties, they had no new recruits to command. These people were still promoted, but the promotions no longer signaled an increased number of men to lead. A general was seen walking the hallways of the Pentagon without a single man to give orders to. An admiral stood on the deck of a destroyer that was still anchored ashore. The giant boat had no one to pilot it.

The other reason there were no more wars was that the world leaders, even the craziest ones, realized there was no point to invading another country if it meant you were helping nature deplete the last remaining normal people. Democracy no longer needed to spread across the globe to ensure future generations could vote because future generations wouldn't exist. Communist countries released their grip, letting people say and hear whatever they wanted because, in the end, it didn't matter what information was controlled if the rulers were already counting down their time. People across the world realized the same fate was in store for everyone else. Borders began to fall. The men who used to carry machine guns took off their uniforms for the last time and became regular citizens who needed to worry about taking care of their families. In America, these former soldiers began assisting with various aspects of the Survival Bill. In other countries, they worked in factories, labored on farms, or just disappeared.

Congressmen, no longer needed to make new laws, said goodbye to each other and flew back to their home states. Only the President felt a need to keep up appearances by going to a secure bunker with his family and a handful of top aides. For all I know they might still be in that hollowed-out mountain. Or, without seeing the sun for a year, they might have lost their minds or opened the hatch doors and wandered off into the wilderness. I would rather be in Camelot with the bears and dogs than be bunkered inside a mountain for the rest of my life. My roof leaks and a bear could easily break through my patio door, but it's a better existence than living inside a fortified mountain. I'm better off than the President! Somehow, that fails to make me feel any better.

December 10

It's difficult to get into new habits. I told myself I would write in this journal every day, but after the chores are finished and I sit in front of the TV with Andrew, it's easier to stay on the sofa and wait for the next day to arrive than it is to get up and go to the computer for the sole purpose of facing the same questions that keep me up at night. It didn't help that Andrew had a bad night and that the next morning I was also feeling under the weather.

At the beginning of her diary, Anne Frank said no one is interested in the words of a thirteen year-old girl. Well, no one should be interested in the words of an eighty-two year-old man either. And even if someone would be intrigued by what I had to say, no one is around to read it. The other houses in the neighborhood are dark and silent. As far as our neighborhood is concerned, maybe even the entire state, Andrew and I are the end, the Omega. I don't know if it's a matter of being pessimistic or simply being realistic, but a whisper keeps sounding in my head: "You have a limited amount of time left. Why are you spending it this way?"

The other part of me says there has to be something after us. Even after Andrew and I are dead, life will continue. Life always continues. Every other species has been unaffected by what is happening to humans. Most have thrived because of our departure. Maybe, millions of years from now, the world will find new ways to create complex life, or gorillas and chimps will evolve once again. Maybe their evolution will create a beautiful new race of creatures that somewhat resembles man, shares man's intellect, but has fewer of our negative traits. They won't be violent. They won't be so eager to put each other down or to rule by fear. Cynicism won't exist. Concepts of slavery and bigotry would seem silly to these complex creatures.

A paper version of the diary would have crumbled to ashes by then. A copy on my computer would be just as useless. Not that I really believe in aliens, but maybe a spaceship will visit our planet, find what has been written, and ensure what happened to us doesn't happen to them. Or, maybe writing this will help me grasp exactly what is happening around me. I convince myself that is why I sit in front of my computer while my brother sits quietly on the sofa and the wilderness reclaims the land around my house.

All I can do is tell what has happened and how we responded to it. It is neither an indictment nor a justification of anything that has happened, especially when it comes to my own decisions over the years. And maybe, with it, I can figure out what to do next. But do I write about those things? Of course not. I decided to write about fake lasagna and wet kitchen floors. If an advanced alien species found my diary a hundred years from now, they would either think my journal to be a joke, or they would think I was the world's stupidest person. What other kind of man would write about pasta instead of the end of mankind?

Each night I wonder what will happen to Andrew if I have a sudden heart attack and die before him. He would have a day or two before his nutrient bag was depleted. After that he would slowly go hungry and become dehydrated until he withered away to nothing. He would never cry out for help or drag himself across the floor to the kitchen; he would simply stay in his seat from one day to the next and starve until his organs shut down. Even if he could yell out, who would help him? Now that the Johnsons are gone, our closest neighbors are probably a hundred miles away—much too far to hear if there was an emergency. One of the greatest luxuries my parents had was the ability to pick up the phone, dial 9-1-1, and have ambulances or fire trucks show up within five minutes.

If only every day could be as good as today. The chores were done by early afternoon, so the rest of the day Andrew and I watched movies. The selections didn't consist of anything too serious, just a bunch of old action movies where the hero always ends up killing a bunch of bad guys before getting his family back or saving the city. I ate popcorn and drank soda until I was jittery from all the sugar. All in all, it was a good day.

Sometimes a scary scene comes on when we're watching movies and I say something like, "I hope you don't have problems falling asleep tonight," or, "I hope that doesn't give you nightmares." Andrew doesn't respond, however, and I know I say these things just to hear what it sounds like to listen to a living person, even if it's just my own voice. Andrew never laughs at the funny parts of the movies or cries at the sad parts. He doesn't get upset when the stubborn hero refuses to change his ways, nor does he cheer when that same hero finally earns his vindication. I cheer enough for both of us.

December 11

Andrew has a slight fever again. He can never tell me if he isn't feeling well—hell, I don't even know if he can feel well or not well—it was only by chance that I noticed his warm forehead this morning. *Nothing has changed just because the Johnsons are gone*, I tell myself. But no matter how many times I say it, it never sounds convincing. If they were here, I would ask them for advice, ask if they notice their sisters getting sick more often as they get older too. Without them, I do my best to take care of a life that can't take care of itself.

After my parents were gone and I inherited sole responsibility of taking care of him, a slew of new habits formed: I checked his diaper for messes, his gums and teeth for infection, his back and legs for bed sores. I do these things partly because he can't tell me if he has a problem, but the other reason is that it became an easy way to make myself feel like I was taking care of him the way I should, the way that would make my parents proud. It looks like I'll be adding 'touching his forehead every morning' to that list.

For his current fever I put a small dose of cold medicine in his nutrient bag. If that doesn't do the trick, I'm not sure what else I can do. The days of going to the doctor are long gone. The last hospitals shut down more than a decade ago. The last doctors did what everyone else did: fended for themselves or went south to join one of the group communities. Everyone panicked the day, years ago, it was announced the county hospital was finally closing its doors. No one thought they would be able to care for their loved ones without professional doctors and nurses around. But not much really changed after the hospital staff quit. People found ways to care for the ones they loved. That's what people do. I probably would have gone to the hospital to have my ankle x-rayed, almost twelve years ago, after missing a step on the way down to the basement. The shooting pain near my foot made me sure something was broken. Instead, I simply iced it and took aspirin. It was back to normal two weeks later. And I probably would have taken Andrew to see a doctor a few years back when I accidently dropped him while moving him from his wheelchair to the sofa. There was never a sign of a bruise, though, so I think Andrew was most likely fine as well. I didn't even know what kind of test I would have asked the doctor to give my brother. It's not like they would have randomly performed x-rays on each part of his body until I was satisfied with the results.

Dropping Andrew that time and not seeing him flinch was a reminder of the tests I used to give him to see if I could elicit a response. There were times growing up, and again after my parents passed away, when I would think of little things to do to see if Andrew could understand something I said or did. During the first years of the Great De-evolution, a small percentage of the new-born children were partial Blocks, a state that left them with normal minds trapped inside useless bodies. They couldn't move or talk, couldn't even blink on command, but a battery of tests revealed they had fairly normal brain activity. These were the bourgeoisie of the Blocks, still motionless, but superior to those with little or no brain activity. Some of these children had microchips inserted into their brains so a small computer could translate their thoughts into words and phrases. Everyone in those days held hope that if their child was going to be a Block, at least it might be a Block with an active mind. They were grasping at straws, but I guess it gave parents the hope they needed to get through difficult times. A lot of parents in those days just wanted to feel like their baby was a continuation of them, not a mannequin with a healthy heart and lungs.

Those partial Blocks only appeared in the first couple of months, and only sporadically, before quickly giving way to a hundred percent of the children being completely Blocked. My parents got irritated with me for holding out hope that Andrew could be one of the lucky few who might be able to understand the world around him. The doctors had already given him the entire range of tests to check for relevant brain activity. He failed every one. But there I would be, sitting on the living room floor, saying something to elicit a response from my baby brother.

One of my earliest experiments was simply yelling in front of him when his eyes were closed. Of course his eyes never gave the slightest flicker of recognition. Sometimes, just to see if he would smile, I held a bowl of ice cream in front of his face or, and I'm not proud of this, told him that doctors found a cure for being a Block. My parents would walk to the edge of the living room and tell me to leave him alone. If I was still conducting my immature experiments the next time they walked past the room, I was given more chores to do.

My father would come in my room on those nights and tell me why the tests weren't important. "Your mom and I love your brother for who he is. It doesn't matter that he doesn't talk or move. He's still our son. It doesn't even matter if he thinks or doesn't think. He's still the same person to us."

"But he can't even blink a 'yes' or a 'no,'" I said, as though that were a factor in how much or how little someone should be loved. My father took the type of deep breath that let me know I was lucky he didn't spank me. In place of stinging my ass cheeks, he walked away without saying anything.

The last time I spoke to my mother, before she went to sleep and didn't wake up, she told me that Andrew was a part of me and should be respected as such. She told me it didn't matter if my brother couldn't laugh at my stupid jokes (she didn't use the word stupid, I added that in) or play soccer with me in the backyard, he was to be cherished just the same. He was my parents' child. He was my brother. As the population got smaller and smaller and the other people I knew from my childhood passed away or moved to the final communities, Andrew was the one person who stayed with me.

My tests with Andrew didn't stop, though, just because my parents told me to leave him alone. They also didn't stop just because I got older, or because I appreciated him as my flesh and blood brother, which I do.

They usually started as part of the boredom that ensued during the one-sided conversations I had with him. Even something as simple as talking becomes a forgotten skill if you have no one to talk to. Sometimes, when I ask Andrew a question, the only noise that comes out of my throat is a slight croak. It sounds like I'm gagging on food before the words are formed. The idea of forgetting how to carry on a conversation or tell stories terrifies me. So I do all of these things with Andrew even though he doesn't understand my words, simply stares off into the distance. His gaze never moves from one spot on the wall to another unless I readjust his head. I like to think he appreciates having different things to look at, but of course he doesn't care.

The easiest of my tests with him was to ask a question and tell him to blink once for 'yes' and twice for 'no.' Needless to say, the doctors' tests were much more complicated and reliable. I always held out hope, though, that their tests were wrong. Maybe the same disease that came over him when he was still in the womb would release its grip as he got older. That was what I tried to convince myself of, although I had no reason to think that would be the case. I'm sure the majority of families held the same hopes for their Blocks. The casual tests on Andrew stopped about thirty years ago when a hopeful breakthrough turned into humiliation and heartbreak.

The night of my final test with Andrew, I asked if he was doing okay. It was the question I asked him more than any other. I never expected a response; it was just something to say before I started rambling. But on this night he blinked when I asked the question. I barely noticed it because I was so used to non-responses or to blinks that didn't mean anything.

"Andrew?"

He blinked.

"Can you hear me?"

He blinked.

"Say yes."

He blinked.

"Say no."

He blinked twice.

I must have screamed and jumped. Miracles were possible! I was out of breath and gasping. Andrew still couldn't move his arms or legs or open his mouth, but he could talk to me with his eyes! He could answer my questions. He could give me someone to spend quality time with. Suddenly, I was presented with someone who could offer advice. He blinked again. Eager to know what he was saying, I asked what he wanted. An inkling of doubt crept into my head, and I found myself holding my breath until I gave the next command and got the next response.

"Say 'yes.'"

There was no response.

"Andrew, say 'yes.'"

He blinked twice, then three times.

And that was it. A moment later he blinked one more time, then shut his eyes for an hour. There had been no rhyme or reason to any of his blinks. It was dumb luck, or, not really luck at all, but me engaging in dumb behavior that eventually mimicked progress. In the end, it was no different than if I had given him a deck of cards and kept guessing which card would be next until, by sheer coincidence, I managed to get three in a row correct.

I always tried as much as possible to keep from being upset in front of my brother. Any time I got mad or frustrated, I went back to my room, shut the door, and turned on music so he wouldn't be able to hear me curse. I knew he couldn't hear me anyway, that turning on music wouldn't make a difference. That night, though, I cried right in front of him. I cried and cried, realizing that the momentary flicker of hope not only made me feel foolish, but reminded me how ashamed my parents would have been of the test in the first place.

After that episode, I stopped sheltering Andrew from my outbursts. The next time I got mad, probably from bumping into a doorframe or dropping a jar in the kitchen, I screamed curses as loud as my old voice would let me. I said every four letter word I could think of in every random order I could think of. There was no apology following my outburst, either. Instead, I walked straight past him to my bedroom and slammed my door.

Slowly, as I grew up, I learned to give Andrew the

attention my parents would have wanted me to give him. Sometimes, when I walk past him, his eyes are open; other times they are closed. It has nothing to do with the environment around him. I can walk past the living room in the middle of the day and his eyes might be shut, just the same as when I walk past in the middle of the night and see him sitting there with his eyes open, staring blankly at an empty wall. I find myself acting as though he's awake or asleep depending on his eyes. There's no difference between the two states, but it makes me feel like he's being given the care he deserves. When I was younger I would even lay him down if his eyes were closed so his sleep resembled normal sleep. My sore back has put an end to that, though.

December 12

Andrew's fever broke yesterday. There's no telling if the medicine I put in his nutrient bag did anything to help or if it was his immune system that finally fought off the cold. To me, the strangest thing about the Blocks has always been that they have regular immune systems and their organs and circulatory system function the same as normal adults, they just don't think or move. Having a healthy immune system is the cosmic joke of the Block's life because it preserves them and keeps them healthy while their lack of mental development keeps them reliant on regular people. Blocks are just like me, except I have free will while they are stuck in motionless bodies with minds that never learned how to process the things going on around them. Andrew has no idea if it's summer outside or if we're in the middle of a blizzard. Unlike every other animal throughout history, he has no ability to adapt. Even a tree's leaves can change color. A flower gives off an irresistible smell. These things further their cause, keep them abundant. For Blocks, it's almost as if nature has said, "Okay, your time is up. No more evolution for you; you've done enough."

The average Block's lifespan is roughly ten years less than a regular adult's. This is primarily because it's not possible for them to exercise the way normal people can, and as a result their hearts aren't as healthy. The timing is a cruel joke: all of mankind will grow old and die at nearly the same time. The last stragglers may live a year or two longer than the rest of us, but there won't be a scenario, like in the movies, where a man wanders the barren land for twenty years as the last remaining member of our species. Who would want to do that anyway? If you gave me the choice between living here for another twenty years after Andrew dies or dying the next day, I would want the latter. My days as a survivor would be spent by myself, re-watching the same movies I currently watch with Andrew. Each day would have one purpose: get through it so I could wake up the next day. Without Andrew, that wouldn't be enough.

At least the weather is of no concern in our ability to keep going. It's probably colder outside now than it will be any other day of the year, and yet it only feels like winter because the calendar says it is. Like the weather in the final settlements, our winters here are nowhere close to what you would find in Chicago or Boston. New Englanders would have laughed at what we call winter. A sweater over the top of my regular shirt is enough to keep me warm. I put a blanket over Andrew's shoulders, even though he has no idea he might be chilly. I think about what it would be like to take care of him during a blizzard if we were living further north. The trash would pile up in my basement until the weather cleared and I could go outside to use the incinerator. If the heater broke, no repairman would be around to fix it. I'd be stuck in the middle of a white, barren wasteland.

Because of this, New England might be void of people already. Probably is. It's hard to imagine anyone being able to survive the winters there on their own. The majority of people were inclined to stay in large groups as the population declined. People in the suburbs packed up their belongings and found vacant apartments in the city in order to join other people already there. That's how Camelot came to be a ghost town.

At the same time, people left unfavorable environments, anywhere with snow and ice, in favor of warm weather cities further south. Florida went from being the punch line to every retirement joke to becoming the lasting image of salvation. Maine and New Hampshire were immediately returned to the wilderness, then

Vermont. I have no idea how many people decided to rough it out on their own by staying where they were. Iowa is probably void of human life. Maybe South Dakota has one man living in a log cabin with his Block brother. There's no way of knowing, just the same as there's no way for them or anyone else (other than the Johnsons) to know I'm out here in abandoned Camelot.

The group community in Boston failed when a blizzard overwhelmed the inhabitants there. A party from the New York collective went up to Boston the next summer. No one was alive. I've heard stories that the same thing happened to the Minneapolis collective, and that the Chicago search party not only didn't find survivors, they didn't find anyone at all. It was almost as if the last remaining Minnesotans simply vanished. I'm not sure if I believe those stories—I don't want to believe them.

Washington and Idaho were affected the same way New England was. People left the suburbs, gathering in Seattle and Spokane first. Then, when their numbers began to dwindle there, the cities were completely abandoned as the people joined up with the community in Portland and Twin Falls. Those communities eventually moved down to join the people already gathered in Los Angeles and Reno. When the Chicago community packed up, it joined with the people in St. Louis. That community ended up joining with the Little Rock community and then again even later with the one in Dallas. The Dallas community is one of the few that still exists.

The journey down to the southern states created one of the enduring images of my life. The very last issue of *Time* magazine ever produced had a cover image of a caravan leaving Winnipeg as it made its way down to Omaha, with the caption: 'Picture of the century: the beginning of the end.'

Each time a group community moved further south they took their Block relatives with them. News reports showed thousands of Blocks being transported in a line of buses stretching for miles on their way to new homes.

Only Philadelphia reacted differently. The people there let their fears get the best of them, or just didn't want to be burdened by people they reasoned weren't really people at all, people who never understood their surroundings or contributed to the efforts going on around them. Some of these people tried to claim the Blocks might get them sick even though the condition wasn't something you could be infected with. They also claimed it was too much of a burden on the outnumbered regular adults to take care of them all.

So instead of taking them to Washington when Philadelphia was abandoned, the Blocks were loaded into a stadium that was then burned to the ground. The evening news provided footage of the fire. The smoke cloud, impossibly big, continued skyward as if it would go right into outer space. The smell of burning flesh was so great that even people ten city blocks away from the stadium were vomiting in the middle of the street.

The anchorman took his reading glasses off before telling his audience: "Reports say that as many as 100,000 Blocks were burned alive in that fire."

No firemen rushed to put out the blaze. Smoke was still pouring into the sky days later when the buses were loaded and the Philadelphians finally departed for Washington. The stench of burned remains seemed to travel with the caravan as it made its way toward the capital. As the long line of buses approached their new home, they were greeted by a blockade and by protestors holding up signs. One of the messages read: *Make love, not fires.* Another said: *You can't drive away from your shame.*

Refused shelter, the Philadelphians were forced to return to the city they had left. A news crew was waiting for them. Footage on that night's broadcast showed men and women crying, not because they were happy to be back home, but because smoke was still rising from the remnants of the fire. And these people could do nothing but look at it and remember what they had let happen.

The anchorman stared into the camera before saying, "Like you all, I am truly saddened to witness a group of people who thought genocide was a better alternative to the burden of unfortunate souls."

As these reports played on the news each night, I thought about Andrew being one of the people in that stadium, packed shoulder to shoulder with strangers he had never seen before. And even though he couldn't smell the gasoline, wouldn't be afraid, wouldn't even understand the simple concept that he was in jeopardy, he was a human being and the last family I had. If he was going to burn in some gigantic man-made structure, I didn't deserve any better. I would have been there with him if it came to that.

I know Andrew can't hear me. I know he has no idea who I am or even that I exist. But on that day, seeing the footage of the smoke rising from the Philadelphia stadium, I sat on the sofa next to him and wrapped him in my arms. I found myself apologizing for all the times I cursed the hassle of taking care of him. I apologized for thinking life might be easier sometimes if he wasn't here. Without him I would be just another man living my final days in New Orleans or Miami without someone next to me that I love.

December 13

I'm able, most days, to make it through the waking hours without going to the window to see if the Johnsons have returned. It's taking a while for it to sink into this old man's skull, but I'm finally realizing they are truly gone. I still hope they return, however, I no longer expect they will.

Until they left, the Johnsons had been doing the exact same thing with their two Block sisters that I'm doing with Andrew. Mark and Mindy were always taking care of their helpless twin sisters. It was a comfort to know they understood exactly what I was going through: changing Andrew's diapers, giving him baths, inspecting each bug bite to make sure it wasn't the beginning of some infection.

In some ways I think I'm the lucky one for not having another regular family member around to see what life has come to in these final times. The other part of me, the part that talks to myself for hours on end, the part that wakes up in the morning wishing for nothing more than another person with the power of speech to converse with, wishes dearly for someone who could answer my questions, laugh with me, recount stories of the old days, and explain the ending of *2001: A Space Odyssey*. Nothing would make me happier at this moment than for someone to appear and begin talking to me. Their words would be better than the best Christmas present I have ever received, each sentence better than the lasagna I had the other night (there I go again, always mentioning the lasagna!). The Johnson's departure must be affecting me more than I thought.

In my defense, though, they lived next to me for the last four decades years, from their forties to their eighties, so having them here one day and not the next should be hard to get adjusted to. For forty years their house was a venue for parties and cookouts. Now it's just as silent as the other houses on the street. They probably decided that a group community was their only option to ensure they were all taken care of if something happened to one of them. Mindy would be overwhelmed if Mark died and she was left to take care of her two Block sisters by herself. If Mindy died and Mark was left to take care of them, he would lose his patience or make a dumb mistake and their house would burn to the ground.

I've considered a shared community too—considered it so many times I might as well have gone—but something has always kept me here with Andrew where we've spent most of our adult lives. This is the home we've made for ourselves. Maybe that's enough of a reason. It's entirely possible that at this point in my life I'm not thinking altogether clearly. I accept that possibility too.

On the days that joining a group community does seem like a good idea, it's usually because I have Andrew in mind. I want someone to be there for him if I die first. The one time I actually put serious thought to leaving the neighborhood, I got stuck trying to make a list of what to take with us. It can't be easy for anyone to choose which possessions they would rank as the most valuable; not many will fit into a car. The rest will be left behind to deteriorate into nothing. Would I be able to leave the family photo albums, even though they provide no practical value for our survival? I already know the answer. That's probably why I'm still here; there's no way I could drive away from this house knowing an album full of pictures of my parents getting married, bringing me home from the hospital, bringing Andrew home from the hospital, would sit in the dank basement until the end of time. And if I did want to take the pictures, something else, something of actual value, would have to be substituted in its place. Maybe one less container of food, one less gallon of water.

It's a decision that makes the romantic in me smile. My mother would be proud. But it's also how I know I'm not capable of making decisions by myself. At least not the decisions that really matter.

The Johnsons and I took turns saying that our decision to stay or leave was made for us in large part by the roads that are no longer suitable to drive on. It was amazing how fast the highways deteriorated once the first cracks and potholes started appearing. One of the provisions in the Survival Bill was supposed to ensure the roads would last as long as people were around to drive on them. This was the least effective part of the government's plan. The resurfaced roads wore down within a decade, quickly becoming too deteriorated to allow most cars to travel safely. The Johnsons were fortunate to have an SUV. My little car wouldn't make it two miles on the old beat-up highways.

The last time I tried to survey the local area I got a mile before making a U-turn. I realized then that was the last time I would ever leave Camelot unless I was a passenger in the Johnsons' SUV. However, instead of sitting down and weighing the advantages and disadvantages of leaving, I did my daily chores until it was time to go to sleep. And then I did the same thing the next day and the day after that. It took a while, but eventually the decision was out of my hands. Life had decided for me.

If Andrew was alert, if he could have spoken to me, surely I would have discussed the options with him. The advantage goes to Andrew in that regard. If something happens to me, or if it doesn't, his life stays the same. He has no idea if I made the right decision or the wrong decision or if I made any decision at all. He stays on the sofa without talking or hearing, unaware of where he is, or even that he has a brother engaging in a daily struggle to keep going on day after day. All of this goes on around him and he never knows. It would be nice if I could be like Andrew and not have to worry about whether or not every decision I make is the right one.

Part of me says, I've stayed this long, I might as well stay to the very end. And anyway, what's the point of going to the last communities, since they too will be extinct in the coming months? The other part of me envisions Andrew starving to death after I've passed away. That's not something I can let happen.

And that's why I'm ready, finally, to leave Camelot. I've always assumed I'm the only living person around for miles, but that might not be the case. If the Johnson's just now decided to head south, maybe there are still others here too. The travelers don't seem to be stopping in Camelot the way they used to, but if I can signal one of them, maybe with a fire, they might come check on me, might see if Andrew and I would like to join them on their way south. If they're attempting the drive, they'll have at least an SUV or over-sized pickup truck, maybe even a tractor trailer. Surely, they will have enough room for two more people. The mild weather has kept me from needing to use my chimney, but I'll use it tomorrow to signal whoever may be around. I don't even care if we end up in New Orleans or Miami. I'm just happy to know someone will be there to take care of Andrew if I'm the one who goes first. Everything will be okay.

December 14

People held out hope for a long time that a cure might be found for the Blocks. This was partly because it was fairly easy for the scientists to determine why the Blocks' brains shut down. They were able to pinpoint the cause within two months of the Great De-evolution being spotted. Year after year, rumors of a new cure gave people hope. Each supposed cure was tested while everyone held their breath. Each solution failed. The scientists slowly got older until they began passing away too.

It's possible that there's still a man somewhere with a microscope and a set of test tubes who refuses to give up hope—that wouldn't surprise me—but I haven't heard of any such person, and even if he does exist, the cure is too late to do any good. We are simply counting down the days.

I can still log on to the internet and see how people are doing in Los Angeles or Dallas, but the news depresses me too much and I haven't bothered to do so in months. Unlike their work with the roads, the government's plan to ensure communications would be available has worked perfectly. The last time I checked there were still small communities located in San Francisco, Los Angeles, Dallas, Houston, New Orleans, and Miami; although, before they left, the Johnsons hinted that no one had seen or heard from the Houston community since October. They are probably gone, another vacant city returned to the wildlife. I'm not sure what kind of wildlife there is in Houston, maybe armadillos, but whatever it is, I'm sure they are thriving.

Each country handled the Great De-evolution differently. All reports indicate that Myanmar refused to acknowledge what was happening and had no resources in place when the population began to decline. The state-run hospitals were crammed with Blocks who outnumbered those willing to take care of them. Riots led to all of the hospitals being burned to the ground. The few hospital workers who managed to escape the flames whispered to reporters that the fires had been started by men wearing government uniforms.

A year after the Blocks started appearing, China changed its one baby law to a zero baby law. The Chinese government soothed tensions by promising the law would only stay in effect until a cure was found. The reassurances didn't prevent protests, but the law did result in a country without a population of Blocks outnumbering the regular adults. One country had managed to avert the crisis that every other country had fallen into. They still have a dying population, that can't be stopped, but the last regular adults aren't worried about taking care of their Block siblings. They aren't wondering who will die first and who will be left until the end.

In Norway and Sweden, Blocks were given every right afforded to regular people. They were allowed to vote, get driver's licenses, and sue whoever they liked. None of this ever happened, but the people there liked knowing their Block relatives had the right to do these things anyway. In Mexico, a drug cartel used the Blocks as drug mules, cutting them open and stuffing them with bags of cocaine.

In Spain, a single nun was taking care of more than one thousand Blocks by herself. She was eighty-three and the rest of her fellow nuns had passed away, leaving her as the only one left to handle all the chores. Seven days a week, from six in the morning until midnight, she walked up and down row upon row of Blocks, making sure each one had enough food and water, clean clothes, and a clean blanket.

Thousands of Blocks died together in India when a

group home was hit by a tsunami. Their caretakers all died in the flood too. In a few moments, that entire area of the world went from being occupied by thousands of humans, to being yet another part of Earth that no longer had a single soul. And so it goes.

December 15

It rained most of the day, which stifled the smoke coming from my chimney. No one will be able to save us if they can't see our signal.

Instead of being rescued by strangers, I spent the day emptying buckets. There are more leaks in the ceiling than I have buckets to catch the dripping water. I frame my memories by how many buckets were in the living room when an event happened. I know if something happened a week, a month, or a year ago depending on if there were twenty buckets, fifteen buckets, or three buckets placed around my house.

I thought Andrew had a fever today until I realized a new hole in the roof was letting water drip right on his face. The house has become too great of a burden. It's not much to ask of someone that they go from room to room emptying water as it fills each container, but it's too much for this old man. Everything, it seems, is too much for me these days.

After it rained, after the buckets were empty, I stared outside my kitchen window at the backyard, at the woods just beyond the spot where our property stops—or stopped, I should say, back when I had neighbors and everyone was careful about the boundaries of what was theirs and what was someone else's. If you had told my parents their kids would one day inherit hundreds of acres of neighborhoods, including a full eighteen-hole golf course and a derelict shopping center, they would have thought we had a winning lottery ticket.

The rain was enough to discourage the wildlife from roaming our streets; the predators stayed hidden the way they used to when Camelot was full of happy families. How long must it have taken for generations of dogs and cats, accustomed to the warmth and shelter provided by their masters, to accept rain and wind as part of their lives? Think about a Labrador and the first time it looked up and saw storm clouds gathering. Did it think to itself, what the hell is going on? Did it look up at the rain and wonder what it had gotten itself into, or was it happy to accept the wet fur if it meant it was truly free to do whatever it wanted without worrying about getting yelled at or slapped? The dogs could bark to their hearts' content without being scolded. They could piss on anything they wanted without fear of being locked down in the basement.

Life had to be a lot tougher, though, once dishes full of kibble weren't pushed in front of them twice a day. Were they skilled enough to hunt down squirrels and snakes, or did they turn into scavengers? A newborn lion watches its mother hunt in order to learn the tricks of the trade. What new habits did these trailblazing dogs and cats pass on to their offspring that hadn't existed in the previous generation? How long did it take for the cats to teach their kittens that hollowed trees were perfect places to sleep during the rain?

Five years ago, when not only the Johnsons were here, but two other families as well, I saw a deer burst out of the forest, its bucking hind legs resembling a stallion's, while a Maltese cat dug its tiny paws into the deer's flank and hung on like it was riding a mechanical bull. The deer kept jumping all over the place until it eventually hopped back into the forest. The cat was still clinging on for dear life (no pun intended) when they disappeared into the trees. An army of cats had been waiting there ready to pounce on the unlucky buck. The next time the deer jumped out of the forest, cats were all over it, bringing it down with sheer numbers and the persistence of animals that aren't playing with little toy mice for fun but are struggling to find food for their survival.

If I left a bowl of food or water out for one of these creatures, would it come up and enjoy the special treat, or would it sniff the bowl and wander back into the woods? If it did eat from the dish, would it let me come out on the patio with it while I drank my morning coffee? It would probably dart away, but if I spoke to it softly, would it let me reach down and pet it behind its ears? Would the animal even know it was supposed to like being petted? Or, more likely, would it think me strange for attacking it in slow motion?

I sometimes wonder what it would be like to have a pet dog. Would it sit at my patio door, barking all day and night at the wolves and bears roaming around outside? Would it wish it was outside with them? Would it think of Andrew and me as its family? If I fed it and rubbed its belly when it lay on the living room floor, would that be enough to override its natural instincts to view us as food?

Every once in a while I catch a whiff of something terrible in the air, the smell of sickness in the forest, and I wonder if it offends these former pets' sensibilities the way our old dog avoided the kitchen anytime my mom made sweet potatoes or the way it slept on the other side of the house each time my dad made a fire in the fireplace. Do the former house pets avoid the awful smells in the forest, or have they forgotten what it was like to have that luxury? Surely they know by now that if there is food to be had, even if it's near an offensive odor, they had better investigate right away before another animal takes it.

The thing that bothers me about this most recent stench is that it's not always there, which makes me wonder if my mind is playing tricks on me. Odors don't just come and go as they please. A lot has changed in the world, but smells don't just enter when they want and then leave after they've outlasted their welcome. If the odor was consistent I would at least know I wasn't going crazy.

Yesterday I was in the living room watching *Revenge of the Nerds* with Andrew when I got into a coughing fit. The smell of spoiled food or decomposing trash was there as soon as I stopped coughing. Five minutes later I realized the smell had vanished again. Can the wind do that? Can the breeze send a smell my way and then retract what had been offered? Some visual proof of the wind would have been nice, but the trees outside were motionless.

"Did you smell that?" I said to Andrew, a question usually reserved for after I've passed gas (no one is around anymore to tell me to act my age).

The smell didn't come back, but I couldn't get the thought of it out of my head. I've never been to a landfill, but that's the image that came to mind. I imagined a heaping pile of rotting trash with birds picking at the remains, bulldozers working the entire time to cover the huge pile of waste.

This is coming from the same guy who, a month ago, was sure he smelled rotten food in the refrigerator. I barely have anything in the fridge anymore since the processor can make fresh food whenever I need it. It's mostly used for storing leftovers. But even with a couple of bins of food stored in there, I was still sure I smelled something spoiled. Finally, I emptied the refrigerator, smelling each container as I put it on the counter. When I was done, the counter was full of plastic containers, the fridge was empty, and the smell had mysteriously vanished.

At the same time I smelled the pungent odor today, I swore a brown bear was roaming in the distance at the edge of the forest. It walked just in front of the tree line, never coming into the open of the community, never disappearing into the forest, always content to stay at the edge of both. It was clearly too big to be anything other than a bear. But then, right as it went into the shadows under a tree, the animal's outline combined with the darkness and vanished. It hadn't gone into the woods. It hadn't rested on the ground. It simply hadn't been. My eyes created the creature, let me follow it through three different yards, then simply stopped letting me believe it was there.

I need to get down to one of the final communities before I lose my mind and my brother is left with a raving lunatic. My fireplace will be going all day tomorrow. It's a matter of time until someone sees the smoke and asks if we would like to go south with them.

December 16

Each day my chimney sends smoke billowing into the sky, but each evening Andrew and I are still alone. Some days, I sit at the window, waiting for a truck to enter our neighborhood and save us. Other days, I try not to think about it too much, try instead to focus on whatever movie happens to be playing. *Don't panic*, I tell myself over and over. It doesn't work.

Each time I need more fuel for the fire, I scurry outside, gather up as many twigs and leaves as I can manage, and then sneak back inside before the animals catch wind of me. The collection does not last long, and I find myself scanning my yard for possible threats before hobbling out and getting another handful. If a bear is out there, or a wolf or a dog, I take apart one of my dining rooms chairs and burn that instead.

More and more of what used to be mine has reverted back to the animals. Already, I'm stuck in my house most days by the predators prowling outside. Recently, though, I have also forsaken my basement. The spiders and snakes rule that portion of my house. It might as well be considered a temperature controlled version of the outdoors, the first part of my house annexed back to the wild.

When I went down there today, spiders were crawling up and down the handrails and walls. Rats were scurrying from corner to corner. A giant black snake, the body of a full-grown rat still in its belly, lurked in the shadows. In the middle of searching for another book of matches, I felt something tap the back of my head. I didn't think anything of it at first.

Then it moved.

"God damn it!" I yelled.

I brushed the bug off my skin, then stomped on it over and over. I was out of breath before I stopped smearing it across the floor with my shoe, my violence a threat to the other creatures down there. A moment later, my attention having returned to the open box I knew contained additional matches, I heard a little chirp by my shoes. A rat was there, nibbling at the laces. That little piece of shit actually looked up at me like I was the inconsiderate one for letting out a yelp. I grabbed the matches and ran back upstairs.

It would be a cat's version of heaven if it ever found its way down there. The lucky kitty would have a smorgasbord to last for years.

I almost burned the entire house to the ground (exaggerating) one day last year trying to lift an old box of Christmas ornaments. Rats had eaten through the box's corners. When I lifted it, everything in the box emptied through the bottom. The rats, it turned out, had also snacked on the Santa costume my dad wore each year. I was furious and wanted to teach a lesson to everything living down there. Fantasies of taking a blowtorch to the entire area quickly popped into my head. I'll never lose myself enough, though, to forget Andrew is living on the floor above this madness.

If the house was big enough, I'd bring everything up from the basement—after disinfecting it and setting off bug bombs—and store it in the living room. The basement door would be boarded up and locked, the little specks of evil trapped down there for the rest of time.

Dread filled me as the logs in my fireplace started to burn out and I realized a second trip downstairs was necessary. The wood I've been putting in the fireplace doesn't last very long and I'm not fond of scavenging for twigs around my yard while the animals lick their lips. On top of this, I can only burn so much furniture before I feel like this place is no longer my home. Already I've burned two chairs, an end table, and a cutting board.

Substituting my old baseball cards will keep me from having to go outside as much. The cards, like stocks and bonds, rare art, and antique furniture, are completely worthless now, good for nothing more than sitting in oversized cardboard boxes that take up space in between stacks of photo albums. The players are all dead now, the last game having been played more than fifty years ago. Most of the cards have been picked apart by the mice and rats anyway. A Ty Cobb card couldn't be traded for a loaf of bread. A Stan Musial card is worth as much as if it were a mere blank piece of paper.

While down there, I rediscovered Mr. Lee's old safe sitting next to a box of cards. The Johnsons and I found it when we inspected his newly abandoned house for anything useful. I asked them if they wanted it, but they both shook their heads.

"What are you going to protect?" Mark asked.

His sister added, "No one is around to steal anything."

They were right, of course. No one new had come to the neighborhood in over two years and there were millions of abandoned houses to pick through. I took the safe anyway. It was something I didn't have, and it serves a purpose different from any of the other things in my house. A sticker on its door said it was both waterproof and fireproof. I guess a part of me liked knowing that, no matter what was happening around me, whatever I selected to go inside the safe would remain protected. Life has a funny sense of humor to give me the safe but nothing worth putting in it. I don't need to protect my birth certificate or social security card anymore. No one is around to steal my mother's jewelry or my father's coin collection. I ended up putting a photo album filled with my favorite childhood memories inside before locking it back up.

After coming back upstairs with a box of baseball cards, I pushed the old rag under the doorway to keep the bugs downstairs where they belong. It would be nice if I could create a similar blockade for everything lurking outdoors, something I could put around my property to keep the predators away.

Standing in front of the bathroom mirror to make sure no bugs were hiding on my clothes, my thoughts went back to my high school cap and gown, which were downstairs in a box between the safe and some family photos. The last time I tried it on, it still fit like a bed sheet, just like the day I graduated. I finished high school fifteen years after the first Blocks were identified and nine years after a hundred percent of new babies wouldn't be able to speak, move, or do anything for themselves. As a freshman, it was the norm to get treated like shit by the seniors. It was quite a bummer not to have anyone to do that to by the time I was a senior. Andrew would have been a freshman that year. If I saw anyone hazing him there would have been problems; no one gives my brother a hard time except me.

My graduation year was noteworthy for being the same year the world's population dipped back under six billion. At that point, twenty percent of people were Blocks. This was reported on the evening news as my family ate dinner, the anchorman saying it with the solemn voice saved for declarations of war or assassinations. My mother seemed to take comfort in the number of people in the world becoming more reasonable. She didn't say anything like that in front of my father, but you could tell she was slightly encouraged by the way she asked us if we would like seconds of the mashed potatoes. My father told us the world didn't feel any more vacant: the roads were still packed during rush hour, the lines still long at the post office. The comment was meant to comfort us.

Those were the circumstances in which I joined the adult world. Although there was a lot of uncertainty back in those days, my parents did let me go to the beach for senior week. It was tradition; they felt like they had to let me go.

The trip was supposed to be my final seven days of carefree life. My friends and I got drunk every night and hooked up with girls just as each graduating class before ours had, but there were also nights out on the sand where we passed jugs of wine up and down the line of friends while talking about the future. The ocean looked black in the night. Waves crashed against the shore while we spoke, causing some of what was said to be missed above the rush of water.

We said the same things that other kids had said during senior week—"You guys are the best friends I've ever had," and "I have no idea what I'm going to do with my life," and "this is our last week of freedom"—but all of these things had a different context from when previous generations had said them. Each time one of my friends said something like this, it made everyone else in our group tear up. None of us made fun of anyone else for crying; none of us even really understood why we were crying, except there was a sense that things would never be the same. Even Trevor Hohntz teared up. In tenth grade, I saw Trevor yawn after his girlfriend broke up with him. It was the coolest thing I had ever seen. And even he cried there on the beach that night. The rest of us didn't stand a chance of not crying.

The kids in our group who had older brothers and sisters told us how other years' senior weeks were different from ours: "The entire beach was packed with kids. Take our group and multiply it by a thousand. There were parties everywhere. Nobody was worrying about Blocks or the end of the world. My brother's greatest fear was getting caught for under-age drinking."

This made some of the girls in our group cry even more because up to that point they felt like they hadn't really missed out on anything, and now they knew that wasn't true. Only four or five years earlier, things had seemed so much more carefree.

Half of our group, myself included, had Block siblings waiting for us at home. We talked about what it would be like for them to grow up: "At least we have this week. My brother will never have a senior week of his own. He doesn't get to do anything at all. When I get back I'll show him all the pictures we took and tell him as many stories from the week as I can think of."

Each of us realized the tradition of senior week was ending there on that beach. But that was only one small aspect of our culture that was fading away as the Blocks began to outnumber the regular adults. A girl sitting across the circle from me sobbed until she had worked herself into a stupor and needed to go for a walk with her boyfriend. My girlfriend rested her head against my shoulder and I put my arm around her. No one snuck away to have sex on the beach. Talking about the future killed any raging teenage hormones we had.

Up to that point I had struggled with the decision of whether or not to go to college. Acceptance letters from each of my top three choices were already hanging on my bedroom wall. Each time a letter arrived my mom asked if that was the school I thought I'd like to attend.

"Mom, dad," I said, upon returning from the beach,

"I'm not going to go to college."

My father frowned, but didn't say anything. My mother squeezed his hand before asking me why I was having a change of heart.

I took a deep breath before saying, "Getting a degree doesn't matter anymore. Nobody needs lawyers or doctors. In a couple of years no one is going to need project managers or tax specialists."

I put my arm around my mom when I said these things. It was important to let her know this wasn't part of an impulsive decision, wasn't me lashing out to hurt their feelings for no apparent reason. Simultaneously, my mom and dad put their heads into their hands. Even then, even for parents who had grown up in different times, it was easy to see that setting a course for your future might be a wasted effort. Too many things were changing.

At the time, the number one book on the *New York Times* Bestsellers List was Steinbecker's "Mapping the Great De-evolution." Each chapter detailed the ramifications on society as the Blocks got older and the last generation of regular adults became senior citizens. Chapter 3 gave a forecast of what life would be like in five, ten, fifteen, and twenty years. The author posed a question to the reader: 'What good is excelling in the business world if the business world is quickly becoming extinct?' Many of the key institutions were already closing shop by that time: there were no more pre-schools or elementary schools, the final classes were being taught in high schools; in a couple of years the colleges and universities would be locked and no one would ever graduate again. The effects were filtering down to the armed forces, Wall Street, and every other facet of society.

"The military isn't recruiting new cadets. And most

companies aren't running internship programs anymore," I told them.

I saw my life as a road in which the end was too far off in the distance to see, and yet I knew there was a clear end somewhere off on the horizon. The same road has been there for everyone; the difference with the road I saw ahead of me was that mine had no forks in which different paths could be taken. There was one path ahead of me and one path only.

When neither of my parents said anything, I added, "My time will be better spent actually doing things rather than sitting in a classroom learning about doing things."

Steinbecker projected that by the time I was forty there would only be two billion regular people left in the world. When I was fifty there would be less then 500 million people left. (The numbers ended up being amazingly accurate.) My parents grumbled and sighed, but accepted my answer. Instead of sitting in a classroom, I spent a couple of years working on a road crew. I got to go all over the country building stronger and newer roads that were supposed to last until my generation was at the end of its time.

Years later, from her hospital bed, my mother told me that she had a long talk with my father the night I told them about my plans to skip college. My dad was having a hard time coming to terms with the decision. He told her how his own father was the first person in their family to get a college degree and how that was always the thing my grandfather was most proud of. He told my mom that he was equally proud of being the second generation of our family to get a college diploma. He couldn't help but be letdown that I wouldn't be the third generation.

She told him it wasn't my fault, just something that

had happened because the world was changing. He understood that, but it still upset him tremendously. My mother said she kissed his cheek before reminding him that she had never gone to college and she had turned out just fine. When he started to protest, she told him Andrew wasn't going to college either.

"I know that," he said and turned away from her.

Knowing her, she would have run her hand through his hair to sooth him. "It just gives the four of us more time to be together." She didn't have to say it was time together before the end.

After that night, whenever my mom saw my dad get frustrated or feel sorry for himself, no matter what it was that was getting him down, she went up to him and told him to appreciate the time the four of us had together. Neither of them mentioned college again.

Three years later, the four of us went to the final high school graduation in our town. My graduating class had three hundred kids. The final graduating class had twenty. None of us knew anyone graduating in that final and compact class, but it felt important to see the last ceremony, to see the last kid crossing the stage with a diploma. The Survival Bill was starting to pick up momentum in those days, so people were openly talking about the end as something that was not only to be accepted, but something to be planned for. All across the country the final high school graduations were being celebrated as an accomplishment that everyone should take part in. Fliers were handed out telling everyone, no matter how long ago they attended high school, to show up to the final senior class ceremony.

An empty field next to the school was transformed into an outdoor auditorium in order to accommodate the thousands of spectators. Balloons were stationed in every possible spot. There was free food. There was an open bar for the adults. Everyone was given a small plaque that marked the date and reason for being there. Door prizes were even given out. No amount of planning for the event to be a celebration, though, could override human nature. The festivities hadn't even begun yet when the crowd found itself grumbling about the armies of gnats and the oppressive heat.

The valedictorian was halfway through her speech when she said, "I'm not sure what the future will hold for our class, but—" and that made her break down in tears. Her parents started crying too.

In between sips of beer, a man in the rear corner of the field yelled, "They sure don't make 'em as smart as they used to!" and a fight broke out.

The next speaker, the principal, tried as hard as he could to remind everyone that the night was meant for celebrating an important accomplishment: "I've seen three additions built onto this school. It has enough room to hold twice as many students now as when I first started." He seemed to consider what he had said, then dabbed his eyes and walked off the stage without finishing his speech.

No one listened to the next speaker; everyone was in line for another drink.

At the end of the ceremony, per tradition, the senior class president invited the junior class president on stage to accept a symbolic key to the high school. There was, painfully, no one there to receive it.

A man in the crowd yelled, "Honey, you got stuck with a lot of book smarts and no common sense."

Another fight broke out.

December 17

The fire has burned itself out for the evening. Another day without being found. Tomorrow, the flames will be rekindled and once again send smoke into the sky. It's amazing how fast my possessions are eaten by the fire. Already, all of the nearby twigs are gone from outside my home, all of the smaller pieces of furniture from around my house are nothing more than ash, and now my collectibles are going up in flames. And still, no one has found us.

The fire goes out at night for two reasons. First, the chances of someone noticing the black smoke against the night sky are not good enough to waste what remaining items I have to feed into the flames. And second, everything I throw into the fireplace burns away too quickly for me to be there all night. I would have to awaken every thirty minutes if I wanted to keep the fire going. If someone drives by Camelot in the middle of the night, they will never know how close they came to saving us.

It's only after the smoke has finished drifting away from my chimney that I write these entries. It's only in the evening, when dinner is finished and the dishes have been cleaned, when darkness is the only thing outside my window, that I turn on my computer and start typing. Why is that? Do my daily struggles and worries need to follow me all day before I can digest them? Do I write about the things that worry me before I go to bed as a way to get it out of my system and have a clear mind before sleeping? It would seem like a good strategy to keep from having nightmares. It doesn't work, though. My first thoughts upon waking are the same as the ones I had when my eyes closed. And the time in between is spent having horrific dreams.

Hundreds of questions keep me restless at night. Is it too late to be rescued? Was the Johnsons' decision to leave better than my decision to stay? Did they make it to where they wanted to go, or did they get stranded halfway there and set up residence in another abandoned neighborhood? What would my parents have thought was the better course of action? Would my mother and father have the foresight to see which destination would give Andrew his longest and safest life? If something happens to me, is Andrew better off living out his last days on the sofa, or would he be better off surrounded by hundreds of other Blocks in a group home?

Perhaps my late night diary entries are the very thing keeping me up at night. They rub my face in doubt, force me to think about my worries. Maybe if I didn't sit in front of this computer and concentrate on what exactly was bothering me I would be able to ignore future problems. It could be nice to let them sneak up on me, to worry about them at the last minute instead of dreading them as they approach. I could go to bed believing my biggest concern is the leaking roof.

A lot of nights, my mind gets the better of me and I end up envisioning how silly I must look typing away on a keyboard—an old man's random ramblings. I'm much too old to be self-conscious. Gone are the days when I got nervous at the thought of asking out the girl I liked. But the silence around me, combined with my loneliness, makes me too aware of my circumstances. If the houses on either side of me were occupied with people throwing parties or having family dinners, I wouldn't feel so anxious being alone in front of my computer. Hell, I'd settle for quiet neighbors playing board games or reading books if it meant I wasn't alone in Camelot.

I fantasize about having a brother who can interrupt my thoughts by barging into my room with pointless banter. I'd act like I was irritated with him, but I would secretly welcome it. My problem—one of my problems—is that I have a brother down the hall, yet I'm still alone. Is it natural for people to put their thoughts and concerns on paper when they get to be my age, or is this something I do because I feel guilty about the way things are turning out?

A lot of my days are spent wishing I could have the same life my father had. He got married. My mother gave him love. He had children. There was always noise and activity in the house. In me, he had an apprentice, someone he could pass along all the things he knew. Each morning he woke up and went to a job he wasn't crazy about, but that offered him yet another constant through the years. It was all a man could hope for, and it's exactly what I yearn for now.

Instead, I have weeds. No wife. No children. Not even a job I would love to hate. Just weeds. Each time I look outside, the weeds have blotted out more of the driveway and the roads and everything else in their path. From my window, the street looks like it's covered in algae, however, I know that when I get closer, the green would begin to distinguish itself into thousands and thousands of individual stalks.

When I see the world as it is today, I'm glad Andrew is the only one here with me. I don't know what I'd do if I had a wife and children to protect. They wouldn't be allowed to play outside; they wouldn't know what it was like to go camping or even waste time in a tree house. I'd lose my mind if I looked outside and saw my son's baseball glove on the ground as the dogs dragged him, still alive and screaming, into the depths of the woods. What kind of life would they enjoy if they were trapped in a house with their father and an uncle who didn't talk or move?

I wish for a life in which I could have settled down with my childhood sweetheart, married her, had two or three children, watched them grow into young adults. I fantasize about being my son's little league coach and cheering louder than any other parent when he gets a game-winning hit. I find myself daydreaming about the interrogation that would take place the first time my daughter brought a boy over to the house. I'd scare that little bastard so bad he'd piss himself right in front of my baby girl. They seemed like stupid aspirations when I was a kid. Maybe I can just get back to the same frame of mind I had when I was twenty and didn't want to be tied down by crying kids or a nagging wife. I used to burst out laughing when my other friends talked about graduating high school and getting married. Get married? Why? But now, with wrinkled skin and no one to talk to except Andrew, I see the value of what I mocked.

That final high school graduation, many years ago now, might have been when the end was truly signaled, at least for me. It wasn't when all of the world's infants were born with non-functioning minds, it was when the other kids around me stopped worrying about what they would be when they grew up and began to focus on taking care of the masses of Blocks.

My mom used to sit by my bed when I was a boy and tell me that anything was possible; I could grow up to be anything I wanted if I just tried hard enough and never gave up. I wonder what kind of message I would tell my own son today—if I had one. It would be a lie to say any wish, any dream, is still possible. Aspiring to be President is pointless because the government disbanded. There are no more actors or baseball players to hang posters of in your bedroom. Astronauts are a thing of the past. As are firemen, lawyers, doctors, and everything else boys used to dream of being at that age when all of life is still ahead of them. There are no more occupations, there is only growing old. You can grow old in empty neighborhoods or in cities that used to hold millions of people and now only hold hundreds, but either way the result is the same.

If the glass is half full: I sort of understand what it's like to raise a child because I've had to take care of Andrew his entire life. I clean him when he needs cleaning, I put him to bed, make sure he's not cold, keep him healthy. There weren't, though, any of the first time experiences a father gets to go through that make fatherhood worthwhile. I'll never get to take Andrew to the bus stop for his first day of school. I'll never sit in the stands during his little league games. And I'll never see him get nervous before his first date. If there is a bright side to be found, I also won't have to go through him resenting me for making him do his homework before he's allowed to go outside and play. I'll never accidently overhear him cursing me under his breath for giving him an early curfew. I get an imposter's version of what it might be like to be a father. I feed Andrew, watch over him, give him shelter, talk to him all day. I get some of the experiences in disproportionate amounts while never experiencing other aspects at all. It's almost like a bad lifelong version of an April Fools' joke.

I have to remind myself that Andrew isn't a child, but my brother. I take care of him, but that doesn't define his life or my own. When you go without many people to talk to, you start forgetting what you really feel. You find yourself hoping someone else can remind you of who you used to be and who you're becoming. Maybe this diary will do that for me now.

December 18

A god damn snake tried to fight me today. The first few boxes of baseball cards didn't last very long, so I went down to get some more to use for fuel in my chimney. I should have known there would be trouble because I sat up last night listening to a mouse crying for help from under my feet. Who would have guessed such a little animal could wail in fear so loud? I wasn't able to find the mouse when I went down there today, it wasn't whining to be saved anymore, so I assume a snake finally flushed it out of its hiding spot and finished the job.

Maybe it was the same snake that attacked me. It wasn't content with attempting a simple striking bite; it wanted a full on duel where only one of us would be alive at the end. I gave a nice cat-like jump away from its strike. After my jump I was only two feet away from where I had started—in my youth it would have been five or six feet—but it was still more than I thought my old body capable of.

The snake moved toward me. When I backed away, it followed. I stomped the ground to let it know a large predator was in front of it, but instead of deterring the reptile, it got more aggressive and came right at me with its tongue firing in and out. It slithered at me faster than I thought a snake could move. I turned and ran back upstairs as quickly as my creaky knees would let me. That fucking snake slithered up the steps, one step at a time, until it was right on the other side of the closed basement door. As I collected my breath, I could hear it slithering there. Waiting. The snake was too big to fit under the gap between the floor and the door. With my foot, I pushed the towel back in front of the door. The snake remained there for a while to see if I wanted to give round two a try, then hissed and slithered off in irritation. I gave it the middle finger as it departed. I've never seen a snake act like that before. I guess all of the animals, not just the wolves and bears, want me for food. Or the snakes are mad that I'm slowly removing boxes from down there.

Without my baseball cards taking up as much space, the basement seems twice as big. I was able to get back into corners of the storage area I hadn't looked over in years. My dad's collection of beer-steins was in a box covered with spider eggs. A box filled with my mom's old sewing supplies was in a corner caked with rat droppings.

There are probably enough cards to last another week. If someone still hasn't found us by then, I'll switch over to my old comic book collection. One of the boxes I found today was of the last set of Topps cards ever produced. There were no rookie cards in that last set. All of the players had been in the majors for a decade by that point.

I watched that last game on TV with my father and Andrew. It was game four of the World Series. There was never another time, either before or after, when I saw my dad get as upset as he was that day.

The talent in those final years was vastly inferior to what it had been when I was a little boy; the youngest players were in their late forties. Most teams had a handful of players in their fifties. A relief pitcher for the Mets was sixty-one. The league had contracted to sixteen teams by that point, but the pageantry of the World Series still managed to make everyone forget the players' ages or that there were only eight teams in the American League and eight in the National League.

It was the third inning. The Cardinals' ace was on the mound. He hadn't allowed any hits yet. My father told Andrew and me that if any pitcher had a chance of throwing a no-hitter in the World Series it was him. A fast ball zipped past the batter for another strike out. And then, that batter walking back to the dugout and the next batter starting toward the plate, a puff of dirt exploded next to the pitcher's foot. No one knew what it was at first; the crowd's cheering had drowned out the discharge. The pitcher looked at his feet in confusion. He knew something had happened that shouldn't normally occur in the middle of a baseball game, but wasn't sure what it was or why it was happening. Then the pitcher's head exploded and his body dropped to the ground. The second bullet had entered through the back of his head and exited by his chin. Parts of his face were scattered across the in-field.

"No," my dad said with a groan. Just a simple "no" as if disagreeing with what just happened would stop it from having happened in the first place.

There was a moment of shock on the field as the players looked around for the shooter. A mad scramble for the dugouts ensued when they realized they could be the next person in the bullseye. Only the shortstop, the pitcher's best friend, stayed on the mound and held the dead man in his arms. There were no more bullets, though.

"Turn it off," my father said. I pointed the remote control toward the TV, but something kept me from making the screen go black. "Turn that trash off," my father said, so softly I could barely hear him.

When the screen went blank he got up and disappeared into his bedroom. My mother went back to try and comfort him. Even so, he didn't come out of his room the rest of the night. She told me later that he wasn't upset because the pitcher was murdered or that it happened at the World Series or even that it was on live television; it upset him that Andrew and I would never be able to have the same kind of awe he had for the game when he was our age. That shot had signaled the end of any hope that we could have the same life, the same possibilities, afforded to my dad. Everything that was great about America's game was gone after that.

Police caught the pitcher's killer later that night. More accurately, he turned himself in after climbing down from the stadium rafters. His job as part of the field crew allowed him to carry an uninspected duffle bag into the stadium. He took it up into the recesses of the ballpark where he assembled his sniper rifle. Reporters were waiting outside the stadium when police escorted him into the backseat of one of their cars. A reporter asked the man why he killed the pitcher. The man turned to the woman holding the microphone and, starting to cry, said he had five children at home, all of whom were Blocks. None of them would ever be able to watch a baseball game, let alone play little league.

"That's not fair," the man said as he was ushered into the back seat of the police cruiser.

At first they talked about playing the rest of the game a week later. Then they talked about finishing it at the beginning of the next season. But after the shooting, after hearing the shooter's motivation, everyone suddenly seemed to notice how old the players were and that with only sixteen teams it wasn't the same as it had been before. They didn't bother playing any more games after that.

December 19

The major airlines were all shut down by the time I graduated high school. To get overseas you had to know a pilot who also had a reason to want to fly across the world, or you had to know how to fly a plane yourself, or be crazy enough to give it a shot even if you didn't know. Private planes were actually more difficult to steal than the giant 747s left at airport terminals because the world's billionaires locked their planes inside steel hangars while the colossal jumbo jets were left at whatever gate they had last arrived at before the airline and airport both closed. Each closed airport was supposed to have at least one security guard patrolling at all times, but sometimes they didn't show up, and even if they did arrive for their shift, they really didn't care about preventing someone from taking a plane.

Every couple of months there was a story on the news of a plane either not taking off correctly and exploding into a nearby field or randomly going down in the ocean when the fuel ran out. These accidents were almost always the result of people wanting to get back to family members living in other parts of the world. You would be surprised how many people attempted to take off from the abandoned airports, having little or no experience actually flying an aircraft, because they thought the plane would basically fly itself.

It was for this reason that I never went to Europe to see the Eifel Tower or Pantheon, never went to Africa to see the pyramids or Mount Kilimanjaro, never trekked across Asia to see the Great Wall or the Taj Mahal. Never, really, did I go anywhere. Not even up to Canada or down to Mexico. My parents always told me I wasn't missing much, but their honeymoon had been spent travelling all across England, France, and Italy, so I knew they were only trying to spare my feelings.

The one time I did leave home, other than for senior week or other random trips with my friends, was the two years I spent on the road crew. My time supporting that aspect of the Survival Bill took me all the way out to Washington State, all the way up to New York City, and all the way down to Texas. I zigged and zagged across the country wherever they needed the roads fortified.

Spokane was a lot nicer than I expected. Being used to mostly flat grounds and fields, I immediately fell in love with the mountains in the distance. Each time we were due for a day off I tried to get one of the other guys to go hiking with me. But no matter who I spoke to they all said they were exhausted from paving roads for six days straight; their idea of fun wasn't walking around in the wilderness with sore feet all day. They would rather, they said, get drunk and pass out.

In Chicago, most of our time was spent repaving the roads leading south out of the city. We never paved roads in any other direction, only south. All of us knew this was because the city's population would only want to head in one direction once the city was abandoned and they joined up with another community further down the road. By the time we arrived there, Wrigley Park had already been converted into a group home for Blocks. Without security guards, anyone at all could walk right in and go wherever they wanted. Of course, that was how I spent my day off. But when I got to the field, instead of seeing the pitching mound and home plate, I saw hundreds of Blocks lined up across the entire ballpark. A massive tarp was tied from the stands on one side of the stadium all the way to the other side. This was to keep rain from landing directly on the bodies. The famous homerun wall was void of its ivy and moss. In its place were hundreds of messages spray-painted by vandals. Some of the graffiti mentioned Block sisters who were supposedly sluts. Other obscenities explained exactly why God hated the Blocks, and still other messages said the Cubs sucked. None of the volunteers bothered trying to remove the graffiti; none of them even seemed to notice it.

In Dayton we came across a bridge that was only half completed. Intended to cut down on commute times, it connected two different suburbs leading into the city. Construction had started right before the Great De-evolution began and then quickly stopped. Even without being told, I could guess the reason why the bridge had a basic frame in place but stopped halfway over the water: everyone started thinking, "Why build a bridge to cut down on our commutes if we aren't going to be here much longer?" So instead of finishing the bridge for them, our road crew repaved the path heading south, and the bridge forever stood half complete and half open.

We never bothered with side streets and auxiliary roads when we arrived at our assigned cities. Each job we started was for the major highways running in and out of the city. We saw neighborhoods similar to Camelot off in the distance, but we only ever paved roads like 95, 495, and 66, the roads that would get the most people going where they needed to go. In almost every city we went to we found people parking their cars on the exit ramps of these major highways. For these people, the people who still had to travel but no longer trusted the integrity of most roads, it was easier to park their cars on the exit ramp and walk a mile or two home than it was to get a flat tire every day. In the time it took to change a flat tire, they could already be sitting on their sofa. And anyway, the supply of spare tires would eventually run out, so why tempt fate?

I got to see the Rocky Mountains and part of the

Appalachian Trail. I got to see the Grand Canyon and the Mississippi River. But although I got as far as Spokane, the road crew I was attached to never went out to Seattle. Nor did they go south to California. I've heard the Pacific Ocean looks exactly like the Atlantic, that if you've seen one ocean, you've seen them all, but I would have liked to discover that for myself. I've seen pictures of Mount Rushmore, but never had a chance to see the faces on the mountain in person. I tell myself I saw more than most people in my generation got to see, but I can't help but think of all the places still out there. Las Vegas and Boston. The California beaches. But at least I got to see some of it. And, I tell myself on the nights when I can't help but think about the rest of the world out there, Tokyo is probably a lot like New York, and the French Riviera is probably just like Ocean City. And so on.

And on the nights that doesn't help, when I still feel like I never truly got to see what the world had to offer, I think about Andrew sitting on the sofa and how he got to see even less than I did. I'm comforted to know that, while I might not have gotten to see the Sphinx or float down Venice, I did see some things. And for the rest, Andrew and I have our movies to take us anywhere we want.

December 20

My yard has no more twigs or sticks. And I certainly won't be stepping into the forest to get more firewood. That would be suicide. All of my dining room chairs have been disassembled and burned, as have my small end tables. My baseball cards are almost gone. In the fire today went my set of 1984 Topps. I threw a handful of cards in at a time. While they are worthless now, I still wasn't able to see my Don Mattingly or Daryl Strawberry rookie cards go in the fire. I set them aside on the end table to be preserved. I did the same with my Bo Jackson and Greg Maddux rookie cards the other day when I set fire to my sets of 1987 Donruss, Fleer, and Topps. The rookie cards do absolutely nothing for me these days except remind me of how happy I was collecting them as a child. When the last of my cards are burned, I'll start burning Andrew's collection. Growing up, each time my parents got me a set of cards for my birthday they made sure to get Andrew an equivalent set for his birthday. The same year I got the 1983 set of Topps, they gave Andrew the 1982 set. When the time comes to burn that box, there's no way I'll let Andrew's Cal Ripken Jr. rookie card go in the flames. I'll set it aside with the small stack of other cards I'm keeping.

Soon, I'll turn to our collections of old comics. Boxes of *Uncanny X-Men* and *Amazing Spiderman* comics will go up in flames. Although I hate to see my childhood collectibles shrivel to ashes, I'm actually quite pleased with the result. One of the chemicals in the baseball cards, maybe the colored ink, gives off a thick black smoke while it burns that the wood wasn't producing. A smoggy version of a lighthouse lingers in the air above my home. Anyone travelling south in the vicinity of Camelot will see the smoke and know Andrew and I are here, ready to be saved.

It will have to happen soon. I don't know how Andrew and I will make it through another year. If the swarms of animals don't get us, old age or sickness will. While my brother has a fever every other week, my old body is growing too feeble to move him to the bathroom when he needs to be cleaned. Burning trash in the incinerator takes me twice as long as it used to. Please let someone find us soon.

All those doomsday movies had it wrong the entire time. Each one that came out through the years imagined a young man or a small group of men wandering the earth in search of another pocket of civilization. Even after the nuclear war or plague or whatever it was that wiped out most of Earth's population, a few still existed here and there. During their travels they always managed to run into attractive young women. They also managed to find evil gangs who thought ruling the few remaining humans was a good way to spend the last years of their lives. How difficult it must have been for the people writing those movies to think of a time when humans wouldn't exist at all. Even in the far corners of their creative, inspired minds, they couldn't think of a scenario where <u>every</u> man was wiped out, just most of them. There always had to be a survivor. Maybe this simply spoke to the optimism of the men writing those screenplays; even with an uncomfortable sci fi plot they had to subconsciously comfort themselves by thinking that at least a hundred people would survive. Someone has to survive.

December 21

When the Great De-evolution began and traditional jobs started vanishing, my parents thought that leaving the city and moving back to the country was the prudent thing to do. Housing prices were already beginning to plummet in the northern states. This was before the housing market vanished completely and you couldn't sell an empty house for the price of a loaf of bread. The fear-mongerers were already calling for the end of the world, saying it was only a matter of time until riots and war broke out and disease and starvation ran rampant. The evening news was filled with these pessimists saying the same thing every night. They were completely wrong: there were never any riots, there were no wars. There were just families wanting to get by as best as they knew how.

We lived, the four of us, a couple of hours north of here until my parents passed away. There wasn't much to it really. We found my father on the ground in the backyard with the lawn mower still running. Heart attacks ran on his side of the family. My mother was already chronically coughing by that time. A year later she died of lung cancer, even though she had never smoked a single cigarette. That was about forty years ago. Andrew and I moved here shortly after, and have lived in this house by ourselves ever since.

Other than the two houses we grew up in with our parents, this is the only house I have ever lived in. Vacant houses were already free of charge by the time Andrew and I moved here, with everyone heading south having the understanding that anyone else could walk right in and start living in their old home, and knowing, too, that they could do the same thing in any empty house they happened to find during their travels. Travelers knew an empty house as soon as they saw it because the mailbox flag would be down. If the flag was up, it meant people were living there already. My own mailbox flag has been standing straight up every day for the last two decades, even though mail stopped being delivered more than twenty years ago.

It was a courtesy during the southern migrations that vacated houses remained unlocked for possible newcomers to take their spot, but if the vacating family was animal friendly they sometimes left their doors open as an invitation to former house pets to enjoy the comforts of a roof again.

I never bothered to ask my new neighbors who the previous owners were or where they had gone. That was the type of question that could only lead to them planning their own departure. No one wanted to be reminded that their new golf community had already started transforming into a ghost town before construction was finished on the final row of houses in the far corner of the development.

And anyway, it was easy enough from the leftover possessions still scattered around the abandoned house to piece together exactly who had lived here prior to my brother and me. Nobody would take the time to package up everything lying around their home, load it into a moving truck, and make sure the house was clean for the next family. Only the most essential items—clothes, food, Block relatives—were valued enough to fill a van with. Leftover were boxes of Christmas ornaments and gardening tools, old magazines and scribbled-on calendars.

As I walked around the house that first day, I found images of a mother and father and their two children. Like my parents, this couple also had one normal child and one Block. The married couple's courtship was recounted in a box of love letters left behind in the attic. The mother's journal said what it was like to finally have the first of many children she had always dreamed of. In later journals she shared her disappointment at having to stop after her second child, four short of the enormous family she had always wanted, because the second child was born without the ability to speak, move, or think. A box filled with military photographs showed a career officer who had never been sent to war, never had a chance to earn medals. The photos of their children showed them growing up from little kids to teenagers to young adults and then, like Andrew and myself, to middle-aged men. The parents' bedroom was still full of clothes. The shirts and pants wouldn't have been there if the parents had been alive when their two children migrated south.

Pictures of the parents and children were still hanging on the walls. The man had left with just his Block brother and not much else. It was impossible to think of this man as ever making friends with the other families on the street, and I couldn't help but feel our new neighbors would think of Andrew and me as an improvement from the pair of brothers who had lived there before us.

We settled in. A year later, the Johnsons moved to our street as well. The six of us—me pushing Andrew in his wheelchair and the Johnsons both pushing one of their Block sisters—frequently toured the neighborhood as the houses on our street became vacant. Each time we surveyed the houses, we walked with bats or golf clubs tucked into the back of the wheelchairs. They were necessary instruments on the days we came across an animal, or a pack of animals, with the courage to attack a group of people.

Even when the neighborhood was still half full, it was common to see foxes that were no longer afraid of humans. Shortly after that, wolves were seen roaming for prey during the daylight hours. One of the few things I remember my grandfather telling me was that it was bad luck to see a wolf during the day because it meant your cattle were going to be killed that night—he either said that or that if you saw a wolf during the day it meant there was also a bear nearby. I can't remember which.

On each of these trips with the Johnsons we found a newly empty house that had once played host to a neighborhood cook-out or New Year's Eve party. Some of the abandoned homes were used as meeting places for everyone in the neighborhood to gather and plan for the future. Eventually, even the people who hosted these meetings disappeared. Some left in the middle of the night because they were ashamed to leave during the day when we could see them go. None of the families could be blamed; everyone had to make their own decisions on how best to care for their families. Some were sick and needed medical attention, others just needed the comfort of knowing they were moving closer to other people.

Now, with the Johnsons' house empty and Andrew and me growing older, I finally see the end that my first neighbors in Camelot must have known was coming all along. There will be a time in the near future when my house, maybe the last house occupied within a hundred miles, goes dark and joins the others. Hopefully, when that happens, I'll be heading south too, Andrew and me taking up space in the back of someone's truck.

Please, we need to be saved.

I stayed at the edge of my driveway for a while today. An invisible barrier, something other than the animals, kept me from walking down the street to the Johnsons' house. I told myself it was because I didn't want to leave Andrew for too long. That isn't true, though. The fear does linger that as soon as I leave him he'll choke on something, gain awareness and be frightened of his unfamiliar surroundings, or be attacked by an animal, but those thoughts don't keep me chained to him. The real reason I didn't want to go down the street was because it would crush me to see another dark, empty house. I don't want incontrovertible evidence that I'm alone, even though I know deep down that I am. The Johnsons' house is just as empty as all of the others, but until I see it with my own eyes I can't be absolutely sure. That's what I tell myself when I want to remember the feeling of being part of a neighborhood, to see men and women driving to work in the morning, coming home at night, taking their dogs for walks, and having barbeques in the back yard.

So instead of actually going there, to the Johnsons', I stared at their home from the edge of my property. At least they were considerate enough to turn off all of the lights before they left. The doors are probably unlocked too. Nobody locks their doors anymore, except in the group communities. Even if a burglar did see my house, I have nothing that he couldn't find in a hundred other homes down the street.

In the entire time I stood on my driveway I didn't hear a single man-made sound. As hard as I strained, listening for the rumble of an approaching truck on its way to save us, I heard nothing. The silence of abandoned houses and empty streets surrounds every corner of the neighborhood so it seems like Camelot was never really a genuine community that hosted hundreds of families, but some sort of studio prop for a failed movie, or a fake development made for an out-of-business amusement park.

When I was little I would lie on the grass at the edge of the driveway with my eyes open and look up at the clouds. Planes would roar in the distance, cars would go back and forth down the road, horns would honk, kids would yell and play, adults would talk about what the future was going to hold. Now, weeds, some as tall as corn stalks, have overtaken any spot where I could put a blanket down and lie and listen to all those sounds. Even if I could lie on the grass, I doubt my back and knees could support me when I tried to stand back up.

Other noises have replaced the planes and cars. Wild dogs bark, flocks of birds squawk, leaves rustle. Ah, the leaves. Without cars honking and TVs blaring, they rustle all day without much else to blot out their noise. They scrape against the ground until they form piles on the side of each house. Every year I see the start of a new tree growing from where the leaves hid an acorn. The side of the Thomas's house broke open because of a tree growing up along its foundation. It didn't take a single day before the house was reclaimed by the squirrels and deer and maybe even a bear. It's only a matter of time until a tree grows straight up through the middle of a house, its trunk coming out through the shingles like a chimney of leaves.

Although it makes almost no noise, the fire I have going creates a nice plume of smoke arcing into the air for a couple of hours each day. Soon, someone will see it, they have to, and Andrew and I will be heading south to join the others. I'm not sure how many people will be there at the group community. Honestly, I'm not sure what to expect at all—I half expect to run into the Johnsons as soon as we arrive at our next destination, an awkward silence ensuing as they try to explain why they left in the night. Different scenarios play out in my mind before I go to sleep. The possibilities are endless.

I checked on Andrew as soon as I came back inside today. I'll go and check on him now too; it's what I do after every entry I finish.

December 22

Andrew has a slight fever again, or the most recent fever never got better and he's been sick all this time. The medicine I put in his nutrient bag doesn't seem to do anything. I often wonder if the fever actually matters; does he feel any discomfort, or is he immune to it because he's oblivious to everything? In that regard maybe the Blocks might be an evolved version of us.

I had another nightmare last night. Gradually, as I have seen fewer living people over the years, bad dreams have become more frequent. In these nightmares I'm exactly like my brother. I watch the world going by all around me but I can't join in on any of it. Kids laugh and play while I'm motionless and quiet (my dreams usually take place back when I was still in school). I wake up having an idea of what it's like to be a Block. It's maddening, truly maddening, when people talk to you and you want to reply but you can't. You have so many things you want to say and no ability to say any of it. I always wake up in a sweat from these dreams.

December 23

I want to tell a good story about Andrew, something that would make my parents smile, something that makes him seem like my partner in crime. No matter how much I try, though, I can't think of one. Every story I think of involves him sitting to the side as a story of my life unfolds. It shouldn't be that way, but it is.

There was the time when I was twelve and I had a crush on Debbie from down the street. She used to come over and watch TV with Andrew and me. The two of us would sit on the living room floor while Andrew sat on the sofa behind us. In between shows I asked her if she would be my girlfriend and she burst out laughing. I think her exact words were, "You're gross." I asked why she was watching TV with me at my house if I was gross and she said she didn't have anything better to do. My face reddened. I wanted to yell at her and tell her I hated her. Behind me, Andrew stared at the TV as though nothing embarrassing had taken place. He didn't smirk at my misfortune the way a normal brother would. He didn't make a fart noise to break the tension. He only stared, the way he always stares. That didn't prevent me from venting to him for an hour after she was gone.

One time, when I was fourteen and struggling mightily with teenage life, I came home with a black eye after getting beaten up at school. All it had taken for me to get picked on was being smaller than another boy. That automatically gave this other kid enough reason to push me to the ground in order to impress his friends. I should have known better than to call him a stupid dick face after finally getting back up to my feet. The stupid dick face punched me square on my cheek, dropping me to the ground again. I still remember that asshole's name: Timmy Bockle. You never forget about people like Timmy Bockle. I ran home crying, and I was still crying when I got in the front door. My parents weren't home yet, but Andrew was sitting on the sofa. Instead of being ashamed to have my brother see me cry, I sat down next to him and sobbed until I felt better. He never made fun of me for getting beaten up. Not once did he hold it over my head by bringing it up the next time I was a brat. I think about the things I do for Andrew now, and nothing I do—changing his diaper, brushing his teeth—will repay what he did for me that day by letting me be upset, giving me someone to share my tears with without making me feel self conscious. For that, I'll gladly take care of him for the rest of his life, or mine, whichever comes first.

I guess if I had to relate this entry back to Andrew, which is what I intended when I started, I would tell the story of the Witherspoons' birthday party for their Block daughter. All of the Blocks in the neighborhood were invited. The parents and regular siblings were invited to "keep the other children company" so I went too. Tracy Witherspoon couldn't blow out the candles on her birthday cake or open her presents. She didn't even know it was her birthday or that her parents were throwing a party in her honor. All of the Blocks sat motionless in a giant circle of picnic chairs.

The thing that stuck in my head about the party was seeing Debbie, the same Debbie who said I was gross, holding hands with her new boyfriend and how it felt to have my feelings hurt again. I went up to her and told her she smelled like fish even though I didn't know what the insult meant at the time, had only said it because I'd heard some of the older boys saying it. She returned my insult by saying she was glad she turned me down because I was too short to be her boyfriend. The boy she was holding hands with laughed and said I would be more likeable if I was quiet like my brother. I wanted to fight him but had a sneaking suspicion it wouldn't end any better than it had with the stupid dick face. So I didn't do anything. The two of them stepped behind a tree in the Witherspoons' backyard to make out. I wanted to smash his face with a baseball bat. Instead, I walked away with my hands in my pockets and my dignity up my ass.

When I rejoined the party, however, I noticed all the Block children were still seated in the same general area of the backyard. None of them were making fun of each other. None of them were saying mean things or trying to ruin each other's self-esteem. In that moment, I was jealous of Andrew. Here he was, with all of these other kids around, and none of them would ever know what it was like to have their heart broken or be bullied. How great it must be to go your entire life without feeling ashamed or embarrassed because someone says mean things just for the sake of hurting your feelings. Blocks were enviable, not only because they went a lifetime without receiving these inhumanities, but also because they didn't know how to inflict them on their peers. What a nice thing it would have been if the older brothers and sisters of all these Blocks were as well off.

December 24

Hours after yesterday's entry, in the middle of the night, I dreamt that Andrew walked into my room and woke me up. Startled, I asked him what he was doing. In my dream I was irrationally alarmed that he was walking around in the middle of the night instead of, appropriately, being shocked that he could walk at all.

He stood in the middle of my room and said, "I remember that girl's birthday party. It was nice seeing everyone come together like that. And I remember that vacation we all went on when I was little, and how Dad held me above the water while the waves broke."

I tried to say something, but for once I was the one that couldn't talk. Andrew smiled, nodded as though satisfied with what he had come to say, then exited my room. My mouth was still wide open as he walked away, not a single word able to escape.

I woke up after that. When I went to the living room to check on him he was lying on the sofa in the exact same position as when I had left him. His eyes were open, so I turned on the lamp, brought one of our old photo albums over to the sofa, and began recounting the old days with him again. Page after page of photographs kept me laughing about something we had done as little kids. When I got to the end I closed the album and turned the light back off.

More and more of our nights are spent without music or movies playing. Andrew and I still sit in the living room, but it seems nicer to leave the TV and stereo off and tell him stories late into the night. Usually it isn't until his eyes randomly shut before I realize I can barely stay awake myself.

It used to be that I would only recount the happy

memories from our childhood: the time I hit the game-winning homerun in middle school, the time I got to meet one of my favorite actors, my senior prom. But now I find myself telling him—I won't say the bad parts—the less favorable stories I used to keep to myself.

I remind him about the time I accidently overflowed the toilet and tried to blame it on him. I'm still ashamed when I retell the story of putting a mouse in the refrigerator so it would startle my mom, but leaving it there too long, and how she found a dead rodent the next morning. I'll never forgive myself for how that mouse died, or for how I acted as though its wellbeing was something I could play with. Some of the stories I recite, like the one of the mouse, don't present me in the greatest light, but they were turning points in one way or another. And they each made me into the person I am today.

With the bears and dogs growing more aggressive every day, and with our health declining, there's a good chance Andrew might feel bad about his lot in life if he could understand the stories I tell. He never takes anything to heart, though. He sits there with a blank expression, unaffected by everything I say. He even sat that way when I told him that our father had passed away. The absurdity of the Blocks is that there will never be a single thing I can say or do that will make one of them gasp with shock or break out in a giant smile. They get to skip the bad parts of life, but they also miss the good parts. Life is neither pleasant nor depressing for them; it passes them by as though everything were a completely neutral shade of grey.

It forces you to ask what the point of their lives is if they can't participate in their existence. Why would nature create life that can't interact, can't do anything? The Blocks are like flowers or trees: they hope for food and water but are unable to ask for either. The end result of their life is completely out of their own hands—like us being found by someone travelling south.

I try not to think about it because I know it's out of my hands. Periodically, throughout the day, I find myself forgetting to keep the fire active, and I know that deep down I'm doing this because I doubt anyone will ever come and find us. For Andrew's sake, I make myself get up and add something else to start a new fire.

December 25

Christmas. Where has the time gone? It certainly doesn't feel like Christmas. Each day takes forever for the sun to rise and set, but then I look back at the culmination of days and it seems like just last week it was still summer. It makes me wonder if Andrew has any perception of time or if his life is one never-ending day.

I am glad, though, that he isn't able to understand the waiting game we're playing. The baseball cards are gone. The supply of comics shrinks each day. Through it all, no engines have approached the community. I would thankfully spend Christmas in the backseat of a pick-up truck if it meant we were on our way to one of the final settlements.

My parents constantly reinforced the idea that Christmas was the most important family day of the year. There were times when my father had to miss my birthday, but he never missed a Christmas. Each year on my birthday, my mother made my favorite meal, but the portions of food she made at Christmas outdid anything she prepared the rest of the year. The bowl of mashed potatoes lasted us a month. The platter of stuffing was high enough to block my view of Andrew sitting on the other side of the table. Now, Christmas is a time for me to sit alone with my brother in silence. Jingles echo in the empty house to remind me of how alone I am. Listening to the carols is depressing, but it's even more disheartening to have silence, so when the CD gets to the end I push PLAY again and listen to it all over.

I used to make a present for Andrew each year. Sometimes it was a decorated picture of the two of us, other times it was a painting I made to give our house more color. Many of these are still hanging in Andrew's bedroom. I rarely take him back to his room anymore, however, so he never sees them. Layers of dust have collected on each one, turning the happy, vibrant colors into muted, historic-looking relics.

One Christmas Eve I found an abandoned kitten on our patio and presented it to Andrew as his present. He stared through me and through the kitten without any reaction. I took care of the miniature cat as best as I could. If I didn't, if I left it outside to fend for itself, it would be eaten by a dog before it ever had a chance to freeze to death. It dawned on me right away that I had almost no idea how to take care of a pet. Pets lost all of their charm sixty years earlier when the first generation of Blocks were old enough to resemble adults. The elderly were bogged down with taking care of thirty and forty year-old Blocks; they couldn't manage, or didn't want to manage, the additional responsibility of iguanas, parrots, hamsters, or something larger. Not many people wanted a dog if they didn't have children to offer as a playmate. Brothers and sisters who couldn't take care of themselves and needed constant attention took the place of needy cats.

It didn't take long for me to come to the same conclusion. Even with a litter box, that little kitten pissed and crapped all over my house. I cleaned up cat crap and then found more of the same in the next room. I gave it a second litter box but it preferred our carpet. Walking past the living room one day, I noticed it had peed on Andrew's lap. I petted the kitten one last time, told it I was sorry, and put it back out on the patio. I returned to Andrew and cleaned him off. When I went back to the patio door the kitten was already gone. I hated myself for knowing how helpless it was, not much different from Andrew when I thought about it, and for what I had let happen.

Each Christmas I still find myself thinking of that little kitten. Was it really so bad to have a kitten's piss around the house if it meant I was saving its life while also preserving a little bit of the earlier life I had known? When I was a boy I never would have put that kitten outside, left it to fend for itself. What's changed since then that now I am willing to?

I tried to think about the cat growing up to be full-sized, tried to reassure myself by saying it never would have been completely tame. It would claw at our furniture, maybe even claw at Andrew when I wasn't watching. It might even nibble on him when it got hungry and he was the easiest thing to snack on. In my heart, though, I know it was a tiny, defenseless animal that just wanted to be loved and taken care of, and I put it out to fend for itself, knowing it couldn't.

That was the last Christmas present I gave my brother. The past few years I've celebrated by making a nice dinner and going to bed early. One of man's last inventions was the creation of flavored nutrient packs for Blocks. Scientists said it didn't matter what the nutrient packs smelled like because the Blocks had no perception of taste or smell, and the food was pushed through a tube going into their arms, not their mouths. But the companies marketing the different flavored packs—turkey and gravy, primavera pasta, and birthday cake—tugged on families' heart strings. It worked. With nothing else to spend my money on in those final days of an organized economy, I ordered a supply of them and still give one to Andrew each Christmas.

The holiday has morphed into a final chance each year to celebrate your family's memory. Not many people bothered giving each other gifts because whatever was given would only bog you down or get left behind when you moved further south to join a group community. Sometimes I sit with Andrew and flip through old photo albums of when our parents were alive and we all spent Christmas together. I laugh when I get to the photo of my mom giving my dad a tie that she knew he would think was ugly. She was right. In the picture, you can clearly see him trying to give his best I-like-it-because-you-gave-it-to-me face, but you can see right through him. That tie is still down in the basement in a box somewhere. It will be one of the many things we don't have room for if someone sees the smoke coming from our chimney and comes to help us get to one of the final settlements. And then there's the picture of my mother sitting on the floor in front of Andrew as she opened his presents for him. No matter how many more Christmases Andrew and I spend together, that photo album will always come up from the basement, and I will flip through it and laugh about the times we shared when we were young and didn't have a care in the world. So in that regard at least, something did stay the same when everything else changed and got out of my control.

Merry Christmas Andrew, I love you.

December 26

The Great De-evolution and the resulting migration south were responsible for the appearance of a new phobia. Where people had once been claustrophobic or agoraphobic, more and more people became unreasonably afraid of not being near enough people. Even people who were in still-populated neighborhoods started panicking. The overwhelming sense held by these people was that a disaster could happen at any moment and they would be too far away from real civilization, whatever that meant, and they wouldn't have the social infrastructure around them needed to respond to a hurricane or earthquake, or in the case of Boston, a blizzard.

They packed up their belongings and moved to a more southern city just because it helped them feel secure. There weren't many benefits from living in Miami that you couldn't get in Camelot, but it made people feel better to be in large groups. I guess that's understandable. And, to be honest, it's probably that exact same fear that has driven me to look for a way out of Camelot. Now that the Johnsons are gone, I find myself afraid, just like the others were, that it's a matter of time until something bad happens here and I'll be stuck without the ability to take care of Andrew any longer.

Mrs. Lee from across the street was one of the most reserved people I knew. She attended every neighborhood cookout but she was always in the corner watching other people engage in conversation rather than participating herself. Then one night, as everyone was drinking beer and all the Blocks in the neighborhood were lined up in patio chairs so they could enjoy the outdoors as well, she asked the group nearest to her if they were worried about being stuck in Camelot when something happened. The group asked her what she thought might happen. She didn't have a clear answer. One of the people in the group said he felt as safe in their neighborhood as he would in a random city. A different woman in the group said she would rather stay in an area she was familiar with than live amongst people she didn't know. Mrs. Lee nodded without saying anything. But later in the evening she asked the exact same question again. Todd (I wish I could remember his last name), from down the street, was in the middle of a big bite of his BBQ sandwich as he laughed away her question.

The next time everyone gathered for a cookout she asked the question a third time. But this time, when people gave the same types of answers, she shook her head and mumbled to herself. Shortly after that she apologized and went home for the evening. Her house was vacant the next morning.

She left her garage door open with a spray painted message for the rest of us: "You're all going to die." I picked up the can of spray paint and blurred out her words so they wouldn't upset anyone else in the neighborhood. Once the message was painted over I added a nice little smiley face on her garage wall. There's no way to know if she made it to New Orleans or Miami, but I hope she did. And I hope she's happier there than she was here.

People like Mrs. Lee left Camelot of their own accord. More often, people simply passed away, their house becoming an unintentional mausoleum. A different woman from down the street, Mrs. Wilson, gradually cut down on the number of cook-outs she attended. It wasn't until she was absent for two weeks in a row that we realized she had finally passed away in her living room. The same thing happened to Ed Whimsley, who lived at the end of the street, and to the Anderson couple one street over.

The bodies could have been left in the house, there were enough empty houses that no one would ever care if a few homes on the street hosted decomposing corpses, but the remaining citizens always took it upon themselves to wrap the bodies in a blanket and give them a proper burial. The Stevensons, from down the road, were in their fifties when they moved to Camelot. Jimmy Stevenson passed away at the age of 78 from a heart attack. His wife followed six months later.

It was a bonding experience for the last of us to dig their graves. The hour of digging was good exercise, and the common effort gave our friends the burials they deserved. Mrs. Stevenson was the last burial we did ourselves. After that we were too old to continue—a bunch of old men in their seventies standing around a hole, each waiting for the next man to pick up the shovel and continue digging. From then on we started using a small excavator to dig each grave. The Dietrichs' front yard became the official spot for the neighborhood cemetery. Later, when the excavator broke down and there was no one else left to repair it, we dragged the bodies out to the back of the Dietrichs' house and had them cremated.

The Johnsons suggested leaving the bodies in the backyard so the animals could have them. Mark told the rest of us: "Might as well benefit someone. It'll keep the animals from trying to eat us."

Harris Chittendon disagreed. "It'll just teach them to eat humans." He cringed when he said this. "They'll get used to the idea real fast."

I disagreed for a different reason; if Andrew died I would go crazy thinking about wolves and dogs taking turns picking him apart. The vote between cremating the bodies and leaving them for the animals came out to nine votes to three. Only Mr. Wong, too in touch with nature to realize that providing animals with an additional food source would encourage them to be more aggressive, voted alongside the Johnsons. The Johnsons were never ones to hold a grudge, though; after being outvoted, they still helped with the next cremation.

I think about how they showed up after Mr. Landers passed away, offering to help with the cremation even though they weren't in favor of it, and then I think about how they drove right past my house in the middle of the night without saying goodbye. Something must have happened to them in those final days to make them switch from the friendliest people in Camelot to the ones who snuck out like felons.

Even though Camelot is empty now, it took a lot longer for this neighborhood to fade away than it did for some of the others. By the time other nearby communities were ghost towns, our neighborhood still had half its lights on at night. I like to think that was because the people in Camelot knew the importance of remaining a close-knit community.

I thought about all of this today as I stared at the Johnsons' house from the edge of my driveway. For a moment, I had the thought that maybe they would come back, that perhaps they had just left to investigate the surrounding areas and would return in a day or two. It was foolish to be hopeful, however, to think of the Johnsons as anything but permanently gone.

In my driveway, in the middle of these daydreams, I heard a soft scuffle against the concrete. A snake was slithering at the edge of the road, only ten feet away from me. I heard a hiss and then, from out of nowhere, a Siamese cat darted from the high grass and yanked the snake off the ground. Its paws batted and scraped at the snake, punishing it anytime it tried to fight back or get away. Finally the snake resigned itself to death and stopped resisting. I must have coughed then or made a noise because the cat jumped straight in the air, its tail puffing to three times its original size. The animal darted back into the weeds without its prize. The dead snake remained motionless on the broken concrete.

"It's okay," I said to the cat, wherever it was. "I didn't mean to startle you. It's all yours."

As I walked back to my house I heard the grass bristle again. It could very well have just been the wind, or it could have been another animal stealing what the cat had worked so hard for. I liked thinking it was the cat coming back to reclaim its meal and that if it ever saw me again it would think of me as the guy who didn't want to get in its way, the guy who just wanted it to be safe as it got along in the world as best as it knew how.

December 27

I wonder where the Johnsons are today. Do they still think about me? Do they have any idea that my chimney has become my last hope for getting Andrew to safety?

I still have a photograph of the six of us—the Johnsons and their two Block sisters next to Andrew and me—on the coffee table. Three of us are smiling in the nice weather while the other three have blank stares. This was twenty years ago, back when I still had a hint of color in my hair and I could grin for a picture without feeling old, without faking the smile. It was before we had to take any subsequent pictures indoors for fear of the wolves and dogs having enough time to form an attack. The Johnsons had a similar picture in their living room.

It couldn't have been easy for them to decide to leave. As I stood by the window the night they drove away, I could have sworn Mark looked over at my house as his Block sisters sat motionless in the back seat. The lights were off inside my bedroom, he shouldn't have been able to see me standing there. Thinking that he had looked my way could very well be my memory playing tricks on me. It's just as likely that he never looked in my direction, that he gazed straight forward as he exited the community.

Maybe he and Mindy frequently discussed if they should stop by and say goodbye. Maybe one of them was adamant against telling me they were leaving, thinking I might try and talk them out of it. I wouldn't have. Everyone is entitled to make their own decisions, to choose their own path. It was also possible that they were on the same side, that they agreed it was best to leave without acting like this was the end of something, even though it was.

After all the times we'd laughed about people

quitting on Camelot, they probably didn't want to hear the same jokes directed at them. I wonder if either of them considered what their Block sisters would have thought of the cloak-and-dagger escape if they had an opinion to voice on the matter. Would Mark and Mindy have been more considerate if the two sets of eyes traveling in the back seat could see what they were doing? If their sisters' eyes were judging what was taking place instead of being silently oblivious, would the Johnsons still have abandoned their neighbor and his quiet brother?

They couldn't be blamed for putting their immediate family before anyone else. The Johnsons were here with me over the years as the neighborhood cleared out and only our two houses were left, but that didn't mean they signed up to be responsible for me or Andrew once the end approached. They didn't have to stay in the neighborhood. They most certainly didn't owe me anything. But even so it would have been nice to give them hugs farewell and wish all four of them a safe journey.

It's a good thing my grandfather isn't still around. To his dying day, he said the Baltimore Colts sneaking out of town in the middle of the night was the sleaziest thing he ever saw someone do.

I probably heard him tell me a hundred times: "Those guys were weasels. All of them. No matter what they did before that night or afterwards, they showed their true colors when they did that. They were rats. Every single one of them. Rats. You don't say goodbye like that. You don't turn your back on people who were always there for you."

He would pause at that point and take a deep breath before finishing his tirade the same way he always finished it: "They can all rot in hell. Rotten Bastards."

That was usually when my father would remind my grandfather not to use that kind of language in front of little kids. But foul language or not, I knew what my grandfather was getting at. It's why I wish the Johnsons had done something as simple as say goodbye, and it's why I'll never leave Andrew. No matter what.

December 28

I find myself trying to keep semblances of our old life together from before we were alone. It used to be that any time I misplaced the remote control I would turn to Andrew and tell him he needed to work on how much effort he put into his practical jokes. If a DVD isn't in the right case I ask if that was his April Fools' joke from the previous year or if a bear snuck in and is playing a joke on both of us. I know I sound like my grandfather when I say these things, but I don't care. So today, when I spilled my dinner, I turned to him and said that was my April Fools' joke on myself… only a couple of months early. He never grins at how lame my jokes are.

I prank dialed 9-1-1 as a kid one time. It was an act done in the name of fun and mischievousness, but in actuality was really more about me just being an extremely dumb kid. I laughed when the operator asked what my emergency was. Being four or five at the time, I'm not sure what I expected to happen next. What did happen was the operator said he was sending a police unit over to the address that the phone number was registered to. There may have been a hint of crap in my pants when he said that. The giggling definitely stopped. Kids aren't known for responding well in the face of panic; my best plan was to put the phone in Andrew's non-moving fingers and hope he would take the blame. Needless to say, my father wasn't amused, nor did he buy that his son, who couldn't say a single word, let alone dial the phone, had pulled the prank. I spent the night in my room without any dinner.

And yet, like the dumb kid I was, I still managed not to learn my lesson because when I was six my April Fools' joke on my mother consisted of sneaking into Andrew's room when she wasn't looking and repositioning my brother's arms and legs so it looked like he was moving on his own. I snuck back out of the room, but stayed nearby so I could see her reaction. It was difficult to contain my snickering. A couple of minutes went by with me laughing in the hallway closet. The next time she went in and checked on him she started yelling. She kept screaming and screaming until my father ran up the stairs to see what was happening. They were the kind of yells I would have expected to hear if someone was holding a winning lottery ticket and their life was changed forever. She didn't have a chance to explain things to my father before I ran into the room and yelled, "April Fool!"

The effect my joke would have was lost on me until it was too late. Until that moment, I had never seen my mother so happy. Immediately afterwards, she had never seemed so defeated. She reached out and balanced against the wall for support so she didn't collapse. My father groaned. Even without an explanation he could guess what my prank had consisted of. He put his arm around my mother but she didn't notice.

As soon as I realized what I had done, I wished I'd been born like Andrew. That way I wouldn't say or do dumb things. Either of my parents could have slapped me across the face. I would have accepted it as fair punishment. Part of me wished that was exactly what they had done instead of simply standing there, devastated. My dumb, little grin vanished as I stood in the doorway. There I stayed, at least a minute passing by, before offering a weak apology. Neither of them acknowledged me. I said I was sorry a second time, but my mother's face was buried in my father's shoulder while he whispered soothing words. Then I walked down the hall to my room and spent the rest of the day there by myself.

Neither of them ever punished me for what I had done. Neither of them even mentioned it that night as we sat around the dinner table. When I asked my mom if I should eat dinner by myself up in my room, she shook her head and, while not saying anything, pulled out my normal chair between her and my father. None of us spoke that night as we ate, and I found myself wishing the entire time that one of them would scream at me, tell me to stop being so stupid and to grow up. They never did, though.

I came to hate April Fools', not just because it reminded me of my earlier idiocy, but because I got paid back for my earlier pranks by falling for every subsequent prank that was pulled on me. My parents and friends knew I was an easy mark so they all targeted me. When I was seven my dad put on a bear costume, stood outside my bedroom window, and banged on the glass. I pissed myself. The last laugh would be on him if he were still around to see how casual the bears are these days. If he were still alive it wouldn't take long before he woke up to find a real bear at his window.

When I was nine my mom said our dog had given birth to puppies overnight. The dog wasn't even pregnant, wasn't even female, but in my youth I didn't put any of those dots together before yelling with delight. When I ran into the living room Oscar was lying on the floor by himself. My mom burst out laughing and yelled, "April Fool!" I don't think I've ever felt so stupid. Although decidedly mean-spirited, part of me thinks she did that because it was the only way for her to get over the hurt I had caused a couple years earlier on the same day.

When I was in high school, a girl I liked asked me out on April 1st. I really should have known better. I didn't even get my answer out (of course I was going to say yes) before she started snickering and then ran down the hall, bursting with laughter as she went. A different girl had to come up and say "April Fool!" on her friend's behalf because the girl I liked couldn't stop laughing.

After I graduated from high school and was working on a road crew, one of the guys on my team buried my lunch in wet concrete. There really wasn't anything to fool me, I knew exactly where my god damn lunch was, but the other guys still chuckled at my April Fools' misfortune. I had to decide if wet concrete on my hands was a bigger hassle than an empty stomach. As far as I know, a perfectly preserved ham and swiss sandwich is still sitting under I-95.

Fortunately, Andrew never conceives of real pranks to pull on me. I'm sure I'd fall for every single one. If the Johnsons were still here and Andrew could be my partner in crime, we might team up by filling a brown paper bag with our feces, sneaking up to their house, setting the bag on fire, and leaving it on their front porch. They would hear me howling with laughter, sharing a congratulatory high-five with Andrew, as they opened the door and had to stomp on it. Lucky for them, they're gone.

December 31

There are only a handful of minutes left until this year passes and the new one begins. Times Square doesn't exist anymore; New York was vacated more than twenty years ago, and even if it was still around, there are no people left to gather, let alone to watch a silly ball drop. I remember seeing the festivities on TV as a boy and laughing at how preposterous it was for people to cheer as the illuminated ball slid down the side of a building. Now I wish I could see it happen again if it meant everything would magically go back to the way it was.

Fireworks, like new movies and little league games, were a part of life that faded away as the last normal generation grew older. People didn't want to be dazzled by explosions in the sky once the end of man was signaled. The bright flashes didn't seem so entertaining when the crowds were limited to fifty and sixty year-olds watching the waves of color blowing up in the sky. Each boom was a tick of the clock, a reminder to the gathered crowds that they had their hands full with Block siblings needing to be fed, bathed, and cleaned up after. No light or laser show could make audiences forget they were getting older one day at a time.

New Year's used to offer a chance for reflection. It used to provide an opportunity to look back at the year and then make resolutions on things you wanted to accomplish in the next one. This New Year's Eve and all the days that follow it are the same as every other day; the calendar resets to day one, but nothing really changes. Andrew will be the same. The animals in the forest will be the same. The only difference over the years is that the neighborhood has emptied out. This year will be noted as the year the Johnsons left. That's all. The next year will be noted as my first year being the last remaining resident of Camelot.

Maybe the year after that will find Camelot as yet another community that was once packed with cars zooming around, but that's now barren, devoid of any people.

The animals that humor me by letting me live near them will finally have the neighborhood back to themselves without that pesky old man and his quiet brother causing weird noises and smells. They won't have to listen to my music in the evenings. When the end does come, maybe I'll leave the doors open so the deer or the wolves or any other creature can more easily make a shelter of what was once my home. It's only fair to turn it back over to where it came from.

The open door could serve a second purpose. In the war movies I watch with Andrew, spies are given a poison capsule to swallow before they are captured, or a soldier behind enemy lines saves a single bullet in his pistol in case he needs it for himself. If the end was in sight for me, the pain or sickness too much, the open door would let all the nearby animals know that the first lucky ones through the door would have a feast worthy of kings.

I need to stop myself. All too often these days I catch myself thinking or writing about the end. Yes, I'm older. Yes, I'm alone. But it's not fair to myself or to Andrew to act like the end is imminent. The end is imminent, I know that, but the power of mankind has always been in overlooking the finality of things and holding onto optimism even when doing so seems foolish. If I start being consumed with thoughts about the end, I might as well walk into the forest right now and let whatever pack of wild beasts is out there have me for their dinner. Better to stay positive and remind myself of everything we still have.

And anyway, the smoke continues to rise each day from my chimney. My stack of old Batman comics was today's fuel. They were the last comics in my collection. Something else will need to go in the fire tomorrow. A band of travelers, heading south to New Orleans or Miami, will find us soon. It will all work out, it always does.

January 2

It's been a month now since the Johnsons departed and I was left as the default king of Camelot. And yet, even after these quiet and uneventful weeks, I still can't bring myself to make the simple journey down the street to check on their house. There are probably a million empty houses for each traveling family to choose from now—if there are any travelling families anymore, which I'm beginning to doubt. Even when the third to last family left our neighborhood—why can't I think of their names right now?—I went with the Johnsons and made sure the empty house had a functioning generator and incinerator and that the doors were left unlocked for anyone who might be interested in moving in.

Making sure abandoned houses were suitable for new occupants ended up being wasted time. What happened more often than not was a window in these houses eventually cracked, or the roof leaked, and the house was eventually opened for the cats and dogs to sneak inside and use as their own. Back when the Johnsons were still here, I would walk down the street to their house and see a pair of wild Dobermans watching me from the bedroom window of the McPhearsons' house. Except it wasn't the McPhearsons' house anymore, it was the Dobermans'. A family of cats watched me from inside the Smiths' house.

Gone are the days of new families appearing out of nowhere on their way south. Millions of Canadians began filtering down the globe to join the New Englanders and Mid-Westerners as everyone journeyed closer to the Equator. Every once in a while a Canadian family would move into one of the vacant houses in Camelot and I would have a new neighbor until they decided to move even further south. One day a house would be empty and the next day a family from Toronto or somewhere else would have a fire going in the fireplace, and I would take them a bottle of wine as a welcoming gift. Two weeks later the house would be empty again. Camelot would go back to being an exclusive resort for me and Andrew and for the Johnsons. I was sorry to see each family leave, as they all eventually did, but it was nice knowing the next day or week a new family could suddenly arrive, and we would have someone else to meet and share stories with.

Sometimes the new families stayed for a year or two before continuing their trip. A house would be abandoned one day and the next it would be a genuine home for a family again. It was a fascinating thing to see. Something I noticed when vehicles came into the community for the first time was that the arrivals never drove up and down the street to find the nicest house. Unless a home was noticeably inferior to the other houses on the street, either because the roof was falling in or because all of the windows were broken out, people were just happy to arrive at a new neighborhood and have a place to live.

As the migration played out over the years I got to meet the governor of Maryland, a pitcher for the St. Louis Cardinals, a senator from Indiana, and some guy who said he won an Oscar for special effects, although I think he was starting to lose his mind and didn't quite know who or where he was. Each family happened upon our neighborhood, raised a red mailbox flag, and made the neighborhood their home for as long as they needed.

The Martins were impossible to forget. The Pelletiers from Quebec, brother and sister and their Block brother, were a blast to have around. Of course I will never forget LeBlanc and her sister. But the last nomad couple that stopped here, what were their names? And how much longer will it be until I can't remember LeBlanc, even though forgetting her seems preposterous right now? Vague memories from elementary school through high school still exist, but I can no longer remember many of the teachers' names or any of their faces. I remember an English teacher who made me smile, a science teacher who always yelled at me, a social studies teacher who always seemed like he wanted to be somewhere else. Each memory is blurred to a shadow, a hint of something that was there but now is unclear.

Will the day arrive when the same thing happens to memories of my mother and father? It has, after all, been decades since they were alive. If I live for another ten years—doubtful I know—will I cease to remember exactly what it was that my dad liked to say before each meal or what my mother smelled like each time she woke me up in the morning?

Will I forget what it was like to live in a normal world where every house was filled with a different family, no two families alike, each one with their own ambitions and goals? Can I even remember what my own ambitions were when I was little? Does it matter if I can't remember?

The migrations did have at least one perk I can't pass up mentioning: it allowed me to lose my virginity. I never had another serious girlfriend after the girl I was dating in high school left with her family, but the stream of new visitors allowed me to manage a couple of flings.

The nice thing about the migratory herds was that people cared less about what they did in a particular town since they would move further south a week or two later. Sometimes the family moving into our neighborhood would have a daughter my age. This was, obviously, back when Andrew and I were still quite young and living in our old neighborhood with our parents. The girl and I would sneak away and do all the things adults did back before mankind started dying off. I know it sounds silly but that's how we felt back then; everyone was still adjusting to the idea that the human race was going to end. It didn't matter that the end wouldn't occur for another sixty or seventy years, after all of us had grown old, died of heart attacks or cancer. The future on the horizon, so foreign from what we were used to, struck a nerve with everyone wanting to make all their unfulfilled dreams come true. The overwhelming sense back in those days was that time was running out quicker than before the Blocks appeared, even though this part of the nightmare wasn't true at all. It just felt like time was speeding up.

The abundance of empty houses made sneaking off for a fling even easier than driving to a make-out spot. All we had to do was walk down the street until we found a house with the red flag down and then go inside. The vacant beds were more of an invitation than I needed back then, although I'm grossed out now at the thought of all the germs that might have been on the mattresses. At the time, however, I couldn't have been happier.

One of the girls I snuck off with asked me if I loved her after we were done having sex. I wish I could remember what her name was. I'm not proud of it now, but I told her what she wanted to hear.

"Say it again," she said.

"I love you."

She smiled. "Keep saying it."

So I did. She could have told me to say I was king of the world and I would have said it. I would have said it with so much conviction that even I believed it.

"We should get married," she said.

My heart skipped ten beats.

Her eyes, glistening with tears of happiness, told me she wasn't joking. My response was based on the knowledge that her family was going to keep moving south in a couple of days. Knowing that, I got on one knee, still naked and with half an erection.

"Will you marry me?" I said.

There was no ring to put on her finger or anyone to witness the ceremony, but she said yes as if that stuff wasn't important.

I don't know why I said those things or why I got down on my knee, other than it made her happy and that seemed important even though I would never see her again. I felt just as silly then while I was actually doing it as I do now when I close my eyes and remember my youthful stupidity. God, I was dumb back then. But it made her happy enough to burst into tears and tell me she loved me, so maybe it was worth it. We made love again while she was still crying tears of joy. I watched from my window a couple of days later as her father drove them away.

Unbeknownst to me at the time, the proposal that day on the dirty wood floor of the abandoned house was for my benefit too. Years later, while staring out the window at a momma bear walking with a young cub behind her, I realized that, for a split second, even though I felt ridiculous being completely buck naked, I had the sense of what the previous generations had. For that one moment I was on the path to getting married and having a family. My life instantly readjusted back to the course that has led me to today, but for that moment, if it could be paused, I had the possibility in front of me of having my parents' life. The life I have always wanted.

A big smile breaks across my face every time I

imagine what that girl's car ride to Miami must have been like. The first time an argument broke out in the minivan she probably dropped the M-bomb and told her parents that she had gotten engaged to a random kid in the last neighborhood and, in her heart at least, was married to him. I doubt either of her parents would have been happy for her.

And like I said, Andrew and I participated in the migration south to a limited extent as well. After mom passed away, a year after our dad had already gone, I looked around and realized our old neighborhood didn't hold anything important for us anymore.

It seemed critical at the time that we move to a different community, not so we could be closer to other people, but so our old house and street weren't the only ones Andrew and I knew. I didn't want to live my entire life in the same place where I was born and where I watched my parents grow old. So I packed up a minivan with our family's belongings, loaded Andrew into the passenger seat, and drove south a couple of hours until I saw the brick sign introducing us to Camelot. The rest is history.

It didn't take long for the same migrations that had occurred in our old neighborhood to start up around us at Camelot. I was still unpacking boxes of clothes when I saw the first pickup truck drive out of the golf community, stacked to the top with suitcases and boxes taped closed, as it made its way south.

A pair of Canadian sisters moved in next door to us when I was in my late forties. I got into the habit of leaving Andrew for a while, getting my fun in, and then returning later to make sure he was okay. It was nice being in their house because it was just the two of them—no Block sibling sitting quietly in the corner to remind us of things we didn't want to be reminded of. The sisters came over for dinner just about every evening. We would sit and talk until late into the night, the three of us drinking wine in the living room while Andrew sat motionless on the sofa. By the end of every night we would be piss drunk and falling over the sofas. Sometimes one of them would stay over, but more often than not they would head back to their house together. Those were some of the best nights of my life.

Every once in a while the sister I was hooking up with would joke that the other Canadian had dibs on Andrew. Any time she said this I felt like she was making fun of him and asked her to stop. To keep them from joking about him being a possible junky, I always made sure he was wearing long sleeve shirts when they visited. If they saw the scattered needle marks around his forearms where I was putting in the nutrient bags they would have made all the same jokes other people made about Blocks needing rehab for their addictions. The jokes got old real fast and were only uttered by people without Block relatives.

Other times they talked about what they would do if the other sister was a Block. I never offered input. I did, though, talk about what I would do if Andrew suddenly turned into a regular person. My take on the idea was that not much would change if he did become normal, but I only said that so he wasn't insulted and so they would respect him as a person.

It was also important to me that they understood he meant as much to me as they meant to each other. They had shared sisterly concerns all throughout their lives, gone on blind dates together, shopped for the same clothes, but I loved Andrew every bit as much as they loved each other. I don't think they were ever able to understand that.

The truth was that if things were different and Andrew could talk and joke around with me, move his arms and legs, help with the chores—really be there (instead of just being there)—there was no telling how everything might be different. I would have someone with me now, someone to share my concerns with. He would be a set of ears to listen and a voice to offer advice. There is nothing I would like more.

Maybe we wouldn't even be here right now if Andrew was normal. Back when the roads were better and my little car could get us out of here, he might have thought joining one of the final communities was the better plan. If he could speak and if he voiced that opinion, we most definitely would have left. The Johnsons would have been the last people in the neighborhood instead of us. But if Andrew was normal and wanted to stay here, we would do that. Maybe the Johnsons would have been more willing to say goodbye if they knew I had someone to keep me company. Maybe they would have stopped by and offered us seats in their SUV if they weren't worried about having another Block to take care of. I would have been more than happy to let Andrew share the middle seat with the Block sisters while I sat in the back with the luggage.

It makes me feel good to think of all the ways life would be better if I had a brother who could experience everything with me. I imagine him laughing with me during our favorite movie scenes. I imagine him sitting up all night talking about what life was like without being able to do anything. The next time a snake startled me, Andrew would chuckle, grab it by its tail, throw it out the window, and make me feel silly for letting such a small creature wreck my nerves.

As much as I didn't want to encourage the Canadians' mockery, I did imagine Andrew going to bed with the other sister. He would be a happy person. I can tell just by looking at him. We would be a team in these final days, instead of a coach and a silent onlooker. There wouldn't be anything the two of us couldn't face.

Unlike the Johnsons, the Canadian sisters came over to have a final meal before they moved further south. Because of the way we got along, part of me was surprised they stuck with their plan to head out of the neighborhood. They asked if Andrew and I would like to come with them, but they weren't sure which community they were going to and everything seemed too unknown, too undecided, to justify submitting Andrew to an adventure that might not be in his best interests. When they were gone it was back to life as normal—as normal as life could be anyway.

One of the photo albums lying around here has a couple of pictures of the Canadian sisters. I'll need to find it tomorrow and look through the photographs again. Andrew will be next to me when I do. When we get to their pictures I'll be sure to remind him there is nothing different about the way the Canadian sisters loved each other and how I love him.

January 3

A yellow Labrador sunned itself on my patio today. I looked out my dining room window, as I do a thousand times each day, and it was lying there on the deteriorated deck without a care in the world. Other dogs were barking from within the forest, but this was the only one out in the open. It didn't look concerned for its safety at all, as though wolves and bears weren't constantly roaming for more food. I loved seeing an animal be so carefree. It would have to be a clever dog to still be alive if it chose to relax in the open by itself. The days of animals respecting the boundaries of each other's kingdoms, even if that rule was limited to the yards where they lived, have been replaced with a daily lottery for ownership.

I told Andrew about the dog as a way to apologize for getting mad at him today. It wasn't anything he did (of course). The fault lies solely with me. All he does is sit in the same spot until I move him to another position, so nothing is his fault. Our situation, our isolation, our ticking clock, is no one's fault really. Maybe that's why I get frustrated sometimes, because there's no one to blame for how our lives have turned out. I wouldn't change any of the things I've done, but at the same time I wish things were different than they are. I have no regrets, but there's also no satisfaction in where I am. I guess that's why I snapped at Andrew today.

His nutrient bag is timed with his body in order to regulate the number of trips to the bathroom, but every once in a while, like today, he goes in his pants at the most inconvenient times. All Blocks wear diapers, but the diapers can only do so much, and Andrew seems to have a knack for defeating them. Everything was fine when I walked by him on the way to the kitchen. The next time I passed, though, the familiar stench of crap was in the air.

It's a particularly putrid smell—something about the combination of chemicals in the nutrient bag really makes a Block's shit smell like… well, shit.

"God damn it," I yelled. "Can't you do anything to make my life easier?" I stormed off before slamming my bedroom door. After finishing a chapter of the book I'm reading I went back out to the living room. The stench was even worse than before. That, too, was no one's fault except my own; it was my temper-tantrum that gave the excrement an opportunity to spread into every inch of open air. And yet I slammed my door again and left him sitting in his waste until another chapter was finished.

Alone in my quiet room, images began filtering into my head of various Blocks being abandoned and left to die while regular adults moved further south. I thought about what it would be like if I just left Andrew there on the sofa, sitting in his own filth, as I packed up my car and made my way south. Andrew would be the last living person in Camelot. It wouldn't take me more than five minutes to pack a bag and get into my car. But within another five minutes at least one of my car's tires would be blown out. There's no way I could make it on foot. Maybe I would reside in one of the millions of abandoned homes between Camelot and the next pocket of civilization. Maybe I would actually get to Miami. But I know I couldn't bring myself to actually do those things. My short walk down the hall to my bedroom, not even enough distance to get me away from the smell of Block feces, was enough separation to make me feel ashamed of how I'd acted.

Eventually I went back out to the living room. I put my arms around Andrew and told him I was sorry. The smell of shit didn't register with me then because I was too embarrassed with my behavior. My cheeks burned at the thought of my parents looking down and seeing me snap at my poor brother. I hugged him as though I hadn't seen him for most of his life, a POW returning home or perhaps a fugitive finally free from jail.

"I'm sorry," I said over and over. "I won't leave you." When I was done apologizing I cleaned him, put a new diaper on him, then a new pair of pants. Upon his return to the sofa, I moved him further down from where he had been so I could clean the soiled fabric on the dirty cushion. I positioned him so he had a clear view of the patio door and of the woods.

A bear came by an hour later. Thankfully, the Labrador was gone by that time. The bear stayed there for most of the night, staring at Andrew through the glass door in a state of confusion. Andrew stared right back at it the entire time, which made the bear feel threatened. The animal didn't know how to take this show of willpower through the glass barrier. It roared, then stood on its hind legs before banging on the doors. I panicked then because it wouldn't take much effort for the bear to smash through the glass panels. I ran to the light switch and turned the lamp off so we were in the dark. Through it all Andrew didn't flinch. The bear grumbled, then walked away, defeated. Andrew was the winner of another staring match!

"You beat him," I said. "You showed him who the boss is around here." I patted his shoulder. "I'm sorry I get frustrated sometimes."

I sat down next to him, where his filth had been. The fabric cleaner was dry now. The sofa smelled better than it had in the first place; even crapping on the furniture can have its benefits. "It's just tough some times," I said.

Our view outside is of a series of houses that were once full of families, the sound of laughter echoing from them. These houses are all dark now, empty. The only house with lights on is the one Andrew and I occupy. That's a lot of pressure for anyone. I guess sometimes it gets the better of me.

"It's just tough some times," I told Andrew again. I laid him down on the sofa, then pulled a blanket up to his shoulders. "Good night." I turned the rest of the lights off. Our house immediately resembled all of the other houses on the street. "I'll see you tomorrow."

I wonder, though, what will happen when the time comes, and surely it will arrive, when I can no longer reposition a soiled Andrew, when I have to clean up after him but can't budge him. Will he just sit in his shit? What will I do when I'm too old and feeble to move him that short distance across the sofa, or to the bathroom? What quality of life would he have at that point? And is there ever a time when his quality of life could deteriorate enough that he would be better off dead than alive, even if he's oblivious while he lives? Surely any normal adult would rather be put out of their misery than sit in their own filth while bed sores spread across the backs of their legs. It would be a matter of days before maggots made a home in his underwear. And I would be helpless to care for him.

Andrew doesn't understand any of these concerns. Is it fair for me to impose my fears and desires upon him? He is my brother. While that qualifies me as the person to best take care of him, there is no qualification that should allow me to make these decisions for him or anyone else. I don't mind being responsible for Andrew's wellbeing, but I don't want to be responsible for deciding what the boundaries of his wellbeing are.

Everything about my existence is a challenge: I don't want to die first and leave Andrew by himself to starve, but I also don't want Andrew to grow sick to the point I have to decide enough is enough. These are the things I never talked about with the Johnsons while they were here. Now that they're gone, I wish they were still down the street so I could finally share the thoughts that keep me up at night.

I've been gone too long, I need to go check on Andrew.

January 4

Alone, the days seem longer than they used to be. Some afternoons, I talk to Andrew all day so the hours seem to pass more quickly. Other times, because I never get a response, talking to him only seems to slow time down.

After twelve years, we finally watched *Ghostbusters* again. The movie brings back too many sad memories for us to watch it on a frequent basis. I've been in the mood recently to reminisce (maybe part of the reason I took up writing this diary), so now seemed an appropriate time to watch as the four bumbling men captured ghosts. As a little boy, it was one of my favorite movies, but when I watched it again as a teenager, the Great De-evolution in full swing, I found myself liking it even more. For a while, I would have said it was my favorite movie of all time. Most movies are the exact opposite for me: I'll watch them the first time and think they're hilarious, tell a great story, or have great acting, but then when I watch them again years later I wonder what I liked so much the first time. I'm not sure if it's part of a normal phenomenon as I grew older, my tastes changing—I won't say maturing—or if the Great De-evolution was to blame for making me realize the childishness of my old tastes.

As a teenager, I watched *Ghostbusters* with Candace, my high school girlfriend, all the time. She liked it as much as I did, so we made sure to watch it at least once a month. We knew every line by heart. By the time she moved away with her family we could perform the entire movie by ourselves. An argument would ensue each time the movie started because we could never agree on who would get to say Bill Murray's lines. I think we liked it so much because it showed how a couple of average guys could come up with a solution to what was terrorizing an entire city. Here they were with this newly discovered enemy to fight, one that wasn't like anything they had seen before, and Bill Murray and his friends stepped up to the challenge to defeat the ghosts. It gave me hope that a couple of average guys could find a cure for the Blocks.

Andrew was always at the far end of the sofa when Candace and I watched the movie. I tried to make out with her a couple of times during our *Ghostbusters* sessions, but she would always push me away, saying it was weird with my brother right there.

"He doesn't care," I'd say, hoping that would be enough to let me touch her boobs. What can I say, raging teenage hormones will do that to a boy. My lines never worked on her.

She had a Block sister at home who she was more mature around than I was with Andrew. Looking back, I suppose I can see how it would have been awkward if I tried to put the moves on her while her Block sister was four feet away. I still apologize to Andrew each time the opening scene starts. That was always when I'd put my arm around Candace and make my move.

"I was young," I still tell Andrew to this day, as if that made everything I did back then excusable. "Young and dumb."

I only dated Candace for two years before she moved, but she was my only real girlfriend. We never even talked about a long-term future or anything like that, but after she moved I had an image of her in my distorted memory as being my last shot at getting married, having a normal family, and growing old with someone I loved. Yes, I still had flings after that, but to me, the prospect of a normal life ended when Candace left. That's what I think about now any time I watch *Ghostbusters*, and it's why I don't like watching the movie very often anymore.

When her family moved I gave up trying to have the same kind of life my parents had. Everyone was starting to pack up their belongings around that time anyway. There was a sense of misplaced urgency in getting to the southern settlements earlier than anyone else, as though the declining population would still somehow manage to overrun an entire city's worth of vacant houses, condominiums, and apartment buildings, leaving no open residences for the last people to arrive. Deep down I think I knew right then, as Candace's father drove her family out of the neighborhood one final time, that I would end up taking care of Andrew by myself until the day I died.

I never did find out if she made it safely to one of the settlements. I never heard from her again at all. What happened to her after her parents took her away? Did she still think about me after she was gone, about the time we spent together in high school and also at senior week? I like to think so. I thought about her.

January 5

The supply of comics is gone. Even some of my old clothes are gone. No one has found us. We're alone. I try not to think about it too much. My dad's Santa costume went in the flames today. I have no idea how many other items are scattered around the house that might serve to keep the fire going.

We need to be found, and we need to be found soon.

It was Andrew's birthday today. As I do every year, I sang Happy Birthday to him. I didn't go as far as baking a cake that he wouldn't be able to eat (although I have done that before) or by lighting candles he wouldn't be able to blow out (I've done that before too). We watched the *Star Wars* trilogy, just like we do every year on his birthday. When the final installment was over I turned the TV off, told Andrew I loved him, put a blanket over him, and went to bed.

There's a framed picture of Andrew and me on my bedside table that never fails to amaze me. My dad took the photograph when I was nine and Andrew was five. Andrew is sitting on the sofa with presents on either side of him while I'm sitting on the floor in front of him with half my presents unwrapped. I don't look anything like I did back then: most of my hair is gone now, loose skin hangs off my arms, and I have more wrinkles than I ever thought possible. But while I don't resemble the happy nine year-old anymore, there has never been a moment in all the time since then that I looked in the mirror and noticed a change from one day to the next. There has never been a startling moment when I saw a reflection of myself and was shocked at the sudden transformation. Andrew is the exact opposite. Sometimes I go out to the living room and can't believe the person sitting on the sofa is the same person from that photograph. Instead of a young boy, I see an old man. When I see how old he looks now, I wonder where all the years went.

As a Block he has always been skinnier than me; he can't do anything to create a semblance of muscle. That's the only real difference between us, however. We share the same brown eyes, the same bubbled chin. I see these characteristics in our childhood photos and I see them in both of us now, but I'm still amazed at how Andrew has progressed from being that little kid, my little kid brother, to an old man with a bald head and grey stubble over his cheeks.

The Blocks were quieter and skinnier than the rest of us, but they went through puberty the same age as everyone else. Each time I had a growth spurt and needed new clothes, my old clothes were perfect for my growing brother. I still remember how happy I was when I finally outgrew a red and orange striped sweater my mother got me for my birthday. It looked like something a kid would wear the day of a family portrait and then hide in the back of his closet. Sadly, my mother expected me to wear it until I finally got too big for it. I giggled two years later when I saw Andrew wearing it for the first time. What I noticed, though, was that it didn't seem quite so bad once I wasn't the one wearing it. It seemed fine on him.

He wore my old sweaters and my old jeans and everything else I handed down. And somewhere along the line, he went from being a little boy to an old, wrinkled man. No matter how many times I see him, I'm still shocked at how he looks because, while he appears to be an old man, he still acts like the same person I've always known. To me, he's still the same Andrew my parents brought home from the hospital that first day, and always will be.

January 6

My old copy of Steinbecker's *Mapping the Great De-evolution*, the book that described what the progression of the Great De-evolution would be like, was in a box in my basement. I flipped through some of the chapters, telling Andrew what the Johnsons might be up to and also what we might expect in the coming days. Part of Steinbecker's final chapter says:

> "The final group settlements will experience a emotional surges each time there is an increase of people due to the migrations. This increase will provide the city with a sense that the urban area is once again bustling, a return to the city they knew in previous years. The crime rate will experience a very slight rise as these people are brought together in the confines of a couple of city blocks. This influx will be limited to minor crimes such as petty burglary and littering. There will be no violent crimes amongst the final inhabitants. Because material possessions will have little or no value, pick-pockets and thieves will become normal members of society. Only the mentally ill will persist in acting out against others. People will notice more revelry and noise in the streets. Drug and alcohol dependence will increase. This feeling will only last momentarily, though. Toward the end, it could last as little as a few minutes or an hour before the emotional surge wears off. The high of seeing new people will be replaced by the low of witnessing another round of senior citizens passing away. The inhabitants of the finals settlements will experience a constant bi-polar swing in which they experience the up of seeing new people arriving to their community, followed by the down of seeing familiar faces pass away. As the Great De-evolution

progresses, and fewer new people arrive to the final settlements, these highs and lows will become less dramatic.

In contrast, those members of society who have remained on their own in the now barren suburbs and rural areas will find themselves experiencing what life was like for the first settlers. These people will witness no influx of visitors, will see no new faces. There will be no crime of any kind, even petty crimes, in these desolate parts. These inhabitants will not go through the bi-polar highs and lows seen in the urban areas. These inhabitants risk isolation due to physical and mental infirmity. Material possessions hold no monetary value here either, but may serve to provide a sentimental purpose for the isolated few. Alcohol and drug dependence could sky rocket. The absence of humans in various areas around the world provides too many variables for the issues these people may experience due to local wildlife. The local predators might become a security threat, while a seemingly ordinary beetle may either become extinct or grow in numbers until it has destroyed the entire surrounding eco-system. The environments are too volatile to determine how the animals might affect each region's transition back to a human-free world."

"What do you think?" I said to Andrew when I was done reading. "He got a lot of things right. But hopefully he got a couple of things wrong too."

I guess we'll see. I wonder what choice Steinbecker made as his own end approached. Did he stay in the home he was familiar with, or did he abandon it for one of the final settlements?

January 7

I've seen too many things in my old age to be afraid of an empty house. I've witnessed the migration of mankind southwards. I've seen countries collapse. I've seen Blocks murdered and abused as though they were mannequins instead of real people with real hearts. I once saw wild dogs drag an unattended Block woman from our neighbor's patio into the woods where she was torn apart without struggling or crying out for help. I cried out for her because she couldn't save herself. There was nothing I could do besides scream. By the time Dan heard me and came running, it was too late. His sister was already disemboweled. It took me a long time to get over witnessing that.

I've seen all of that, yet each time I try to convince myself to go down the street to check out the Johnsons' house, I can only make it to the edge of my driveway before I become stuck. The first night, I turned back without needing much convincing. Last night I was all set to go down the street when I thought I heard a pack of dogs in the woods. The late hour meant too little sun, too much cover of darkness for the nearby animals. The bat I had with me would do little good against a pack of feral house cats, let alone a pack of Dalmatians or Labradors. There was a time when I used to be too proud to back down from a band of kittens! Now, though, I concede they would get the better of me. And then there are the wolves and Rottweilers—the animals I thought I heard growling from the edge of the forest—that I was never foolhardy enough to think I stood a chance against.

From somewhere in the forest I heard a roar that made me think of a Tyrannosaurus rex, a roar much too great for a bear or even a pack of bears in unison. For a moment it made sense: the world had become so unbalanced that there might in fact be three-story tall monsters roaming in the woods. Anything was possible. Just as quickly, I had the thought—I'm not sure why—that the sound was either a normal growl, one that hadn't been nearly as menacing as the one I thought I had heard, or else the roar had never sounded at all, my mind had imagined the entire thing.

The odor from down the street, the smell of filth and sickness, overwhelmed me then, kept me planted at the edge of my driveway. Like the roar, the odor might not be real, might only be a figment of my imagination, some peculiar display of my nervousness. Maybe if I become even more worried and anxious I'll begin hearing voices. I'll know the end is near when all of my senses are being tricked. Sometimes I have to remember I'm an old man. Kids never get scared. Old men get nervous; they get paranoid. Their minds are overactive like their bladders.

I still wonder what could make the Johnsons feel like they had to pack their things, buckle their sisters into the backseats, and sneak away without saying where they were going. Each time the Johnsons and I discussed the possibility of leaving Camelot, they were the ones against going. Maybe, when it came down to it, they had one priority: taking care of themselves and their Block sisters, not taking care of an old man and his Block brother.

It's also quite possible they were deceiving me the entire time. Andrew is the only person I spend my days with and he's incapable of telling a bold-faced lie or even a little white lie, so it's definitely feasible I'm just not used to sensing when someone is swindling me. It's possible the Johnsons gave every indication that their intentions didn't match with what they were saying, but I never picked up on it. They could have been passing knowing looks back and forth in between bites of pork chops or chicken wings. If all of those conversations were replayed again, maybe I would pick up on how their tone didn't match their words or how they never looked me in the eye when they said they were staying in Camelot to the very end.

After they left the neighborhood I rewatched every mobster movie in my collection. Each gangster movie had a scene where one of the criminals was being lied to, recognized the deceit, and did something about it. Every time I tried to identify the same telltale signs that the gangster noticed when being lied to, I thought the other character had been telling the truth.

Of course it's also possible that the Johnsons weren't lying, that they really did want to stay in the neighborhood, but an emergency made them leave as quickly as they could. If that happened it wouldn't matter if it was the middle of the night when they needed to leave. If Mark thought his sister was dying, he would have packed his three siblings in the SUV and raced as fast as he could toward one of the settlements where better care awaited them.

So now that I'm the only one left, what keeps me from going six doors down the street to their old property the way I did for a hundred other houses? It's a simple thing to do. And yet I remain at the end of my driveway, staring down the street at the Johnsons' two-story Elizabethan as though just looking at it is the same as going there.

I'm reminded once again of my neighbor's Block sister who was dragged into the woods and eaten by dogs. The funny thing is, after it happened it was the Johnsons who pulled me aside and told me I did the right thing, both for myself and for Andrew. I got the feeling Dan had expected me to go into the woods to try and save his sister, to put his family's wellbeing above my own responsibility to Andrew. I could never put someone else before my brother. Dan left Camelot a week later without saying another word to me. The Johnsons repeatedly told me, both before he left and then again after he was gone, that they would have done the same thing if they were in my place. That was how I finally came to terms with what I saw that day, because the Johnsons made me feel I hadn't done anything wrong. So how did things change from them being the ones to reassure me when I had doubts, to being the ones who left here so suddenly it was almost as if one more day spent in Camelot would mean their downfall?

January 8

My mom used to tell me the Blocks appeared because there were too many people on the planet. "The world has a way of restoring its natural order. Earth was never supposed to have this many people."

Knowing my father didn't approve of her telling me that sort of thing, she always made sure to make these comments when he wasn't around. The one and only time she said something like that in front of my dad when I was there to hear it, he told her not to say such things. Then, later that night when he and I were watching TV with Andrew and my mom was somewhere by herself, he told me the world didn't work that way.

"Your brother isn't a Block because the world is trying to even things out. That's ridiculous. I love your mother but when she gets scared, she says things she doesn't really believe." He raised his voice when he told me that, I think, because he hoped she was listening nearby.

So after that, instead of not saying those things, she just didn't say them around him. But me, I got to hear all of her thoughts on how it was a matter of time until God or the universe or nature—the exact force behind it depended on her mood that day—decided to balance things again. That explained the history of great diseases and plagues throughout the centuries.

"How many people did everyone think could inhabit the earth?" she would say. "People are just too selfish. If you dropped a couple of billion people on earth out of nowhere, everyone would see there wasn't enough room for everyone, that the world wasn't supposed to be filled with buildings on top of buildings and roads dividing every section of land, people shoulder to shoulder no matter where they stood. But because it was a gradual increase, slow enough that schools could always have additions built to make room for more students, more houses could be built for families to live in, people never noticed. Everyone was living for the day. No one cared about the future. Sure, your father and I could have had ten kids, but is it fair to have ten kids living where the previous family had two kids? Imagine if everyone did that. What were those parents thinking when they had kids that often, that they were building armies? There's no need to have ten kids. What's the point of having more than two or three?"

When she went on this version of her rant, I never interrupted. The Dixons were the only family I knew that reproduced like bunnies, and most of their seven kids were assholes, so I liked hearing her talk bad about them by association. And I knew what she meant about not noticing something was going bad if it built up slowly. The old stories of people going into debt never had them jumping immediately into bankruptcy; they built their debt slowly so it seemed manageable at first, something that could be corrected. Gambling addicts didn't just go from not having a problem to betting their entire livelihood in one hand; it took a series of ups and downs to make it seem like there might be a time when one final bet could fix everything. Most problems were that way. Hell, that's how I ended up alone with Andrew in Camelot. If I went from being with my parents in the lively neighborhood of my childhood, then got transported here—no one around, my old body deteriorating—I would have immediately put Andrew in the car and we would have been driving to New Orleans. But because the isolation built up slowly, a single family leaving one month, then another the next month, my knees creaking just a little bit more each year, I never became shocked at my own situation. So yes, I can understand what my mother was trying to say.

It was her other tirade I didn't care for so much: "If

it's not war or famine, it's disease. There will always be something to control the human population, some natural mechanism that saves people from their irresponsible selves. I love your brother as much as I love you or your father—he can't help what the world has done to him—but the Blocks are just another attempt by nature to bring the world back into synch. People got too good at curing all the other diseases the world passed our way. Scientists got too good at prolonging the average lifespan. People who were supposed to die kept living. People who were never supposed to have children started having eight or nine kids. It doesn't take a genius to figure out that you can only tinker with the natural order of things for so long before nature gets the last laugh. Say a scientist figured out how to stop aging forever—I wouldn't be surprised if people were so short-sighted they all didn't just go on living, having kids, acting like there would never be any consequences. How long would it have taken for the world to realize there were just too many people everywhere? Would ten billion people have been too much? Twelve billion?"

I never bothered to tell her that people said similar things all throughout history. In some people's minds, the bubonic plague had been sent to punish everyone. Same with malaria. I never bothered to tell her that all the wars men engaged in—one of the ways she thought the world controlled populations—only resulted in population increases, not decreases. Sure, there was a lot of death on the battlefield, but then all the survivors went home and made as many babies as possible. I saw a story on the news one time that said the world's post-war population was always back up to pre-war numbers within nine months—nine fun months—of soldiers returning home.

I never asked her how she could claim to love an embodiment of the current plague, as she saw my brother, as much as she loved my father and me. I didn't ask because I knew she really did love him as much as the rest of us. And I knew what my dad said was right: she was just saying these things because she was scared, and scared people don't really mean what they say, they're just looking for ways to rationalize everything so they have someone or something to blame. They need to have a reason for what's happening because when they have that they can take comfort in knowing it's out of their control.

While my mom was sneaking in these monologues any time my dad wasn't around, my dad was doing things my mom wouldn't agree with when she wasn't watching. He knew, as did I, that zombie movies irritated her. She saw the mindless bodies marching down streets, terrorizing people, and thought it was, in its own way, insensitive to her as the parent of a Block. It wasn't just her. It seemed that half the people I talked to in those days thought zombie movies were in poor taste. Any depiction, she would say, of a mindless person wandering neighborhoods for brains to snack on should be banned from homes where Blocks reside. When I reminded her that zombie movies existed well before Andrew was ever a sparkle in my parents' eyes, my father shushed me and said he was sorry. Yet, every time she was gone and Andrew was in his room, my dad and I would pop on a zombie classic and share some father and son time. It wasn't tossing the baseball in the backyard or going fishing, things he probably did with his father when he was my age, but it was nice—we watched people get their brains eaten.

A big part of what offended my mother was a new breed of the zombie movie genre in which the mindless bodies weren't like traditional zombies, they didn't turn into zombies once their brain was eaten by another member of the undead. The new breed of zombie was born deaf, mute, and motionless, until one day they woke from their slumber and began eating the brains of the very families that had been raising them.

"These movies are awful. Do they really think Andrew is going to wake up one day and try to kill us?"

"It's just a movie, Mom."

"Just a movie? Just a movie? They're making fun of your brother and people like him."

She didn't have to say anything else. My father turned the movie off. The evening news took the place of what we had been watching.

"That's better," my mother said, smiling. My father returned her smile. That evening's news reported on a police raid on a prostitution ring in which the cops found twelve Blocks lying on top of various mattresses in an Atlanta basement. All of the Blocks had AIDS and a slew of various other STDs by the time the cops found them. The next story recounted how a group of boys, only slightly older then myself at the time, had made a game out of setting a Block on fire in the woods behind their house. That was in rural Kentucky. The next story focused on a grandmother in San Francisco who could do nothing but watch in horror as her house burned to the ground while her two Block grandchildren sat motionless in an upstairs bedroom. She hadn't been able to move them before needing to escape the smoke. The Blocks were engulfed in flames by the time the fire department showed up.

"Christ," my father said. "Turn this trash off."

The next time my mother was out running errands and Andrew was upstairs in his room, my dad and I watched another zombie movie until he heard the garage door. Then he clicked it off.

January 9

The Labrador sat outside my patio door again today, panting on the welcome mat like a throw-back to the days of house pets wandering in and out of homes. The dog is like the ones you used to see chasing down tennis balls at the park, or in the backseat of a car with its head hanging out the open window to get fresh air. I caught myself glancing over at Andrew to make sure he wasn't scared, but he was sitting there with the same blank look he always has. I've spent my entire life with a brother who doesn't talk, hear, or move, yet I still catch myself telling him something and then half expecting a response. We could live for another hundred years and I would still say things just to comfort him.

Of course, the things I say are to settle my own nerves too. More and more I find myself checking to make sure Andrew isn't scared when the lights flicker or when a bear lumbers up to the patio and sniffs around. He has never been scared of these things, so my motive for checking must have more to do with me than with him. Still, I can't help myself.

The dog sat there for a while, resting on the warm wooden planks as though there weren't predators all around. It tilted its head side to the side a couple of times, amused by my interest in it, before repositioning itself to watch me through the glass. Other times, it had its back to me so it could watch the woods, make sure it wasn't attacked.

If it was domesticated—if there were still pets—I'm confident I could have brought it inside and it would have sat next to Andrew. It would protect my brother from anything that could cause him harm. I thought about leaving a bowl of water for it or using the food generator to make it something that resembled dog food, but when I came back from the kitchen it was gone. A while later I heard barking from the forest and found myself hoping it wasn't that same dog because what ever dog was making the noises was soon yelping and crying before going silent. A pack of wolves howled then. I knew they had made a meal out of the unlucky animal. The only way I'll know if it was that dog or a random Dalmatian or Pit-bull is if the yellow pup comes back to my patio again tomorrow or the next day. I have to admit, I hope it does. Having the dog around makes me feel like things could go back to normal if I could just get through this rough patch.

I don't like mentioning it, but I'm almost out of books to burn. After the books, there won't be much of anything left to set on fire. I refuse to sit at the window all day with the hope that a truck will pull into our community. I do, though, find myself turning the TV's volume lower just in case an engine announces our salvation.

January 11

Why do I sneak off after dinner each night to record my thoughts? Is it merely to keep track of them?

There are probably thousands of similar diaries scattered around the country, in every abandoned little Midwest town, in every metropolitan area, and all the places in between. Before the Great De-evolution, diaries were passed down through the generations. Mine will stay here without anyone to inherit it. But mine is no different from thousands of others. There are forgotten pages all around the world, abandoned, each one containing stories of what their daily life was like, of dreams that were longed for, some achieved, others left to remain fleeting fantasies. All of them will go unread.

How many other prized memories around the world are being forgotten on a daily basis? The last of my books are gone. My baseball cards and comics were already turned to ash in the fireplace. Is this what other diaries talk about?

For the first time in three weeks, I didn't start a fire in the chimney today. No one has driven past to investigate the home with two men still living in it. Other than the Johnsons' SUV, I doubt a car has come within a hundred miles of our house in the time I've been setting fire to my old hobbies.

I thought I heard an engine the other day, but when I opened my front door there was no noise and I realized the sound must have been my furnace. An hour later, I thought I heard an airplane flying overhead. From the low rumble, it sounded like a giant 747. Planes haven't taken flight in years, though. Especially not something enormous like the one I thought I heard today. Even as I was listening to it, I knew it wasn't really there, that the sky would be empty if I went outside and looked up at the clouds, that my ears were just transforming another noise from my house into something that might offer hope.

I considered scavenging the house for other materials to burn, maybe blankets or boxes of Christmas ornaments, but even if someone did spot us, why would they do anything to help? Even if they did see the smoke in the distance, why would they risk going out of their way with the roads in their current condition? They would already have enough problems of their own. Everyone left is either living in one of the final group communities or they are like me: dispersed throughout once-bustling neighborhoods, taking care of their Block relatives and themselves as best as they can after everyone else has left. Why would they want the burden of taking Andrew and me in as well?

For this reason, I've come to realize the option of leaving Camelot doesn't exist for Andrew and me the way it used to. By watching movies with him I tried to make it seem like any other day, but I found myself thinking about what we would do tomorrow and the next day and the day after that instead of paying attention to what was on the TV. If I can act like it's just another normal day, maybe I can start believing it.

Even if I wanted to take Andrew away from our home to join one of the last communities, we would have a flat tire after a quarter mile. The last thing I would need is to get stuck out there. The bears would get me unless the dogs got me first. I like to imagine, if our car did break down, that I could throw Andrew on my shoulder and begin south as though the car was a luxury. The pair of shotguns I would be carrying would leave a trail of animal carnage hundreds of miles long. I would only stop long enough to reload new shells. And when the hike was completed, I would let Andrew gently slide from my shoulder into the waiting arms of caretakers who are ready to ensure he had the care and attention he would need if anything ever happens to me.

Ha! Wishful thinking.

I return to the question of why I am driven to write down my thoughts and actions each day. Am I returning, in a way, to being an overwhelmed child, feeling the need to fill a page's lines with my daily worries the way a lovesick elementary school girl might? Unlike my youth, when I simply felt like no one else understood the things that troubled me, I now only have the choice between confiding in my Block brother, who can never offer a reply, or confessing to a blank screen. Anything said to a Block, even my dear Andrew, is gone as soon as it leaves my lips. Things written down at least have a chance to leave a soft echo of what had been.

January 12

There's no telling how old the current oldest living person is. I wonder how close I am to taking their spot on the podium. Maybe there's a woman in Japan who has me beat by twenty years. There could be a man in India who makes me look like a youngster. But what happens when they both pass away? What happens when the oldest woman in Italy dies? All of it puts me one step closer.

There used to be a website that tracked the oldest living person. It was intended to give people inspiration, the thought being that even if they felt old by the time they were seventy or eighty, there was always someone out there who was their senior; life wasn't as close to ending as it sometimes seemed. One of the things no one thought of when the Blocks appeared and the last regular generation got a little older each year was the effect of only being around other old people. My grandfather, sent to an old age home by my father the year after I was born, is probably laughing his ass off right now. If all you see are old people, you feel older. Another person you know dies every day. Everyone around you is complaining of arthritis and talking about the good ol' days. Sometimes they die of cancer. Sometimes they die of a heart attack. The end result is always the same. That was why the website tracking the oldest living person didn't work: because it was one name one day and another name the next day. The following week there was yet another person listed. Each name change made everyone else feel like they were one step closer to the end. It was easier to grow old when the end wasn't flaunted in your face. When it could be ignored.

A similar website tracked the youngest regular person. It was even more of a disaster than the site for old people. The youngest boy was born in Sweden nearly six years after Andrew was born, when 99.999999% of children born were Blocks. His celebrity had nothing to do with hit songs or athletic accomplishments. He became a celebrity solely because he was the last normal person who would ever be born. That's a lot of pressure—the children of celebrities had nothing on this kid. The boy had a difficult time adjusting to his fame because his stardom was a reflection of man's final hope for a normal life. In an interview on the evening news one night, the kid said he despised the stares he got everywhere he went. Senior citizens routinely asked for his autograph. By the time he was in middle school he was hooked on every kind of drug a Swedish boy could get his hands on. By the time he was in high school he had nearly died three different times from overdoses and was admitted to a drug rehab facility. Four years later, he was found in a bathtub with his wrists slit. A note on the bathroom floor didn't try to apologize or explain: "Now you can find someone else to put your hopes on."

The website held a contest to find the next youngest person but no one cared. Everyone had bigger concerns at that point than if a woman in Moscow was a day younger than a woman in Panama City and three days younger than a man in Vietnam. People realized they didn't want to see what was, essentially, a clock counting down humanity's last days.

It's been forty years since I thought about the youngest living regular person or the oldest. But now I find myself wondering how many of the thousand or so people left are younger than I am and how many are older. Am I smack in the middle of the group or am I leaning closer to the oldest person than to the youngest? Does it really matter if I'm closer to one side than the other? Part of me feels it does. Or, at least, it should. I would like to think everyone remaining is older than I am. At least that will give Andrew time to pass on before me.

January 13

A crippling chest pain racked my lungs today, throwing me into another coughing fit. It was impossible not to think I might be having a heart attack. I'm not even sure what it actually feels like to have a heart attack. That said, at the time, I was sure I was having one. I grabbed my chest where the pain was. No matter how many times I tried to let new air fill my lungs I just couldn't make it happen. The pain kept choking me. I went to the kitchen and got a glass of water. The pain faded a minute later. After it was gone I felt fine again. If the Johnsons were here and I told them about it, they probably would have joked that it was just indigestion.

Andrew sat on the sofa the entire time I was grabbing my chest. He didn't budge as I struggled to breathe. His eyes, closed, never once flickered. Out of instinct I called to him for help. Even in my pain I blushed from embarrassment after forgetting my predicament.

The pain came back an hour later, even worse this time. Only when the pain subsided a third time did I realize it really was nothing more than a bad case of indigestion, or, at least, I started to realize it was closer to the symptoms of indigestion than what I knew about heart attacks.

There was a time, not long ago, when I could do sit-ups while telling jokes, or pushups while people sat on my back. Tonight I was almost crippled by indigestion. How painful it is to get older. Not just in my joints and my bad back, but in the knowledge of all the things I could once do that I no longer can.

I never used to get headaches; now I get them all the time. Of course, I also never used to have chest pains, stomach pains, an aching back, knees that grind and feel like they're going to explode when I crouch down, or a constant cough. Somewhere up there, every senior citizen I ever smirked at when I was a kid is returning my smug look now that I know what it's like.

At various times throughout the day, a wave of pain hits my heart, making it impossible to breathe. Each time this happens I feel like I'm one step closer to dying. It's as though I have a limited number of times I can have that chest pain before I count down to zero and drop dead. Part of me wishes I knew what that magic number was so I could relax all the other times the pain comes. The other part of me is glad I don't have a set amount of days to count down, to worry about what will happen to Andrew when my cold body starts rotting on the kitchen floor.

Oh, what it was like to run sprints in high school and feel fine afterward, to play hide-and-go-seek and never get tired, to play capture the flag like it was guerilla warfare. As a kid, I used to scale fences, jump off rooftops, and swing from trees—all in the name of childhood fun—without a single worry given to my wellbeing. I remember one time after high school, I put Andrew on my bike and guided it back and forth across the driveway so he could experience what it was like. My mom watched from the living room window, one of the biggest smiles I've ever seen stretched across her face. There's no way I could get Andrew on a bike these days, and absolutely no way I could keep him balanced on it. If we tried that again now he would fall on his side and break his hip. The effort might even give me the heart attack I fear is on the horizon.

I was young once. I was invincible. I just need to keep reminding myself what it was like.

After the pain had gone I went to the sofa and took a seat next to Andrew. His eyes were open again. I tried to make a joke out of it by telling him he slept through the whole thing. Even if he could have, I doubt he would have laughed.

I do everything in my power to ensure he stays healthy and has a long life. But while I do this, I also don't want him to outlive me. Even with lingering fears of dying first, I can't do anything other than take care of him as best as I can. Doing anything else would go against what my parents wanted. So I base my day around his needs. When he gets sick, I take care of him. When he has an accident, I clean him up. And I would gladly do more. If a bear got in the house I would stand between it and Andrew and fight it to the death in order to protect my brother. He doesn't know what's happening to him; he doesn't know me from the Johnsons or anyone else; he doesn't know anything. And yet I love him so much it hurts.

It's times like this, when I think about our eventual fates, that I can't help but imagine us joining one of the communities. Andrew would have a support group in case I did pass away first. The worst part of Andrew's lot is that his fortune is tied to mine. It seemed like the best course to stay where we were, to stick it out. Why pick up and move when we were in a familiar place, in a house we loved? Now, alone, all I can do is hope my decisions don't cause Andrew undue pain, that if the end does come for him, it comes because it's his time and not because I'm dead on the kitchen floor.

He has never said or done anything hurtful toward anyone else. He has never neglected anyone. He has never done anything except grow older in peace and quiet. If there's a better candidate for who deserves a long and healthy life, I don't know who it could be.

The role of caretaker is not one I fancied playing as a little boy. If you told me then that I would have to clean my brother's ass each day, I would have laughed and yelled, "Gross!" the same way I did the first time an older kid from down the street said I should try to kiss Megan Simpleskin. Now, I don't think twice when I wipe the crap off Andrew and get him cleaned up. There's no grudge to hold with him for any of it. This goes beyond his being a Block; it's just part of getting older to have to take care of someone that way.

My mother once told me a story of a time when my dad was bedridden with the flu. They were newlyweds, still young and energetic. In the middle of the night, as he shivered in his sleep, he accidently soiled the sheets. My mother said she told him to stay under the warm blankets, moving him just enough so she could clean the dirty part of the bed and then also his dirty backside, and then she had him roll back over and go back to sleep. My father, she said, was in such a bad state that if she didn't clean him, he would have lain in his own shit until the fever broke. She loved him, and that's what loved ones have to do eventually. It took me a while to grow up, but I finally learned that for myself.

Cleaning familial crap is one thing, but I still wonder what I would have done in our younger years if I was bathing Andrew one night and he got an involuntary erection. It wouldn't be because of anything I was doing. He wouldn't even have the where-with-all to be embarrassed by the display. Maybe I would ignore it and finish shaving his chin as quickly as possible, another chore completed. Maybe I would leave the bathroom and come back when it was gone. How did the siblings of female Blocks handle it once a month when they also needed feminine caretaking? Thank God Andrew never had those problems.

I only have one brother, yet I find myself exhausted each evening from taking care of him. I find myself bringing his toothbrush into the living room and brushing his teeth there. My shoulders ache from the simple act of keeping the electric shaver running back and forth over his cheeks. The days I skip shaving him he actually resembles a man going through the normal stages of life rather than someone drifting along for almost eighty years. When I was younger I could yank him up from the sofa and carry him in my arms to the bathroom. At the time, I liked thinking it must have resembled a scene from an old movie in which a firefighter was the protagonist. My mom used to laugh hysterically when I would carry Andrew under my arm like he was a heavy suitcase. Now, though, on the few occasions when I still think it worthwhile to move him, it takes me the better part of an hour to keep repositioning him off the sofa and onto his wheelchair.

Oscar, always more observant and passive-aggressive than we gave him credit for (he was, after all, the same dog that routinely crapped on the carpet if he felt slighted), would have been jealous of the treatment Andrew receives. The dog wasn't allowed on the sofa, let alone allowed to sleep and crap on it.

This just goes to show how my priorities change depending on my circumstances. Fifty years ago I wouldn't let my dog jump up on the sofa because I didn't want to get fur on the fabric. Now I let my own brother sit on the same sofa that he has shit on a hundred times over. If you had told me back then that this is how things would turn out I probably would have joined everyone else in New Orleans or Miami. It's amazing how much one person can stand if there are only small changes from one day to the next. My circumstances here don't seem too terrible today because I saw what it was like yesterday and the day before that. Changes to Andrew, to me, to our house, to the neighborhood, are all at a snail's pace. If I could magically go from how life was forty years ago to how life is today, I would pack my things as quickly as possible and see if I could get to the settlement before the Johnsons.

I can't imagine what it's like for the caregivers at the group homes where three or four regular people take care of thousands of Blocks. How do they do it? I saw one of the group homes on a webcast a few years back. It was the Cleveland community before they packed up and joined with the Cincinnati group. Their group home was a converted incinerator factory, which, in turn, had been a converted elementary school at one point. The entire inside was gutted, so there was nothing resembling classrooms, a gymnasium, or a cafeteria. Instead, the brick walls became one giant coliseum of Blocks.

Thousands of them were arranged on the floor in neat rows, each one with a blanket underneath its motionless body so it wasn't directly on the hard concrete. The video showed a woman talking and smiling to each Block as she made sure their nutrient bags were full. A different woman, this one in the background, could be seen wetting a sponge and rubbing it on the lips of the motionless Blocks. It was supposed to show how humanely the Blocks were being treated. Aisles provided the caretakers with paths to walk up and down the different quadrants of the facility. The camera panned back and the hundreds of Blocks on the screen became a thousand, then five thousand, then ten thousand. It was one of the most horrifying things I've ever seen.

The thought of Andrew becoming just another body in a giant mass of nameless people was enough to never let him out of my sight. I didn't mind the thought of the Johnsons taking care of him if I died first, but leaving him in the middle of that gigantic horde of lifeless people seemed like an injustice. Worse, it was something my parents would have abhorred. These rows of men and women were people's sons and daughters. They were people's brothers and sisters. And they were just abandoned. I thought back to the way my mother answered my questions when I was a boy—about taking Andrew on vacation with us if he didn't know what was going on around him—and I understood that her worst nightmare would have been seeing Andrew lined up as part of a row of a hundred Blocks.

When I think of whether or not I made the right decision for Andrew, I remember that footage. It was impossible not to imagine him as a random body—line 17 in row 57—surrounded by people he didn't know, and I tell myself he would rather be here with me, even if it's just the two of us fending for ourselves. If he could have heard the way my mother and father spoke about him, about the importance of family, if he could have seen my father holding him above the waves as they crashed, there would be no other place my brother would want to be than right here.

January 15

I have casual thoughts (very quickly discounted) about leaving Andrew outside to fend for himself. They aren't serious ideas, just whimsical I-could-do-this kind of thoughts that are gone as soon as they arrive. Like driving head-on into an approaching car, or grabbing a cop's gun out of its holster. Leaving him outside is the same as turning him over to the dogs and vultures. The thought makes me sick to my stomach. Andrew will never be able to smile at one of my jokes, know the highs and lows of growing older, or be able to put a hand on my shoulder and tell me everything will be okay, but I'll never leave him to that fate. It doesn't matter if he can't understand his surroundings, he's my brother and I'll stay with him to the end. Better this than to have him surrounded by people who could take advantage of him.

There have always been people who said Blocks weren't really people at all. They argued Blocks could be left outside to die because they don't know and don't care what happens to them. The people saying this would have made great Spartans since the ancient army was in the practice of throwing deformed babies into a chasm, but they also forgot about the potential of those wasted lives. These people tried to equate an indifference to Blocks as being no different than thinking abortions were okay. A regular fetus, they argued, probably has more sensory capability than an adult Block, it's just that Blocks have the advantage of looking like the rest of us. I never thought this was a well-reasoned argument. I was swayed, though, by an old woman I saw on TV one time who asked if we would be indifferent to Blocks if one of them could hold the key to fixing the Great De-evolution. Surely, she said to the studio audience, we have to be around Blocks, we have to understand them, if we want to have any hope of correcting the problem.

There were more stories than I care to remember of people abusing or abandoning Blocks. Blocks were cursed from birth by being easy to abandon, but as they became teenagers and then young adults, more of their numbers were left to the abuses that normal people could impart. Some of these Blocks eventually ended up at the front doors of group homes like the ones who were abandoned at birth, most arriving either beaten or diseased. Newborn babies could cry for attention. Little kids could hold onto their parents' clothes and beg not to be abandoned. The Blocks, though, could be abandoned just as easily when they were teenagers or senior citizens as when they were first born. They were further cursed by not being able to state their case for why they shouldn't be left behind; even a newborn baby could reach out for its mother. Any parent struggling with the decision to abandon a Block child would never be swayed by pleading looks or tear-filled eyes. They could load middle-aged Blocks into the backseat of their car and leave them any place at all, even a landfill. The Blocks would never cry or ask where they were being taken. They wouldn't try to hold onto the safety belt as they were dragged out of the backseat to be left on the roadside. Even a kitten would do more to preserve itself.

All across the country Blocks were stolen or specifically raised for unspeakable purposes. Some were prostituted as sex slaves, others were used as punching bags until they died. Little boys, teenage girls, every type of Block adult, were, at one time or another, found by police raids in dirty houses owned by sex offenders. Some of the Blocks found by police had blisters and sores covering every inch of their bodies. Some had been beaten so badly it was surprising they were still alive. And yet these beaten and abused Blocks never uttered a cry, never tried to fight off their attackers, never knew what was happening to them. During their trials, the men who took advantage of them complained that it wasn't rape because the Blocks never said no, that it wasn't any other crime because the Blocks didn't understand pain or fear. Communities all across the world, even in Philadelphia, were outraged. The offenders were either sent to prisons or were executed. The punishments handed down didn't factor in whether or not a Block could feel pain or humiliation. Rightfully so. It was blind justice in the most beautiful sense possible. Most of the rescued Blocks had their injuries and diseases treated. Some were so badly beaten they were euthanized in order to put them out of the misery they would have felt if they could acknowledge pain.

One controversial part of the Survival Bill was its proposal for how prisons would be handled. Traditional prisons wouldn't work as the inmates and guards became geezers and the last convicted felon, initially a kid who had murdered an old woman when he was eighteen, grew up to be an old man. Congressmen relied on a group of sociologists to come up with a viable solution for handling those citizens deemed unsafe within the general community. After much debate, the solution they came up with was to redistribute the inmates to different prisons based on the type of crime they had been convicted of. Murderers were sent to the same prisons. Arsonists, robbers, and those convicted of vehicular manslaughter were handled the same way. Pedophiles and rapists were sent to prisons with the murderers. Each prison was given food generators, electrical generators, incinerators, and anything else they needed to survive. Once each prison was fitted to be a self-contained facility, the inmates were left to fend for themselves. With the gates sealed but each individual cell unlocked, the inmates spent the rest of their lives in prison the way they had been sentenced. The inmates at each facility were left to create their own rules, to govern themselves as much as their various dysfunctions allowed. The saner of these inmates were quoted as saying they missed the days when security guards would break up fights and confiscate any shanks they might find. Without a security presence, inmates quickly began walking around with knives and axes in clear sight. Some of the prisoners might have escaped the madness by living in nearby abandoned homes, but all of the stories I heard had the inmates staying on the prison grounds in a daily fight to rule the facility. The prisoners at one prison burned the entire building to the ground while they were still inside. Everyone died. The inmates at another facility formed into two armies that fought until every single person was dead.

Rumors got out in various internet chat rooms that all the prisoners in a facility in Minnesota had escaped and were beginning to filter into the general population. Similar rumors were sometimes heard about a prison in Kansas or one in Maryland, and always seemed to coincide with the migration talks going on in those places. No sooner would a city, already in favor of joining a more southern settlement, begin having talks about abandoning their homes than more rumors of freed convicts would begin slipping out. It took one person to say something—the supermax jail was empty after everyone escaped—and no matter how unreliable the rumor was, no matter how little evidence there was to support it, the whispers scared people into wanting to head south to the final communities a little sooner than they would have before.

There was talk of re-opening the infamous Alcatraz and sending California's deadliest inmates there. The abandoned jail would be a perfect place for these men, capable of hurting anyone around them, to be isolated from the general population. And while they would have an opportunity to swim to safety, none of the inmates had the stamina anymore to make the swim across the channel. One of Alcatraz's historians actually laughed when asked if senior citizens, albeit senior citizens who happened to also be serial killers, could make the swim back to the mainland. The bodies of seventy and eighty-year old inmates would be found off the banks of San Francisco's settlement, the historian said. In the end, they decided it wasn't worth the hours of labor it would take to install power, a food generator, and incinerator, and the idea was scrapped in favor of shipping the inmates off to a maximum security prison in Nevada.

In Russia, there was talk of transporting violent offenders into the middle of Siberia, then building a giant wall around the frozen tundra so they couldn't rejoin the general population. The idea was discarded once plans for the wall illustrated how resources were already becoming limited. Not to mention there was a noticeable shortage of middle-aged men willing to spend their time constructing a wall hundreds and hundreds of miles long if there was nothing in it for them.

As for the Blocks who were taken advantage of, I can't begin to imagine which is worse: being a molested Block who doesn't know what is happening, or being a regular person who can fight back, but also has to deal with the pain and fear that is forced upon them. Would I rather be tortured and abused my entire life without understanding what was happening, or would it be better to have the chance to fight back even if the abuser was still successful in his attack? If I had to spend the rest of my life living with the pain of what had happened, would I rather not be aware of it at all? In all the years I've thought about that question I've never been able to determine that one might not be as bad as the other.

I don't want to imagine those things happening to Andrew. I can't help myself, though. My love for him forces me to think about what I'd do if he was taken from me, inducted into a sex ring, or stored away in the damp basement of a man who abuses him every day. It makes me want to give Andrew a hug that lasts for days, a hug that doesn't have to end and that can protect him for the rest of his life.

January 16

One of the bushes behind my house actually has the beginnings of some leaves again, a sign that the mild winter has subsided. There wasn't much of a winter to speak of, except for a couple of days seeming a little chillier than the others. The bare limbs will eventually give way to bright green leaves. My pessimistic side views spring as the time of year when the leaves keep me from seeing into the woods for animals that might be lurking out there. I can still hear them, know they are there, but can't see them until they are less then twenty feet away. At that distance they would chase me down before I could get back into the house.

The weeds didn't die during winter, but they did have a momentary pause in their expansion. In a couple of years, the weeds will come up through the kitchen floor and the living room. When that happens my home would become a glorified tent rather than the solid, impenetrable house it was meant to be.

Every year I am surrounded by more wildlife than I was the year before. I'm sure it's the same feeling the animals had each year when they saw more people plopped down on top of already overcrowded cities and streets. Every rabbit and squirrel that watched as car after car passed by on newly-widened roads had to be asking itself, "When will the madness finally end?"

There was a time when my front porch was reserved for quiet nights for Andrew and me. This, of course, was back when it was easier for me to move him around. And before the animals learned they didn't have to fear us. We would sit there on the wicker chairs, noises all around us from the woods and golf course. A howl from one part of the forest would be followed by some barking from another direction. After the barking quieted down a cat would meow or a bear would growl. The animals are the last orchestra the world will know. I sipped iced tea while the music went on around us. Andrew had to be sprayed down with insect repellent before he was allowed outside. The bugs used to love having something sweet to bite that didn't swat at them.

Now, instead of going outside, we sit at the patio door when we want to watch the wildlife. The other day I saw a pack of house cats that must have been fifty or sixty strong. They grazed on bugs hiding in the tall grass and then fled when a pack of fifteen Rottweilers came charging out of the brush. Today, a bear roamed onto our yard. It sniffed around the incinerator, then wandered off. A couple of minutes later, a squirrel stayed in the open grass for too long. We saw it get snatched away from the ground by a hawk. Its little legs flailed as the hawk carried it to the top of a tree and, presumably, tore it apart. I know that happens all the time—the hawks and owls have to feed on something too—but I had never actually seen it happen with my own eyes until today.

I turned to Andrew as the hawk was soaring back into the sky and said something stupid like, "Holy shit, did you see that!"

A little bit later a pack of dogs squared off against a couple of wolves. The dogs consisted of a German pointer, an Irish setter, two cocker spaniels, and two Labrador retrievers. In the end, both sets of animals thought better of actual bloodshed and were content with displays of aggression such as growling and raising their hind fur. The two gangs eventually backed away from where they had come.

"Wow, that was amazing," I said to Andrew.

I repositioned him to face the TV. *The Silence of the*

Lambs played on the television the rest of the night. I like to envision Andrew as even more dastardly than Hannibal Lecter, the ultimate evil mastermind, secretly biding his time by pretending to be comatose, then one day taking advantage of his situation by becoming the new leader of the neighborhood. He would be like Keyser Söze, but pretending to be motionless and mute instead of having a limp and a bad hand. At the same time, when watching Indiana Jones with Andrew, I imagine my brother swinging from a whip and finding rare archeological treasures, so the idea of him being super evil doesn't reflect on how I feel about him personally.

As I was writing this I heard another animal howl from inside the forest. I've gotten pretty good at determining which animal is being killed by the sound it makes as it dies. Sometimes I can even guess which animal was doing the killing. Tonight it was a fox being eaten. Probably by a pack of dogs. The terrified wails made me go back to the living room to make sure Andrew was okay.

On nights like tonight I turn off the lights in my room, power off my monitor, and close the hallway door. My bedroom is thrown into complete darkness. At the window, I have a perfect vision of the woods. The moon decides how much of the surrounding wildlife I get to see. If the clouds are out I can barely make out the outline of the trees or see where the branches end and the sky begins. But if the sky is clear and the moon is full, like it is tonight, I can see animals pacing back and forth at the edge of the woods. If I stare long enough, a series of eyes will line up at the edge of the trees and gaze back at me. One pair of eyes will be there first. Then two. Then three. One time there were eight sets of eyes, all lined up behind the layer of brush at the edge of my lawn, staring at me through my bedroom window. I couldn't tell if it was a pack of wolves or dogs; they are more similar these days than they are different. The eyes peeking out at me become green or orange depending on the moon's light. All of them remained there to see if I would be foolhardy enough to leave my house after the sun had set.

It's funny how differently the animals act during the daylight than when it's dark. If I stepped outside at night the animals, dogs and wolves alike, would run toward me at full speed. My dead body would be dragged back into the forest within seconds. If I went outside right now I might as well jog willingly into the woods to make it easier for them. If it was daylight, though, and I went outside, the animals might growl and hiss at me, but more often than not they would remain at the edge of the woods. They might pace back and forth but they wouldn't make a move while the sun was out unless they were particularly desperate for food. But my circumstances are no different between day and night. Maybe they think I can see better than them during the day, or maybe they think my neighbors will come to my rescue (little do they know my neighbors are all gone!), but none of this is true. If a single animal out there, their blazing orange eyes tracking me, was smart enough to realize the sun doesn't hold special power, they could have me for a meal.

A good bet would wager how many more days I can go to the incinerator in my backyard before one of the animals is willing to dart out of the woods and attack in the sunlight.

January 18

I don't want to think about being trapped in this neighborhood. I know we're stuck here, but everything might be okay if I can just keep thinking about better times. It's becoming more difficult, though, to act like everything will be fine. Instead of focusing on the end, I find myself reminiscing about the relics scattered around the house.

One of my favorite pictures of Andrew is from an amusement park when I was twenty. The trip was a mini-vacation to celebrate his sixteenth birthday. All things considered, I wasn't sure how much of an event it could be, but my dad shocked us by saying Andrew should ride one of the roller coasters. My mother didn't want her son getting on that kind of ride but my father convinced her it would be okay. I soothed her by saying I would be next to him the entire time to make sure nothing happened to him. She didn't stop worrying, she was a mother after all, but she relented and let him go on the ride.

The roller coaster took forever to climb the first steep hill. The frantic whispering of people in front of and behind us grew louder as the train of chairs made its way up the sharp incline. Each yard up that giant hill meant the ride would be that much more ferocious as soon as it started speeding down the other side. It took forever to get to the top. Even I was getting nervous. The anticipation created by these rides always made my nerves worse than they needed to be. There would be loops and rolls until everyone could barely breathe. There would be spins and g-force until everybody wanted to throw up. I tensed all of my muscles so the shakes weren't noticeable. This also helped keep my jaw from clattering. A girl behind me was crying. We were only five feet from the top. My fingers were clasped tightly around the chest guard that held us all in place. Just then, right as we got to the very top of the mountain, not a single thing higher in the sky than us, I turned and looked at Andrew. There was comfort to be found in how serene and unconcerned he was. His eyes were perfectly at peace. He was the only person on the entire ride who looked like he belonged there. Everyone else was screaming, or trying to scream, while he just sat there and let the roller coaster take us in three consecutive spirals followed by four consecutive loops. Each change in course made me feel like I'd been sucker-punched, but Andrew took it all in stride. He never moved so much as a finger, never made a single noise. When the ride was over he was in the exact same position as when it started. His hair was standing almost completely straight up because of the g-force, but other than that he was an angel.

After the roller coaster, we went to one of those cutouts where you stand behind it and put your face through a hole to make it look like you're the one flying a jetfighter, driving a race car, or otherwise doing something more spectacular than you would normally do. My father held Andrew where his head could stick out of one hole. I stood next to him with my head out the other hole. And just like that we became professional baseball players. Andrew was the catcher for the hated Chicago Cubs while I was the all-star slugger for the St. Louis Cardinals. I still laugh at the contrast in our faces. The hitter should be focused and calm, but I was hamming it up by making a face like I was going to charge the mound. The catcher, usually busy giving signs to the pitcher, looked like he was sound asleep.

The picture has been on my bed stand ever since. As much as it was the perfect photo of us as brothers, it has somehow become even more than that for me now. I find myself staring at it for what seems like hours before I go to sleep. Some nights I'm still smiling when I close my eyes.

I still constantly mention that picture to Andrew.

Sometimes I bring it out of my room and show it to him to remind him how we spent our time as a family. It's important to show him that, even if it was only for a moment and only for a photo, he was the catcher of a professional baseball team (it was the Cubs, though, so just barely a pro team). Sometimes, when I'm feeling lightheaded with the responsibilities of our lives, I tell him I ended up getting a homerun that day. Other times, when I realize he's all I have left, I tell him he gave the pitcher good signs and I struck out.

My favorite t-shirt is also from Andrew's birthday that year. It doesn't fit anymore, but I still pull it out of the closet occasionally just because it makes me smile. The shirt has a picture of a sixteen-year old Andrew sleeping (his eyes are closed) with a thought bubble showing that he's dreaming about walking on the moon. I like to think there were options for what the dream's picture could have been about—leading an army into battle, being at the beach with a swimsuit model—but that was the one my mom thought most fitting for him.

Three months after Andrew's birthday we were invited to a sweet sixteen party that one of our neighbors was throwing for their Block daughter. A hundred other local Blocks and their families were invited. All of the regulars celebrated this girl's sixteenth birthday by going to the park and eating hot dogs and flying kites while the birthday girl sat under a tree so the shade could keep her cool. She never played games, she never rode on the merry-go-round. Nor did she magically become a professional athlete. She remained motionless and quiet the entire time just like all the other Blocks, until the party was over and the Blocks' parents loaded them back into cars and took them away. It was a nice party but it could never compare to my parents and me taking Andrew to the amusement park.

January 21

The amusement park I wrote about the other day, the one from Andrew's sixteenth birthday, is no doubt dilapidated and abandoned now. Without men there maintaining the rides, acre upon acre of manmade structures, designed for the sole purpose of entertaining families, would slowly rust, the overly fun characters and graphics plastered all around the park withering away to look like vengeful demons painted all over the rides.

How long would it have taken for the metal pins holding the rollercoaster's tracks together to rust and snap? That first hill at the very top of the ride seemed impossibly high when I was young—ten stories, maybe twenty? After falling that far to the ground, I can't imagine what kind of noise it must have made when it landed on the concrete below.

What a waste it was for everyone to take time out of their lives just to buy cotton candy, watch teenagers parade around in preposterous costumes, and wait in line for rides that were over a minute later. Even the most deluxe of haunted houses from my childhood must pale in comparison with today's abandoned theme parks. Those houses just had cobwebs and spooky noises, maybe scarecrows and fake blood thrown on the walls. The ghost town theme parks didn't have any of that, but they did have bird shit covering every place where children used to laugh on their way to the next attraction and vultures perched at the top of each deserted ride waiting for the next wolf to leave a little bit of bloody guts from a vanquished cat.

The ticket booth has a colony of thirty mixed-breed feral dogs living inside it. You couldn't pay me to go there now. The screams of dying animals would echo across the empty park. Instead of little kids waiting impatiently for the next ride, kittens and puppies hide from the bears and wolves while they wait for their momma to come back with food, if the momma can avoid the hundreds of other animals and return at all.

Everything has gone to hell. The happiest places on earth have become littered with animal carcasses. Random bones scattered in random places. If I hadn't spent the day cleaning up Andrew's shit and feeling sorry for myself—no one is coming to save us; we are truly alone—I might be writing instead about how nice it would be to imagine a bear and a dog having their picture taken in the same cutout where Andrew and I once posed. It's just not one of those days to be writing about happy things.

I lost my patience with Andrew again today. He chose the exact moment I was repositioning him on the sofa, with one of my hands around his shoulder and the other under his leg, to crap himself. It squished against my palm. Pieces of liquid shit pushed through the cotton khakis he was dressed in.

"God damn it!" I yelled.

At that moment I swear I would have fought him if he had turned toward me and said, "Stop you're whining, it's just a little bit of crap."

I paced back and forth across the living room while Andrew remained motionless and speechless, devoid of any embarrassment at the mess he had made.

"Son of a bitch," I screamed, not at him, but at the neighborhood in general. It did not make me feel any better.

One glance at my helpless brother was all it took for me to feel ashamed of my outburst. There was nothing he could do about changing his circumstances. I washed my hands before apologizing to him.

It took all of my strength to get him back into his old position on the sofa. And when it was done, I was out of breath and desperately in need of a glass of water. My chest was on fire. I felt lightheaded.

I sat next to him on the sofa until I stopped shaking. "I'm really sorry. I shouldn't have snapped at you like that."

I wouldn't have yelled at him if the Johnsons were still here, or, at the very least, if there was a chance someone might find us.

January 22

Andrew and I are over another round of colds. One reason Andrew is lucky: he doesn't have the reflex to cough. He gets all the same colds I get, but as I walk from room to room announcing my presence and departure with long strings of hacking coughs, he sits perfectly still as though the frogs in his throat don't exist. Perhaps the frogs in his throat are Block frogs.

The days have become difficult for all of us. Andrew's arm shows signs of irritation where the IV for his nutrient bag goes in. He hasn't had an infection there since he was a baby. Either he is growing weak in his old age or I'm not doing as good a job of disinfecting the needles.

Andrew would think me insane if he knew what I did today. He would break out of his spell long enough to say, "You're crazy if you give that dog water. You're just encouraging more animals to come up to our house."

I don't even know if that would be his opinion or not, but it seems like something my parents would have said. I transfer their voice onto him since he doesn't have one of his own. Each time a voice in the back of my head reminds me to get the day's chores done before I relax in front of the TV, I think it's something my parents would have said to me when I was younger, and because of that I think of it as something Andrew would say to me now. The same thing happens when I hear a tiny voice reminding me to clean the food processor before going to sleep. A clean kitchen keeps bugs away. "Yes, mom," I would have said as a kid. "Okay, Andrew," I think to myself now.

In an attempt to gauge my brother's reaction, I look over at him each time the dog arrives on our porch. On the days when I'm in a bad mood, Andrew would tell me to leave the dog alone. When I've had a good day, Andrew would say it might be fun to have a pet; it would be like old times.

The dog gave cautious sniffs while approaching my patio. The bowl of water, it seemed, might be a trick of some kind. It's possible the dog caught my scent on the bowl and questioned if it could trust this strange creature that lives inside a house while the other surrounding animals all live in the woods. Its head rose then, expecting an attack party from the woods, but for the moment at least there was nothing around to harm it. It didn't stay for very long after having the water. I blame the constant shuffling of unknown predators lurking in the forest brush.

I have to admit part of me would like the dog's company at the edge of my driveway while I'm staring down at the Johnsons' house. Its tail would flap against my leg. If the dog got nervous because of the smell, if it whined and wanted to retreat to the woods, I'd know I shouldn't walk down the street to investigate. But if the dog panted and sniffed as though the smell wasn't any worse than walking in the woods and coming across a huge mound of bear crap, I'd know it was okay to venture down the street.

The dog will quickly get used to the water I provide. After drinking today, it looked at me through the glass panels, its head cocked sideways, a look that makes me think it was wondering where the food dish was that belongs next to the water.

I've begun talking to it the way I would if it was next to me on the floor, my hand rubbing its belly, instead of us on either side of the glass door. It has learned not to be bothered when I make movements on my side of the glass. When I placed my hand on the glass today, it looked up casually, then rested its head again. And for my part, when its head darted up because of a sound from the forest,

I didn't accidently jump in my seat the way I would have a week ago. I knew it was reacting to something behind it, something it considered a threat, not to me, the man who sits and talks to it, gives it water. We were perfectly happy with each other's company. Andrew had no complaints either.

I was in the middle of my blabbering, one-sided conversation with the dog when a fox appeared at the edge of the woods. Immediately, the Labrador was on all four feet, the hair on its back standing straight up. I couldn't believe the same dog I sat and relaxed with could growl so ferociously. It bared its fangs and saliva spilled out from between its teeth. I was amazed at how sharp, how long, its teeth were. They were the same teeth that every pet dog had, but as a wild beast they looked deadly. It was hard to imagine those same daggers retrieving a twig in a game of fetch.

The fox was smart enough to stay at the edge of the forest. It crouched low to the ground but was also curious at this dog and man sharing a day together. Its teeth still bared, the dog took a small step toward the fox. Then another. The movement was so slight that I would have sworn the Labrador was in the same spot as before if I hadn't personally seen it move. It repeated this miniature step again. I knew it was going to make a mad dash at the fox. Just then, the fox jumped higher than I would have thought possible, vanishing into the trees.

The dog's fur was still sticking straight up, its teeth still on display. Nothing else dared to approach. After a minute it relaxed and turned back toward the spot it had been occupying on my welcome mat. It grumbled a little, then went back to resting in the sunlight, giving a single whine in my direction as though apologizing for the outburst.

"I'm sorry," it was trying to say. "Nobody is more embarrassed by my behavior than I am, but I have to act like that if I want the other animals to leave me alone. It won't happen again, I promise."

I tried to go back to my meaningless conversation with it, but I couldn't get the image of it—ready to chase down another creature, dig its teeth into the other animal's throat, disembowel it—out of my head. The moment between us was ruined. The dog was on its side with its belly facing me. It gave me a carefree, happy glance, as though I was supposed to join it in acting like nothing had happened. I couldn't think of it the way I had five minutes earlier; I couldn't nurture it like it was my pet.

It struck me as odd to think of the Johnsons at that moment, but that was exactly what I did. They had been my best friends. My only friends for the past two years. And then, just like that, they were gone. I had an idea of them that was based on nothing more than time spent together, and that understanding of them and who they were had been completely inaccurate. It took much less time with the dog, but in the end I realized the same thing. My romantic notions will be the end of me.

I leaned over to check on Andrew. He was, as he always is, perfectly unaffected by everything that had taken place. When I walked by the patio door again the dog was gone.

Now that I'm over the most recent bout of coughs and fever, I'm not going to wait any longer to find out what's causing the smell down in the neighborhood. I wouldn't be surprised if the Johnsons' incinerator broke in the weeks leading to their departure, and instead of simply walking to one of the other working units in the neighborhood, they let a landfill build up behind their house before leaving Camelot.

People always used to say that serial killers seemed like normal people; you would never suspect one of foul behavior because they presented a sense of normality in order to hide their insanity. I feel that way about the Johnsons now. These people who I spent thirty years next to, who I discussed the fate of our neighborhood with, not only snuck out in the middle of the night without saying goodbye, but they didn't even burn their trash before they left. No matter how long someone lives down the street from you, you never really know them.

My only concern in getting down the street is protecting myself from the animals on my way there. I was going to take a golf club with me but imagined it breaking in half after the first time I hit a dog (as if I can actually swing that hard anymore) and then being left with a useless grip to defend myself with. Instead, I'll take a baseball bat. It's heavier than I wanted, but it won't break. And I'll keep a knife in my backpack. And I'll wait until the sun is at its highest. That's when the animals are most likely to stay in the shadows. If I attempted the walk in the middle of the night I'd never make it past my driveway.

To combat the smell, a bandana will be wrapped over my nose and mouth. That's my plan. I'll put it into action tomorrow.

I like to think the Labrador will walk with me on my way there. I might cry if a dog actually did accompany me down the street like pets used to do. Maybe I would throw a tennis ball ahead of me and it would go and get it and bring it back. That's a nice thing to think about as I fall asleep.

January 23

Getting down to the Johnsons' wasn't as easy as I thought it would be. I was all set: my bandana and bat in hand, a knife and a water bottle in my backpack. But when I opened my front door a bear was sunning itself in the Matthews' old driveway. I could have tried to make a run for it, but I would have been out of breath and hobbling after twenty feet. I once saw a black bear chase down a Rottweiler that had gotten separated from its pack; I wouldn't have a chance of making it. And with the roads overgrown with weeds and broken up into rocks and potholes, I would have twisted my ankle before I could break a sweat. The bear would have all the time in the world to walk up and tear my guts out.

I considered sneaking out the patio door and walking behind the houses until I was at the Johnsons', but if the bear caught one sniff of me it would have been over just the same. There was also the risk of some other creature waiting for me at the forest's edge. One of my greatest fears these days is being dragged into the woods by some monster that has a hold of my leg. No matter how much I would struggle, the animal would drag me away until I was enveloped by leaves and brush. Not soon after I would be eaten alive. Maybe I could hit whatever animal came at me with my bat, fight it off, but if it was part of a pack there's no way I could take them all on. A pack of ten feral dogs would make short work of me. One of them would easily pounce and knock me to the ground. As soon as I was down I would never be able to stand up again. There would be an army of wild dogs ensuring I stayed exactly where they wanted me. And to think they used to bark ever so cutely and play fetch.

My plan will have to wait until tomorrow, when the bear is gone.

January 24

One of the most amazing days of my life. I scanned the neighborhood for animals before leaving my house. The streets were clear. My supplies were in hand. The sun was directly overhead. I was sweating even before I stepped into the open air. At the end of my driveway I stopped to make sure no animals were getting ready to dart out. A trickle of sweat ran down my back. Even from the end of my driveway, the smell coming down the street made me want to gag. That was how my journey down to the Johnsons' house began.

It took me longer to make my way down the street than I thought it would because the grass provided cover for each pothole. Some of the crevices are the size of human bodies. I had just gotten past the Mackenzies' old home when I saw it out of the corner of my eye: a tiny grey blur. Staring toward the bushes where the movement had been, I stopped in the middle of the street. Everything was still. I kept staring at the bush without seeing anything move. Eventually, I realized I was an old guy standing in the open, welcoming any bear or wolf to a surprise present. As soon as I turned to start down the road I swore I saw another flash of movement to my side. But when I looked at the shrubs, there was nothing. To the extent possible, without tripping on the broken road in front of me, I kept my eyes toward the Jeffersons' overgrown bushes. I got halfway between the Jeffersons' home and the Gladwells' house when I saw it. It darted out of one bush and ran to the next as quickly as I had ever seen anything run in my life. A house cat. It was grey and fluffy, the type an old woman would have pampered with expensive cat food and demeaning costumes.

It was hunting me.

My eyes stayed on the bush it was hiding in. After a

couple of more steps, a second cat appeared. This one was grey and white with a stripe of orange down its face. It trailed ten feet behind the first one. Another one, this one completely white, darted out of the bushes in front of the first. By the time I got to the next house there were four. Then five. I was closer to the Johnsons' house by that point than I was to my own. I paused in the middle of the street to consider my options. It took me one look back at my house to determine I'd gone too far to turn back. A collection of eight cats was meowing and hissing to each other, trading tactics on how best to approach their prey. I shook the bat in their direction. They didn't back away or seem threatened at all. Then there were nine of them. Then ten. An army of white, orange, grey, and black fur watched me from the edge of the Balmers' former garage. They kept my pace so they were always the same distance, parallel with me on my journey. Unlike me, having to constantly look down to make sure I didn't turn an ankle, they never took their eyes off the animal they were hunting. Every time they hissed in my direction or licked their lips, I shivered and gripped the bat tighter. I couldn't imagine a worse way to die than being eaten alive in the middle of the overgrown street in Camelot. It wouldn't be a quick death; those tiny little mouths and centimeter long claws would take a long time to kill me. I would be alive for a good part of the day while they snacked on my flesh.

Up to that point, the cats had taken my mind away from the growing stench I was trying to find. As soon as I attempted to calm myself by taking a deep breath, I gagged, almost throwing up all over my feet. The smell was overwhelming. It was amazing that the cats weren't gagging along in unison. Trash shouldn't smell that bad. Five years of dirty Block diapers shouldn't smell that bad, not even if I was standing in a pile of them. Once the odor was in my nose it was all I could smell anymore;

repositioning the bandana in front of my mouth did nothing to help.

I looked back at where the cats had previously assembled, then stumbled in shock when I realized they were now only ten feet away from me. Dispersing from a group and encircling me like I was already defeated and didn't know it, they seemed to have sensed my weakness. I could have taken a swing at one of them with my bat, but thought better of it; if I did swing it might not scare them away as I intended, might only provoke them to start their attack even sooner. They circled and hissed, circled and hissed. It was difficult to keep track of the ones that went behind me; no matter where I looked they were all around. I was drowning in cats. One of them got too close and I swiped at it with the Louisville Slugger. The wood hit the edge of the cat's butt, causing it to bounce off the road and skid back to the other waiting kitties. It righted itself and hissed at me so fiercely that I felt like I was pitted against ten mountain lions instead of ten tiny cats. It was a sad state of affairs that I was over-matched by little things that used to love scratching posts and licking cat-nip.

Another cat lunged at me. With the bat's end I poked it in the face. It limped away for a moment, then rejoined the pack. Another one sprang at me. Then another. One bounced off me by sheer chance without me intelligently defending myself. Another one was hanging from my shoulder by its front paws, swinging back and forth behind me as I tried to swat it off. They were all biting at my ankles now. I finally grabbed hold of the tail of the one on my back, its claws embedded in my skin. When I threw it in the air it had pieces of my flesh on its daggers, my blood in its fur. I was swinging my bat wildly now, not even aiming. The bat hit square across one of their faces. The little animal remained motionless in the middle of the street as its companions kept trying to bring me down. If I stumbled they would have jumped on me and I would never stand upright again.

Right then, as one of the cats reared up and hissed at me, ready to jump at my face, a roar came from my side. A pair of golden retrievers was there, only five feet away from me. I'm not sure why, but I laughed. It wasn't a mild chuckle either, but a full burst of the loudest laughter I was capable of mustering at that moment. Part of me felt like they were my teammates in this mighty injustice and had finally come to be tagged into the match. I snapped out of this fantasy when one of them brushed against my leg. It had been focused on the cats until it touched me. Then it turned and growled, only two feet away, so that my heart stopped beating until its eyes focused back on the cats. One of the cats tried to dart away. It was in the mouth of one of the dogs, however, before it could go anywhere. The dog bit down. A loud crunch signaled the cat was dead. The dog dropped it on the road before swiping at another one. The second cat skidded sideways through the weeds. By the time this cat realized which way it wanted to run the dog's teeth were around its face, throwing it back and forth through the air like a doll.

I backed away from the fight. The Johnsons' house was only one driveway away. I wasn't interested in it any longer, though. Thoughts of Andrew flooded into my head—my brother sitting by himself in our house. The urge came over me to go back and make sure he was okay. The dogs had four of the cats dead on the ground with the other cats retreating to the forest. If I would have turned and run toward my home the dogs would have chased me down too. Instead, I walked slowly, keeping my eyes on them except when I needed to check the uneven ground under my feet. The pair of golden retrievers stuck with the food they already had. One of them growled at me when I kept my eyes on it. It only did so because I was making it nervous and it wasn't used to the feeling.

Back on my porch, I turned and looked at the battlefield one more time. The Johnsons' house looked like it was on the other side of the country even though it was only a hundred yards down the road. In my childhood I could have sprinted there and back without breathing heavy. Hell, I could have carried Andrew on my back and not broken a sweat. Now, my clothes were soaked, my knees were shaking. And I was lightheaded. Worst of all, a pack of house cats had almost gotten me! The neighborhood was already overgrown, barren, and worn down, but at that moment I realized I wasn't any better off than the neglected golf course or the broken road. The only difference between me and the rest of the neighborhood was that Andrew was sitting inside waiting for me to take care of him while the rest of Camelot had no one to watch over it and keep it maintained. Other than that, Camelot had as much to envy as I did.

I was getting ready to close the front door when I heard another roar, a different kind of roar, from down the street. This one was deeper and more measured than the one given by the dogs. The golden retrievers stopped eating. Their heads were directed at a giant brown bear lumbering down the road. The hair on the back of the dogs' necks stood straight up as they snarled in anger. Deciding that another fight wasn't a good idea, each dog took a cat in its mouth and jogged back to the edge of the woods to eat in peace. Two dead cats were left for the bear. The giant brown animal took one of the furry, little bodies in its big paws and then the cat disappeared into its mouth. Happy, the bear rolled on its back and scratched itself against the warm, rough ground. Eventually it got up and dusted itself off, then grabbed the other cat in its paws and shoveled that one into its mouth too. The army of cats, just like that, was reduced to half its number. And I had a pair of dogs to thank for being alive.

As soon as I got to my kitchen I filled a glass with water. The bat and bandana were sitting in the middle of the floor. With my breath back, no longer shaking, I sat on the sofa and repeated the entire story to Andrew. I'm sure he wouldn't have believed a single word of the amazing turn of events unless he saw it with his own two eyes.

He probably would have listened with a straight face until I was finished, then said, "A pair of dogs saved you from a pack of cats? And then a bear challenged the dogs? Yeah, right."

I haven't given up on going down to the Johnsons' house, but it can wait for another day. It will take at least that long for my nerves to return. The next time I head down there I'll take a better mask to block out the smell. And I'll take a hammer and gun to fend off the animals. The bulky bat was too heavy to be effective. The cats must have known I would be an easy target.

January 25

A pack of wolves roamed the neighborhood today. Instead of getting down the street, I watched the animals attack anything they could find.

The dog still comes to the edge of my patio. I make sure it has a full bowl of water every day, even though it arrives inconsistently. He goes for a stretch of days without appearing, then the next week he's at my patio door every afternoon. I leave water every day because it wouldn't be fair to suddenly stop providing for it after it has come to rely on me. Somehow, even though I have my hands full with Andrew and with keeping up our house, I found a way to add even more responsibility to my plate. When everyone else is looking for a way to do something as simple as ensure their own livelihood, I'm the only person stupid enough to add another living thing to my list of obligations.

As the list of luxuries I'm able to provide Andrew is reduced (simple trips to the bathroom, a good night's rest in his own bed), I should spend more time ensuring he has the other types of care I can still offer. If I can't carry him to the bathroom for a proper bath, the least I should be able to do is sit by his side and keep him company instead of talking to some mangy animal from the forest.

I try to feel like I'm doing both things—taking care of my brother and providing for the dog—by including Andrew in the conversations I have from the sofa.

"How do you think he would have gotten along with Oscar?" I ask my brother. When I don't get a response, I add in, "They would compete for who got to snuggle up with you on the sofa each night."

Outside, the dog stares at me as if it too is pondering the question while also considering who this mysterious Oscar might be that I always mention.

"You could have protected Oscar from the other animals out there," I say to the dog. "You could be his big brother and watch over him."

The dog yawns, then rests its head on the deck again. Andrew blinks. "Wouldn't that be nice?" I say to him. "Everyone deserves to have someone there to watch over and protect them."

The dog also appears in my sleep each night. In my dreams, it talks to me telepathically, telling me what it's like to live in the forest where every animal is trying to outsmart and outlast everything else. I sit there, fascinated, while it breaks from its stories just long enough to lap up more water. The dog and a pack of its friends, it says, have faced off against a pack of wolves. The dog tells me the story as though it's the forest's version of gang warfare. It also tells me of fights between bears and wolves. It swears an adult bear will never lose a fight against two wolves, but will never win against three. I don't know if this is true; I take the dog's word for it since it's from the forest and I'm not.

In these dreams, I find myself fantasizing about the dog eating me. It wouldn't be anything violent where I struggle while it growls and fights against me. The feast has nothing to do with it holding me down as I gag on my own blood. I would simply be living one minute and the next minute the dog would have me as the source of food it needs to continue its daily struggle. The entire episode is very peaceful. In the dream, the dog senses what I'm thinking and laughs at how silly I am.

"Don't think such foolish thoughts. I'm your friend." It says this in a whining howl that I trust.

I want to tell the dog what it's like to be alone now

that the Johnsons are gone, but even in my dreams I can't bring myself to give up hope that someone else might come by and save us. Each time I open my mouth nothing comes out. The rest of the dream is spent with the dog waiting patiently for me to continue. I'm left to tell stories I don't feel like telling because I can't get the words out to describe what really bothers me the most.

I ask the dog if it was watching as the cats attacked me in the street. I get an affirmative nod. "Why didn't you come help me out?" Its only response is a shrug of the shoulders. It can see I want to talk about something else.

The old pains come back as soon as I wake up. Old injuries are flaring up again as though they never fully healed. I broke my right arm in middle school during a game of neighborhood football. It was in a cast for a few weeks, but when the cast was taken off my arm was as good as new. It was fine for another seventy years before it started bothering me again recently. At various other times in my life, and for various other reasons, I broke my left foot, my left collar bone, and my nose. None of the injuries seemed important at the time except for earning me sympathy from girls. In contrast, Andrew has never broken a single bone or sprained an ankle. He has only ever had the bruise on his hip from when I accidently dropped him.

My entire body might ache, but I only recognize the pain in places that have shown me pain before. When it's cloudy out, ready to rain, I swear my forearm warns me of the oncoming thunderstorm. Or I'll wake up and my ankle will be sensitive when I put weight on it, and I know the temperature will be slightly chillier than normal.

If he could talk, Andrew's response would be predictable: "Yeah, and every time there's going to be a thunderstorm my butt hurts from where you dropped me, you jackass."

What would our founding fathers have done if they knew the world would turn out this way? Would they have bothered fighting for freedom, would they have bothered with a Constitution, would they have bothered with any of it if they knew it was going to turn out like this? If they knew there would only be a United States for three hundred years, would they have done what they did, or would they have put up with tyranny for themselves, their children, their grandchildren's children, until the end of man played out? Would tea have been thrown in the harbor? Would armies have gone to war? Maybe they would have calculated that years of war and death weren't worth freedom if it was only going to last a couple centuries, but I think they would have done everything just as they did. That's what made them so great: they weren't concerned about themselves, they were concerned with ideas that were worth fighting for, regardless of how long they lasted. There's no chance Jefferson or Washington would have said, "Well, it will only be a great country for a while, the struggle isn't worth it." No, they would have assembled their friends and said, "It may only last for three hundred years, but for those years, it can be the greatest country we've ever known."

Would the first men have done the same thing? Would the caveman who created fire, struggling to live amongst animals twice his size, have fought to survive if he knew mankind would eventually die out no matter how much he personally fought to persevere? Of course he would have. The same omniscient voice that might have whispered "three hundred years" in Washington's ear would have whispered "hundreds of thousands of years" to the unshaved man in the cave. If you told me Camelot would only be around for another hundred thousand years I wouldn't worry about anything for at least 99,000 of those years. A safety net of a thousand years! An eternity!

More recently, would men have bothered with billion-dollar sports stadiums, bridges across lakes in China, or expeditions to space? Maybe not. Maybe, if you told someone that the end of man would occur in another hundred years, they would have thought to use those billions of dollars for another purpose, something better than getting people more quickly from point A to point B or rocketing chimps into outer space. Greater men than myself would have to worry about those things. I worry about simpler things: getting through another day, getting Andrew though another day. When life is simplified to this degree, worrying about anything else seems silly. So I try not to think about anything other than how to get Andrew through another year, knowing that for him to get through it, I must do the same. That's all. The men who spent millions on fancy monuments or oversized shopping malls are welcome to look back and reassess if that was worth their time and money now that we are all getting a little older, fading away a little more.

I like to think the truly great men would have not only done all the same things they did, knowing the end was approaching, but maybe they would have fought even harder if they knew there was a clock ticking in the distance. Maybe Washington would have told his men, "We have to get it right, this country, before the end. A constitution of men has been forming in our collective minds for thousands of years. Let's do it now and show everyone what we were capable of all along." Maybe Tesla would have said, "Only another century? Then I'd better conduct even more drastic experiments so they can benefit people as long as possible."

January 26

It's been a long time since I was singularly fixated on something like I am these days with getting to the Johnsons' house. In elementary school I had my heart set on getting the G.I. Joe F-14 for Christmas. In High School I had a terrible crush on Christie Elendorf. For the past fifty years, though, I've been happy to just live my life day-to-day.

Each day I wonder if I'm exaggerating the monstrous smell or if it really is as bad as my senses tell me. It could just be my nerves playing tricks on me. Other people hear imaginary voices when they have mental breakdowns, maybe I smell imaginary odors. I ran (hobbled quickly) to the window yesterday because I was sure I heard a car driving down the street. With a clear view of the neighborhood I realized there was no vehicle to speak of. The sound vanished in the clamor of me getting to the window, much the same way the smell fades away when I'm completely engrossed in taking care of Andrew.

The stench reminds me of when I was ten and a small mouse died behind our kitchen wall. It was amazing how terrible those three inches of dead rodent could make the entire house smell. Spraying air freshener every day didn't do anything to conquer the stench of its rotting flesh. Opening all the windows did nothing. My father couldn't get rid of the tiny carcass without tearing open part of the wall, something he wasn't crazy about doing. After a couple of days we were eating all of our meals on the porch because the smell made us sick to our stomachs. All because of a tiny mouse. When we absolutely had to be in the kitchen, we covered our noses and mouths. The smell snuck in anyway. One tiny mouse was capable of polluting our entire home with the smell of death. It only took six days before my dad hammered a hole in the kitchen wall and found the dust-covered rotting carcass. Two days later everything went back to smelling fresh again.

The task of getting to the Johnsons' home mocks me with how simple it is. All I have to do is walk to the end of the street, not journey to another community. Yet it's still inaccessible because the neighborhood has been handed over to the beasts. The other reason for my difficulty has to be acknowledged: I'm an old man.

I pissed myself a little bit yesterday. How's that for old age? Andrew was all cleaned up for bed when I realized a little bit of my own urine had escaped. My pants were stained at the knee. It must have run down my leg without me realizing it. How is that possible? Andrew was on the sofa, still as clean as when I left him; I was the one who needed to change into new clothes instead of my invalid brother.

None of that will stop me from getting to the Johnsons' house. My hammer and gun are ready. I didn't want to have to take my pistol but the cats outnumber me by too much. I have one of those little white masks that people use for painting. Hopefully that will keep the smell away. I even have a sandwich in case I get hungry while I'm there. If I read this entry tomorrow I'll laugh at how it sounds like I'm heading out for a day-long journey instead of a simple walk down the street.

As soon as the sun is peaking in the sky I'm going to leave Andrew once again and make my way down the road. I refuse to let this neighborhood have the final say in my life. I refuse to let it become a place where I'm afraid to leave my own home. I won't prove the Johnsons right in their belief that I was too scared to leave my house. That was probably why they didn't say goodbye, not because they were rude, but because they felt bad for me.

I made myself laugh last night thinking about how I would react if I was in the Johnsons' home when they came back. They would open their front door after an extended family vacation, or maybe they would get to New Orleans, realize it wasn't what they expected, and drive back to Camelot. There I would be, standing in the middle of their kitchen, eating a jar of peanut butter, a guilty look plastered on my face. We would stare at each other in astonishment, and then we would burst out laughing and I would welcome them back to the neighborhood with hugs.

Even if they were lucky enough to make it all the way to a group community, though, they would never make it back here again. No one's luck is that good. More likely, they would have broken down somewhere along the way and been forced to settle in someone else's abandoned house. Their SUV's tires would go flat before they could make it halfway. An axel would get irreparably bent.

Their house looks just like all of the other empty houses now—like it has been abandoned for years. Bird crap covers the entire roof, making it look like a watercolor painting of whites, grays, and blacks. The windows are all cracked. It's possible that it always looked that way, that the only difference wasn't how it looked, but that I knew there were people inside. It's possible that's the reason the Johnsons left: because their house was already overgrown and abandoned, it just took them a while to realize it. And it took them leaving for me to realize it.

None of that stuff matters right now. The sun is coming out over the trees. When it's directly overhead I'm leaving for the Johnsons' house. This is the first time I'm writing one of these entries in the morning instead of at night. That has to be a good omen. The sun is almost overhead. It's time to go!

January 27

I made it to the Johnsons' yesterday. Words can't describe what I saw. How did things get to this point? Staying here in Camelot with Andrew was the wrong decision. I understand that now. We should have gone to one of the final communities a long time ago. The Johnsons have shown their true colors.

Why did I insist on staying here? Because it was a continuation of the life we had before everyone grew old and died? Or was it because, a long time ago, it was the type of neighborhood my parents always dreamed of living in? Most likely, it was because I was scared of change and of the unknown. As long as I stayed in this neighborhood, in our home, I felt like I could hold onto that old life for one more day. I'm disgusted with myself and with the Johnsons. I would never sit down for a meal with them again. I would never talk to them or so much as look in their direction. But they're gone, so at least in that regard they were smarter than I am.

January 30

What's this journal for if it's not for capturing the difficulties we face? I certainly didn't feel the need to write down the day's events back when everything was okay (relatively speaking). That's why I'm going to write about what happened at the Johnsons'—not because I want to, but because not writing about it would only keep me up at night.

I can't guess how many times I went there as a friend while they still lived in the neighborhood. Now the only thing I can think about is that last trip. I wasn't prepared for what was there, and quickly became overwhelmed by everything around me. That much I can be sure of. Maybe my eyes didn't really see the details I thought they saw. Maybe the smell wasn't as bad as I made it out to be. The air seemed so putrid that even its taste made me gag. But was it really that bad, or did I merely think it should have been that awful?

I should have known something was amiss when there wasn't a single animal to threaten me in between my house and the Johnsons'—a bad omen if there ever was one. Looking back, I imagine that the pack of house cats from my unsuccessful trip down the street was trying to protect me rather than eat me. They didn't want me to see what had happened at the Johnsons'. The entire walk to their house, I looked around, continually expecting a former house pet or a forest predator to be hiding at the edge of a bush, crouching and ready to attack when I least expected it. I even stopped halfway there and then again at the edge of the Johnsons' driveway, but no animals were to be found.

The painter's breathing mask, intended to provide peace of mind, made me feel like I was suffocating. After a couple of deep breaths I decided I could get by without it and took it off. With it off I actually looked like a normal guy walking down the street instead of somebody from an old apocalyptic movie. By the time I got to the Johnsons' house, though, the smell had intensified again. At their driveway, the stench seemed as bad as it ever had. The breathing mask went back on.

Most of the windows around their home were cracked. The gutters were clogged. Those things were to be expected of abandoned houses. But then I looked back at my own house and was shocked at how dilapidated it also was, especially compared to the vision I had of it. In my mind it was the only house left on the street that could still be considered attractive and well kept. The impression stuck in my head, however, was of how the house looked when we first moved into it. An outdated image if there ever was one. It looked this way in my thoughts, not because it was my house, but because it was the only house remaining that had living people inside it. My roof was identical to the others, though. My windows were cracked too.

The Johnsons' garage was in front of me. The garage door was closed. I stepped up to one of the small glass panels to see what was on the other side. The fogged panes only allowed me to make out vague shapes. I saw their car leave the neighborhood, and it had never returned, yet something, the same basic shape of a car, was there in the middle of the garage.

I bent down to peek through the hole where the garage handle had been. Just from bending slightly, my knees creaked and my back hurt. The only thing through the hole was darkness. Just then, as I was starting to pull away from the makeshift peephole, the hissing, angry mouth of a cat snarled against the hole, an inch away from my face. I nearly shit myself. If the garage door hadn't divided us the animal would have had a clean shot at my face. I yelled a curse before falling backward.

There was a tiny hole at the corner of the garage where an animal had broken through. I never would have noticed it unless I was sitting on my ass like an idiot when the cat darted out. It hissed the entire way from the Johnsons' house to the woods.

If I had tried to stand up right away I probably would have stumbled like a punch-drunk fighter and fallen right back over again; it was better to stay on the concrete, let my heart slow back down, and let my ass stop hurting before I tried to move.

Not a single dog came out of the forest to inspect the silly, old man on the ground who was nearly scared to death by a cat. For a moment it was almost as though all of the animals decided to pack up and leave Camelot, just as all the people had. Then, from far off in the distance, I heard a roar that made me break out of my stupor. It took the remainder of my old man's strength to stand up again. Sliding my fingers under the bottom of the door and lifting, the garage was suddenly filled with daylight.

The Johnsons' old kitchen table was in the middle of the space where I thought a car might have been. It was a big rectangle of wood, oak I think, right there as though people should dine next to their cars. A large white blanket, maybe a bed sheet, was crumpled in a pile on top of the table. The sheets were stained through with blood. I'm proud of myself for not gasping at what should have startled me. In fact, I almost touched the sheets out of simple curiosity. My hand hovered over the fabric until my better judgment returned and I realized it wasn't a science fair project but someone's or something's blood that I had no explanation for.

Other than the table and bloody sheet, the rest of the garage looked normal. Their collection of camping gear was missing from one of the corners. The sleeping bags, tent, lights, and axe were all gone. It was safe to assume they took it all in case their SUV broke down and had to be ditched. A spare pillow had been left behind, but a cat or some mice had torn it apart. I assumed at first that it was random destruction before finding tiny bits of blood and bones and realizing a family of mice had made it their home before being ambushed by the cat. The constant reminders all around me made it impossible to forget that every living thing was one step away from being eaten by something else.

I opened the door leading from the garage to the house. A stench hit me. Even after putting the painter's mask back on, the odor was overwhelming. I found myself gagging in the same hallway in which I had taken bottles of wine over for dinners. And to think I used to take my shoes off when they were wet to keep from tracking dirt into their house! It reminded me of the smell of lima beans when I was a little boy. As soon as I got a single whiff of them I was conditioned to gag because I knew that was what I would do when I put them in my mouth.

"Hello?" I said, even though I knew the house was empty. I don't know what compelled me to say that other than dumb, old habits.

There were no sounds. Everything was still. With the blinds down I could see the dust floating in the air. Part of me expected a pack of German Shepherds to appear out of a bedroom doorway, but the house seemed free of wildlife. Like everything else in the neighborhood, it was a matter of time until the animals penetrated the walls and the Johnsons' house became just another extension of the wilderness.

The kitchen left me as confused as the garage. A large butcher's knife and a smaller serrated knife were in the sink, both covered with dried blood. The flies had long since feasted on anything of value. The only explanation I could think of was that the Johnsons cut packs of raw meat before leaving so they were assured of not running out before they got to New Orleans or Miami.

The living room carpet was also covered with blood. As was the sofa. I started wondering if a band of murderers hadn't made their way into our neighborhood and, left with the choice of two houses to pick from, randomly selected the Johnsons' house to butcher everyone. Then the murderers had taken the Johnsons' SUV and left. I kept that thought in mind until I got to the steps leading to the front door.

A note was there. Of course they would have thought I would enter through the front door. I picked up the piece of paper and mumbled the words out loud.

We're very sorry for not saying goodbye, but we couldn't stop by your house on the way out of the neighborhood. We knew you wouldn't understand. We barely understand it ourselves. I know it's impossible, but please don't think any less of us. Times have been difficult on everyone, but tougher on some than on others. You always seemed to take everything in stride. We were always jealous of the way you made it seem easy to take care of Andrew. We always wondered how you did it.

PS: We thought about just burning the place down.

That was the entire note. I wished they had known how much I struggled to take care of Andrew by myself. One of the dinners together would have been better spent talking about how discouraged I got by growing older and not being able to take care of my brother as well as I used to. Maybe that would have changed things. Maybe they would have sympathized with the sadness and anxiety that comes from being forced to make every decision for yourself and for another person, a person who is always affected by your plans but never has a say in them.

I went to Mark's bedroom. The drawers and closet were empty of clothes. I went to Mindy's room. It was in the same condition. The only bedroom remaining belonged to the Block twins. At that point I still thought Mark's note was apologizing for all of them leaving the neighborhood without saying goodbye.

Then I got to the last bedroom and saw the twin sisters. The girls were lying on their beds. I thought of them as girls, even though they were Andrew's age, because I had known them for so long and because they had to be taken care of as though they were little girls. The blankets were gone from the beds. Only a thin sheet covered each girl up to their shoulders. My hands involuntarily clenched. It was only then that I realized my knees and hands had been shaking ever since I'd entered the house.

Their skin was rotting. Maggots were slithering all over them, making it look like their flesh was twirling in small circles, a thin sheet of life draped over the remains of a person. Both twins were in the same condition. Seeing them made the smell even worse. It's funny how that happens.

I gagged again. Positive I was going to throw up, I bent down and put my hands on my knees. Nothing came out. I still didn't understand where all the blood had come from, so I took another step toward one of them—I couldn't tell which because they looked as much alike as deteriorating corpses as they had when they were alive.

"You poor thing," I said to one of the bodies.

But when I took that step forward I must have stepped on the edge of the sheet because it tugged slightly against the body underneath it. I bumped against the bed frame. In the short moment it had taken me to forget I was an old, bumbling man, I quickly remembered. The Block's head was jostled toward me when I bumped against the mattress and frame, causing it to turn to the side as if it were going to look at me. The momentum carried it even further, though, and before I knew what was happening, the head slid completely off the edge of the pillow and fell to the floor. It thudded against the hardwood like a coconut. I'm not even sure which curse words I yelled. The head ended up on its side, staring blankly at the wall across the room.

Everything made sense: the table in the garage with the bloody sheets, the knives in the kitchen sink, the note. I pulled the sheet away from the body to make sure. The girl was cut into pieces: foot to knee, knee to hip, torso, arms, head. Something must have made the Johnsons decide to move to one of the group communities. Maybe the Blocks were already sick at that point and the Johnsons didn't know how to take care of them. Perhaps they didn't want their Block sisters to suffer. One of the Block sisters could have already passed away and the other was growing sicker every day.

Whatever it was that happened, the Johnsons thought their Block sisters would be better off with a quiet death rather than struggling to continue. Once the decision was made, they must have thought it would give their sisters a more dignified burial if they could sleep in their beds one last time. But how to get the bodies up the steps? Mark and Mindy were as old as I am. They would never, even as a team, be able carry the sisters up the steps. They had long since gotten into the habit of keeping their Block sisters downstairs on the sofas the same way I did with Andrew. One of them must have come up with the idea to cut the bodies into smaller pieces that could be carried more easily. Maybe the Blocks were already dead when they were cut to pieces, but maybe they were still alive, unable to cry out or ask why their brother and sister were doing this to them. Once upstairs, the bodies were reassembled. It would be important to Mark and Mindy to see their Block sisters look peaceful one last time. The look of serenity as the sisters lay on their own beds would give the Johnsons a sense of comfort.

Luggage and clothes must have been filling the backseat of their SUV as they drove away that night, not bodies. My mind saw whatever it had hoped to see.

I threw up then. The urge came over me before I had a chance to take off the breathing mask. The cotton protector around my nose and mouth filled with vomit before the rubber band broke. The mask, along with my throw-up, splashed all over the floor like a carelessly tied water balloon. Vomit covered my face, making me want to throw up again. I wiped it away with my hand, but chunks were still in my mouth and nose.

The Block sister's head was at my feet. It too was now covered in my puke. I gagged on my way down the steps and out the front door. I stumbled and choked the entire way back to my house, not a single thought given to being attacked by animals.

The first thing I did was get myself cleaned up. Without the smell of vomit following me everywhere, I went and sat next to Andrew. I stayed by his side the entire night. All night, there was only one thought that circled in my head—what could make them decide that was their best course of action? Until then they had been no different than me. Every time we sat down for a dinner together they understood my goals and the things that worried me. I understood the same things about them. And yet, when the time came, they gave up and decided enough was enough. Neither of them had ever made the slightest comment, even a joke in passing, to hint this might happen. There was never a Freudian slip or a troubled look to tell me they were capable of killing their Block sisters and leaving the neighborhood.

I thought about going back down the street, picking the head off the bedroom floor, and putting it back on the mattress where it belonged, but I couldn't bring myself to leave my house again that day. It was sunny and bright outside the following day. The light was rude; anything other than rain clouds seemed inappropriate. I couldn't bring myself to open my front door that day either. When I did eventually go outside it was only to walk around my lawn in circles. The smell, even though it had to be out there still, no longer registered with me, and I wondered how much of it had been real and how much my mind had exaggerated.

January 31

How did the Johnsons come to their decision? How can I ensure I don't go down a path that leads to the same conclusion? I'm a normal guy. They were normal people. Will illogical thoughts start creeping in until I pay them too much attention and end up doing something I would never have thought possible? Is this what happens when you're isolated from other people for too long?

My goal is to go back down the street and burn the entire house down. I'm rational enough to realize the wind could catch the flames and set the next house on fire, and then the next house, and then the next, until suddenly my home is on fire too. Andrew would be burned alive. If that happened, I would be okay with it because I would be there next to him. At least I would be with my brother at the end. At least Andrew would have me sitting on the sofa with my arm around him.

It didn't dawn on me earlier, when I had these thoughts, that this line of thinking could have been exactly how the Johnsons morphed from normal people to monsters.

February 1

I made my way down the street again today, this time to do what the Johnsons should have done. The jug of gasoline in the wheel barrel was part of my final reserves from the days when I thought I might still leave Camelot. It sloshed the entire way down the street as if complaining that it didn't want to be used for this purpose. A book of matches was kept safe in my pocket. If the animals decided to attack me, my only defense would be splashing gas in their general direction. A large dog watched me from down the street. It must have sensed I was on a mission because it seemed nervous and chose not to approach.

I only managed to circle the garage, front porch, and the side of the house before the gas was gone. I left the plastic container on the ground where some of the gasoline had pooled. The book of matches gave a scratch when I rubbed one of the sticks against its side. A small flame appeared. Then the line of gasoline burst into flames. The fire, unlike everything I had seen in movies, was slow to spread. At first I thought it might put itself out. Hollywood had taught me the house would explode into a ball of fire with me ducking for cover.

I knew I could have burned the house down more easily if I went inside and poured the gas there, but nothing could have made me go inside again. Eventually, the flames got bigger, crawled up the side of the house. Happy with my work, I walked back down the street, to my home and to Andrew. From my porch, I watched the fire spread. It only took a couple of minutes before the house was completely engulfed in flames. After half an hour it burned to the ground. The other nearby houses never caught fire. No sirens sounded. No fire trucks arrived. No other neighbors came out of their houses to see what was happening. I went back inside after the house collapsed on itself. The fire kept burning for another three hours after that. It is still smoldering.

February 2

As happens so frequently these days, the Labrador arrived on my patio again this afternoon. It sat on the other side of the door as though expecting to be let inside. Its scarred flanks, a reminder of what it does when it isn't relaxing on my deck, were highlighted pink under the sunlight. As I stood by the glass door the dog panted and stared at me the same way Oscar used to when he had finished doing his business and wanted to come back inside. My initial reaction was to do just that, to open the door and let it in. Anything else seemed neglectful of the dog's wellbeing.

I'm not sure why I feel like its health should fall on my shoulders. Minus the scars on its side, it looks like an animal I would take for walks, let sleep at the foot of my bed. But it comes from the forest, a grey wolf stuck in the adorable yellow costume of man's best friend.

"What's it like out there in the woods?" I asked it. I gave a pause for a response that would never come. "Do you run into a lot of bears out there?" Another brief pause, another non-response. "If I didn't think you'd bite me, you could come inside and get some food."

It drank from the bowl until there was no water left. It did seem like a happy animal. A pleasant vision—the dog becoming the third member of our family—often makes me smile, as it did at that moment. It would be a perfect pet. I was broken out of my fantasy when the dog growled at a noise coming from the woods. The true scenario, if this animal were let into our home, would be discovered the next morning: I would wake up with a justly deserved premonition of violence, go out to the living room to check on Andrew, and find him in the middle of the floor with the dog on top of him. The animal would be feasting on my brother's intestines after tearing open his stomach. Andrew would still be alive, just barely, while all of this was happening. He would never be able to scream.

"You almost tricked me," I said to the dog, the closed patio door still between us.

A noise must have sounded that the animal could hear but that I could not because its head bolted upright and its nose pointed toward the forest wall. It stayed perfectly still for a second, then jumped over the patio railing and disappeared into the trees. A moment later, from a different corner of the yard, a brown bear lumbered out of the woods. It walked across my lawn until it was in the middle of my backyard. The bear looked at me, then at the forest, curious as to which way the dog had vanished. I got the feeling the bear was reminding the nearby animals that it could go where ever it wanted. It was nobody's servant. I opened the patio door just far enough to bring the water dish back inside. It was important to make sure nothing outside would entice the bear to stay any longer than it already wanted. The last thing I needed was a pet bear in addition to my new Labrador.

I turned toward Andrew. "He seems like he would make a nice pet, don't you think?"

Andrew stared straight ahead. I'm not too senile yet to forget the Labrador will do whatever he needs in order to survive. Sure, he would probably rather be sitting in the air-conditioned comfort of my home, eating processed food and enjoying the protection that the walls and roof provide, but he obviously has the skills to survive however he needs. I like to think my new friend is civilized, but I wouldn't be shocked if he came to my patio door tomorrow with another animal's blood plastered to his fur. If that's what the dog has to do to survive, then more power to him.

The dog is undoubtedly doing a better job of

surviving out in the wild than its old masters would have. Throw me out in the woods and see how long I last. Even if I had a backpack filled with flint, beans, a tent, and a blanket I still wouldn't last longer than a week. Give me an additional assortment of survival tools—a knife, a compass, a canteen—and I might last a month. Every predatory animal would laugh hysterically at my attempts to pitch a tent or catch food once my can of beans ran out. It would be funny enough for them that every enemy would put down arms for an hour, a sixty-minute truce, in order to enjoy my performance. A fox would sit next to a pit-bull. On its other side would be a pack of cats. Then a bear. All of them would be united by this ridiculous newcomer, grey-haired and wrinkly, that snores during the night, whose tent falls over when the wind brushes against it, whose knife sits unused. The poor old guy would have no chance at all.

This animal, whose great, great grandparents used to lie on someone's living room carpet and sleep all day, has only itself and other like-minded dogs to rely on, and yet they thrive in the woods as though the bears and wolves should have taken them more seriously all along.

February 4

Of all the times people looked to religion for support, none was more important than when the Blocks started appearing: humanity's future was in doubt. Instead of giving a unified message of comfort, though, each religion stumbled. Some ministers stuck to the same stories they always told, saying it had to be part of God's greater plan. No one wanted to hear that. Some rabbis continued saying the Lord works in mysterious ways and who were we to question his will? People groaned when they heard this. Some priests told their followers not to question how God works. This brought another round of sighs.

The most common reaction was for church, mosque, and temple leaders to throw their hands in the air with exasperation. What kind of joke was being played on them where the end wasn't approaching with horns sounding from the heavens but with the birth of people who couldn't hear or say prayers, couldn't attend church services, couldn't pass church doctrine to another generation? What were the clergymen supposed to do with these people—they were still God's children after all. The Blocks didn't attend mass, they didn't read the Bible or Koran, they didn't attend Sunday school. How were the churches supposed to accept the Blocks if they preached that regular people were supposed to do all of those things, all the while knowing Blocks couldn't do any of them? Some leaders from each religion modified their teachings to accommodate the Blocks, but mostly the religions turned their backs on these people. The Blocks were left to find salvation for themselves.

A few clergymen, not satisfied with the speed of their congregation's discontent, took a proactive approach to alienating themselves from their followers. Some said stupid things (that Blocks didn't have souls) that enraged every family with a Block child. Seeing as how a hundred percent of the children were Blocks when this outrage was spoken, huge portions of each congregation stopped going to church, quit volunteering their time, and withheld donating a portion of their income.

There were people, however, who didn't care what negative things were said about the Blocks, they simply cared about getting their own ticket to heaven. Other people, people like myself and my parents, saw how concocted these holy men were and stopped paying attention to them. Attendance at churches and temples plummeted. People stopped praying for something to save them or to change their circumstances. Religion went from being the second most important social influence in the world (nothing could ever topple the family unit as the most important), to becoming completely irrelevant.

I think about how I reacted in those days and about how the people around me reacted. We could have given up and started feeling sorry for ourselves, it would have been understandable to do so—there was a noticeable spike in suicides—but most people, myself included, accepted what was happening and continued on. I played on the neighborhood baseball team until we didn't have enough players to play anymore. I went on with my life as I would have if there were still kids in the neighborhood. I acted like Andrew would answer me when I asked him questions.

Nothing changed just because the minister down the road was one of the first people to leave Camelot in favor of New Orleans. The rest of the neighborhood woke up the next day and continued with their lives just as they had the previous day and just as they would until they passed away or joined the minister at the group community. That was all.

A year after the minister left, a family from

Michigan moved into his old house, took down the few religious relics that had been left behind, and made it their own home. Life went on.

I wish the Johnsons could have remembered that.

February 6

Without a hope of someone new coming to the neighborhood, I catch myself creating imaginary friends much the way I did when I was four years old. I could go online right now and chat with someone from San Francisco or Dallas, inquire about how they're doing. Do I really need to see and hear other people going through the same thing, develop a bond with a random someone on a random Saturday, get to know their life and their struggles, just to have them pass away days or weeks later?

So I create people that will never have to die. Most of the time these friends are newcomers to Camelot who saw the lines of empty homes on their way to one of the final communities, thought the area looked nice, and decided they would stay for a while. I imagine them being happy to listen to my stories while I prepare dinner. There's more to making a good meal than pressing a button on the food processor; you still have to get the seasoning right and serve it with a nice wine. When I venture down to the basement, these new visitors provide an extra set of eyes to look out for bugs. I prepare a list of things to tell them about while they sort through random boxes like curious kids.

"That box? That's filled with notes I passed my girlfriend in class when we were seniors… That picture? My mom painted it… She was quite the artist. I wish I had more of her paintings."

I don't actually say these things out loud. When I imagine friends spending the day with me, I think about the conversations we would have but I keep the actual words to myself. If he was alert and could hear my voice, not even Andrew would know I was spending my day talking to people who aren't there. I do talk to myself as much as I ever have, I can't help that—I even find myself mumbling these words out loud as I type them—but when I talk to myself, it's more about acknowledging my thoughts than it is speaking to someone who isn't really there.

I'm left wondering why I would create additional make-believe people in my life, none of whom can talk or provide me with feedback, when I already have Andrew in the other room. Here I am with a brother who's alive and breathing, has been with me through the worst times, and I could talk to him from the moment I wake up until the moment I go to sleep. I don't, though. He would never get bored with me or yawn and tell me to give it a rest. Maybe it's because Andrew already knows all the things that worry me, has already heard all my stories.

Looking back, that moment when I went from sharing all my daily concerns with him, to protecting him from them, was the point when I went from feeling like Andrew was helping me carry the hardships to feeling absolutely and completely alone in a wilderness that had grown up around me.

Something inside me wants someone new to share these things with. Is that human nature? If I suddenly did have new people in my life, would I crave different people as soon as I had once again exhausted my stories with the people around me? If Andrew passed away, would I have a make-believe version of him that appeared in my thoughts to keep me company? And if this is the case, why aren't I out in the living room talking to him right now instead of muttering and typing? Something has to take my mind off the animals that intrude on our property. Something needs to take my mind off our house, which is falling apart while we still call it home.

There is the dog, but even he reminds me of my predicament. That dumb animal could probably read me for a sucker from a mile away.

“Look at that old man,” it was probably telling its friends. “I’m going to go on his patio and he’s going to give me water every day, just because he’s lonely.”

“No way!” the rest of his pack would say.

“Oh yes,” the dog would say, a canine grin spread from one side of fangs to the other.

“No human is silly enough to befriend a dog anymore,” the other dogs would say. “Those days are long gone.”

“Oh yeah? You sit and watch. And you know what? I’ll even get him to pet me like humans used to.”

February 8

My dreams with the dog kept occurring night after night. It was only normal that I developed a kinship with the animal, even if the relationship I nurtured was based upon dreams and from outdated ideas of how man and animal could get along. It knows me as the thing that gives it water; it has no idea I dream about it every night or that I share a bond with it because it talks to me when no one else can. Looking back, I guess I can understand why it was puzzled when I opened my patio door earlier today after it had arrived for water. Hindsight being 20/20, I should have seen that it was a bad idea. Whether it was because I'm alone or because of what I saw at the Johnsons' house, I didn't act the way I normally would—with caution. It's clear as day now that I should have stayed on one side of the glass door and it on the other side.

Not trusting me, it backed away at first, prepared to flee at any sign of danger. I stood in the open doorway. We stared at each other like that for a while. Then it blinked. Once our tense stare-down was broken it remembered the water and its daily habit kicked in. When the dish was half empty, its head rose and looked at me again. I was still in the same spot. This calmed the dog, and it seemed to begin trusting me. I started talking to it then.

"Hello, little guy… are you okay?… What did you do for water before I started leaving it here for you?"

It didn't answer back the way it had in my dreams, but it also didn't growl. The dog simply stayed. It stayed like dogs used to stay when they were pets, staring at me as if waiting to be given the okay to move again. If I'd had a milk bone in my hand I would have whistled, and the dog would have eaten it out of my palm.

That was probably why I did what I did next: I

stepped forward and joined the animal on my deck.

I offered reassurances to soothe the dog's nervousness. "It's okay, little guy. I'm your friend. I give you water. I'm your friend."

It stayed where it was. It had some brambles caught in the thick part of its fur. I reached down to pet its head and stroke the brambles off its back. It was easy, after decades of not having a pet, to forget how to treat animals. Instead of leaving my hand out to let the dog smell me and get used to me, I reached straight for its fur.

The Labrador wasn't used to the idea of humans the same way I wasn't used to the idea of pets. It didn't even growl before its teeth were deep in my hand. As soon as it reacted, out of fright at first, its instincts—those of the woods and the pack doing what it must to survive, not those I associated with being man's best friend—took over and it was growling furiously and throwing its head back and forth from right to left without letting go of my hand. My arm jerked every direction the dog's mouth went.

I cried out to Andrew for help. He remained motionless on the sofa without even looking in my direction. Pain and fear overrode any normal thoughts. I would have yelled curses if I could have formed real words; the only noises I could make were stupid and nonsensical. Finally, it let go of my hand, but only so it could lunge at me. I staggered backwards into my house. My arm must have flailed for something to grab because the next thing I knew my elbow had smacked into the patio door causing the glass to shatter. Half of the broken pane fell on the patio, the other half just inside my house.

The noise startled the dog. Maybe it thought I was capable of giving more of a fight than it first suspected. If it did think this, it was wrong. If the dog had continued forward it could have killed me on my living room floor before moving on to Andrew, who was sitting peacefully on the sofa the whole time. More likely, it had never heard something as unnatural as glass breaking and was startled by this new kind of thunder. We faced each other from opposite sides of the broken patio door. Then it looked back at the trees and at a noise coming from somewhere in the woods. Its eyes narrowed and it turned and darted into the forest.

I kept looking at the woods until I was sure the dog was gone. Afterward, I stayed there a little longer to make sure something even bigger wasn't on its way. With the woods quiet, I looked down at my hand. It was covered in blood. So were my shoes and the floor where my hand was dripping on them. I held it in my other palm and ran to the kitchen to rinse it off. Red water drained down the sink. When I squeezed my wrist blood squirted out of the giant puncture wounds. I kept squeezing because the pressure kept the water from stinging as bad as I knew it could. I wrapped a towel around it, then moved to the bathroom where the antibacterial creams were. There was no one I could see for treatment if my hand became infected. The only thing I could do was sit and tolerate the pain. I forced the white cream into the holes in my hand, but it came back out as a watery pink mixture.

It was surprising, though, how fast the bleeding stopped once I wrapped a bandage around my palm. I expected the bandage to become stained through with red before dripping blood onto the floor, but it continued to be the same ugly beige I had started with. I flexed my fingers to make sure I still had full movement in my hand. Keep in mind, there was nothing in my life that required me to have full gesticulation. It wasn't like I had to go back out on the mound and throw curveballs or sinkers; all I had to do was refill Andrew's nutrient bag and clean him each day. If necessary, I could do those things with one hand. Even so, it comforted me to know I wouldn't be handicapped.

There was a noise at the broken patio door. Having completely forgotten the dog and the shattered glass, I quickened my pace to see what the noise could be. Andrew was still sitting on the sofa, his eyes closed. Something out of the corner of my eye moved. A cat darted out of the kitchen, trying to sneak back through the broken door. It was either a lucky shot or anger clearing my head because my shoe caught one of its back legs perfectly so the animal went flying through the air and over the deck's handrail. Field goal! If it had bounced against the living room wall instead of out the patio door, I would have jumped on it and beaten it to death. I would have clawed at it and screamed with such rage that no other animal would ever dare come onto my patio steps again. I would have left it dead in my yard as a warning to every other beast in the forest.

The defeated cat didn't pause to turn and hiss at me. It bolted into the woods and disappeared. I kept screaming curses at it, taking all of my rage at the dog, the Johnsons, and the empty neighborhood out on the little cat that tried to take advantage of an opportunity to steal my food. I was lucky it chose to inspect the kitchen instead of nibbling on Andrew's eyes or ears. I don't know what I'd do if I went back out to the living room and one of Andrew's eyes was hanging out of its socket while an orange and white cat purred and licked the dangling, gooey ball.

The broken glass crackled under my shoes when I walked to where the patio door had been. There was a seven-foot by three-foot opening where the glass previously kept my house closed off to the outside world. Now, wind was hitting me. Fresh air blew against my face to remind me my house was one step closer to being annexed by the forest. I stood there amongst the broken glass trying to think of a good solution for sealing it. I turned every once in a while to make sure Andrew was okay. Sometimes his eyes were open, staring blankly at the wall. Other times they were closed. If I had a big piece of plywood I could have nailed it against the door's frame. I wouldn't be able to look out at the forest behind my house or watch the dog's disappointment the next time it came to find an empty water dish, but I don't have any wood that large anyway. A plastic tarp would work to keep the wind and bugs out, but I don't trust that it would keep a larger animal from getting in if that was what the creature wanted. There were too many horror stories as I grew up of people going camping and having a bear claw at their nylon tent. Stories like that stick in your mind forever. I wouldn't let my house be seen by a bear as being nothing more than a luxurious tent.

It crossed my mind that I could simply move next door or to any of the other abandoned houses in the neighborhood. They would all serve as suitable shelters just as well as our house does. It would also mean that I'd be making a hundred trips back and forth between the houses to move all of our family photos and belongings—unless I gave up on all of it and left our family history in this house. I knew I wouldn't be able to do that. Andrew's eyes were open again. I brushed the glass off the bottom of my shoes and took a seat next to him.

"What should we do?" I asked him. "Should we move next door? Should we stay here?"

We stayed on the sofa like that for a while. Another cat came up to the patio door. Upon seeing me it hissed and the fur on its back stood straight up. I hissed back even louder and more ferociously, but it was already darting off.

"I wish you could tell me what to do," I said to Andrew.

I took a deep breath and said I should stop feeling sorry for myself. Andrew did not disagree with this. One by one, I took everything off the dining room table and placed each item on the floor. Then I sat on the edge of the table so it leaned in the air. It was easier to move once it was off all four legs. It more than covered the open hole to my patio. The blood and glass were still on the floor underneath and around the table. I thought about walking next door to get Mr. Lee's patio door. It would make a perfect substitute. But the thought of taking tools to his empty house, detaching his old door without breaking it, and somehow dragging it back to my property made me cringe. I had better odds of playing eighteen holes of golf without an animal tackling me and tearing my neck open. If I was younger I would have at least tried to get the replacement door, but being old and tired, and yes, lazy, I was content with a dining room table where my old glass door had been.

I don't know why I insist on staying in this house. I don't know if it's that I'm too stubborn for my own good or that I feel like a vital piece of me will die if I give up the way everyone else has given up. Even if my move is only one house down the street, I would be admitting I can't live here anymore. If I confess that, I'm admitting I'm too old to take care of myself and my brother; I'm admitting I made the wrong choices; I'm admitting our last days are closer at hand than I'd guessed. I refuse to acknowledge those things.

My own health and safety are of minor consequence—my idiocy with the dog proves that much. I refuse to give up because my brother deserves better. He deserves a brother who protects him until the end, so that's what I'll do.

A week after seeing the Johnsons' table turned into

a butcher's cutting board, my own dining room table has been transformed into a protective wall. My hand hurts like hell. The Johnsons are gone. But Andrew and I will make our way the same as we always have. A squirrel could burrow through our roof and open a new route for the animals to get in. I would have to lay poison in my attic. Maybe a pack of wolves will try tearing out the weather screen on our front door tomorrow. If that happens, more of our furniture will be used to keep the outside wildlife away as we slowly barricade ourselves from the outside world. But no matter what, we will not give up.

My hand hurts worse and worse as the night goes on. It's taken me twice as long to type this entry as it has the others because I'm only using my index fingers. It didn't hurt at all right after it happened. Now, it hurts too much to curl my fingers. I'm afraid to take the bandage off to inspect the wound because I don't want to see an infection beginning, so I leave the bandages where they are and ignore it as best I can. I thought about pouring alcohol on it the way I have always seen in old movies, but I have no idea if that would actually work. And I'm in no mood for the searing pain that the actors always let the audience know they are feeling immediately after.

February 11

Holy shit, my hand hurts. Between what happened at the Johnsons' house, the dog's betrayal, and the terrible pain in my hand, it hasn't been a good couple of days. Don't feel like writing anything else tonight.

February 12

Two empty bottles of wine take up space next to the kitchen trashcan. For the first time in what seems like ages, I got piss drunk last night. The Johnsons and I enjoyed glasses of wine during our dinners together, sometimes to excess, but that's vastly different from last night's episode of drinking for the sake of getting bombed. I'd forgotten what it was like to have a blazing headache the next morning. My forehead feels like it's stuck in a bear's jaws. Closing my eyes does nothing to make the pain go away, only reminds me how nauseous I feel. If there is a gold lining to my current agony, it's that I live in a perfectly quiet house with only the hum of the power generator providing any sound. I don't have to worry about a rambunctious little brother running into my room and waking me up just to ask how I feel after a night of drinking. I don't have to worry about walking into the living room to find the TV turned up louder than usual, or neighbors throwing loud parties.

Every once in a while a dog gives a blood curdling scream that makes my shoulders rise involuntarily to my jaw. No animal should ever have to make a noise like that. It's safe to assume the animal was announcing to the rest of the forest that its time was at an end. I wonder if it was the dog that visited here each day before betraying me. That dog seems like it would be too crafty, too resourceful, to get trapped by a pack of lowly wolves.

That dog is probably a hero to all the forest animals by now. All the other animals celebrate it as the creature that not only had the man in the last occupied house in Camelot providing it with water each day, but also ended up catching the old man when his guard was down. Whereas the cats, the court jesters of the community, came up short in their attempt, the dog was successful in its try.

That damn dog is probably the president of the forest by now. All the other animals step aside when the victorious Labrador walks through the rows of trees. All the other male dogs wish they were him. All the female dogs give him googly eyes. That damn dog. God, my hand hurts. My fingers are purple.

Although I can blame the animal for my hand, I can't blame it for my headache. I wonder if I would even have a hangover if I was still young and had regular drinking buddies to waste time with. I looked over at Andrew sitting on the sofa while I was sloshed and thought it was only appropriate that he join me in the festivities. After all, he has to live in the same abandoned neighborhood, put up with the same leaking roof and howling animals. I put my glass of chardonnay up to his mouth and gave him a single sip. When I woke up this morning with the headache to end all headaches, I took four aspirin for myself and put part of a ground up aspirin in Andrew's nutrient bag just in case he had a slight headache too. I always want to make sure he's given the consideration he deserves even if he can't ask for these things and probably doesn't even recognize the need for them.

At the same time, I wonder what kind of treatment I would get if our roles were reversed. If I was a Block and he was born normal, would Andrew go out of his way to make sure I was comfortable and provided for, or would I lay on my bed every day without so much as a, "How are you doing today?" even though he knows I won't be able to answer his rhetorical questions. Or would he sit on the sofa next to me and keep me company while the same old movies play again and again? Would he give me a sip of whatever he was drinking so I could experience it too, the way my parents took both of us to the beach when we were little even though only one of us could build sand castles and splash in the waves?

More importantly, would I like my brother as much if I got to know the real person who's hidden away somewhere in his head? If he suddenly broke out of his stupor tomorrow, would he give me someone to joke around with and share my concerns with, or would he be an asshole and tell me I was the least funny person he ever met. Would he leave the toilet seat down when he peed because he didn't care if I sat in his piss? Would he function as the family I don't have, giving me presents at Christmas and baking me a cake on my birthday, or would he be more concerned with his own life and immediately begin planning a trip to New Orleans or Miami? Would I have the same connection that I have with him now, even though all he does is sit next to me when the sun rises in the morning and sets in the evening?

This hangover makes me think stupid thoughts. I need to go be productive. I'll make sure Andrew isn't lonely.

February 14

A scenario is constantly playing out in my head where I eventually have to watch Andrew pass away. It isn't something I want to happen. On the contrary, it's exactly what I've been fighting against my entire life. But because I'm sick more often than I used to be, not to mention feeble in my old age, I know Andrew's time has to be coming up as well. We are linked together; what happens to one of us will most likely happen to the other. The clearest indication of that is the infected needle mark on his forearm that refuses to get better. I've put the nutrient bag's IV into his arm a million times, but only recently, after nearly eighty years, is he showing the first signs of irritation since he was born.

At least if Andrew were my older brother I'd have the reassurance that he would be the first one to go. Whereas Andrew quietly passing away would be my best-case scenario, me being the one to die first is my worst case. It would leave Andrew by himself, unable to refill his nutrient bag. He would sit alone until he died. What if Andrew is the exception to the Block's lifespan? What if he has an exceptionally healthy heart and lungs that would let him live another ten years if it wasn't for me dying and leaving him to wither away? That's why I should have made the trip to a group community when I had the chance.

The easy bet for my downfall would have been a heart attack or sickness, maybe being surprised by a pack of wolves. Nothing so simple as a dog bite. I cried out when I finally took the bandages off my hand this morning. In the light, some parts of my hand were white with puss. Other parts were purple where the blood was pooling under the skin. It took all of my might to clean it again and put more antiseptic on it.

I re-bandaged it as quickly as possible so I didn't

have to keep looking at it. Although there isn't a single scene from a movie that makes me look away, I have always avoided the pains of real life. My mom and dad would have been reminded of the little boy who refused to play in the backyard for a month so I didn't have to see the place where Oscar was buried. By the time I did go in the backyard again, the grass had grown back and I didn't have to know exactly which segment had been given to him.

It's all but impossible to make a fist now. Pressing my fingers against the keyboard is excruciating. There is, obviously, no one to blame for all of this but myself. I was the one dumb enough to trust that dog and treat it like a friend. I was stupid to give it water in the first place. How many other animals were drawn to my house because they saw the water dish or noticed one of their own kind coming to my door every day and being treated like a prince?

Chalk it up to a long line of idiotic mistakes I've made, the worst of which was staying in Camelot when everyone else filed out. One by one, the houses emptied as their owners drove past me on their way to a better (at least in their eyes) destination. The entire neighborhood was full at one point. How many evacuating people would it have taken in the neighborhood before I finally changed my mind and joined them? If the neighborhood had two hundred houses instead of one hundred, would it have made any difference? If they had all left at the same time instead of slowly trickling away, would I have packed my bags and loaded Andrew in the car so I could be a member of the caravan? If these same people were evacuating from a building during a fire alarm I would have surely joined them, so why did I sit idly by as they left this neighborhood? I wish I knew the answer—just as I wish I knew how the Johnsons could do what they did.

The horror replays itself in my head. I wish I could

forget it. I wish I had never gone down the street. I wish I had left the neighborhood a long time ago. I wish, I wish, I wish.

February 15

With the last of the real wine gone, I had to switch over to the food processor's version. Something amazing: you can barely tell the difference. The only thing that makes it feel unnatural, I suppose, is that there's nothing romantic about pouring yourself a glass of wine out of the same humming processor that gives you shrimp pasta and tenderloins, not compared to the splash of pouring from a nice bottle. The Canadian sisters wouldn't have been so carefree if they had to get up from the picnic table every time they needed a refill from the processor. It was much nicer passing a bottle around the table anytime we wanted more. It was exhilarating sitting with the two of them each time a new cork popped free from its bottle. It meant more talking. More laughter. You didn't have to leave your friends, even for a second, to get another glass. Each trip to the kitchen would have given an opportunity to feel wobbly, to think about the chores you had to do the next day, to break up any chance of continuous conversation. But for a party of one, which I am these days, I guess it suffices.

The nice thing for me, the silver lining in my situation, where I drink by myself to let the alcohol dull the pain in my hand, is that I have an endless supply of whatever type of drink I want. Cosmopolitans, martinis, Long Island iced tea—you name it. I can let the food processor start another batch while I'm emptying the first dose. The processor will click shut, beep twice, and then start humming. The creation is finished before I can empty my previous glass; I'll never be able to drink faster than the machine produces. Imagine if farmers had the same problem! Before they could harvest their crops, the field would be full of fresh, new vegetables. It's like looking down into a crevice and knowing no matter how long you listen for the rock you dropped to hit bottom, it never will.

You keep listening and listening but nothing ever clanks. You keep drinking and drinking but the glass is never empty. It's an easy way to lose yourself and wake up with a blazing headache. Three of the last four mornings have seen me wake up with a fire alarm going off inside my skull.

It would be nice if the food processor could create me a batch of aspirin. I guess if I was crafty enough with manipulating the pre-set commands I could get around the built-in settings that prevent medications from being generated. There are probably a hundred different suggestions online for exactly how to hack into the food processor's settings so you can make whatever you want: aspirin, antibiotics, laxatives, heroin.

I still laugh when I think about the public outcry that took place when it was announced the government issued food processors would be able to recreate alcoholic drinks but not medicine. Heaven forbid we should be able to relax and enjoy a beer while we watched the human population get older and fade away. The same people who found a reason to protest everything the government ever did, every ruling the Supreme Court ever made, every bill proposed by the Senate, found time to hold up signs protesting machines that could get you drunk but couldn't address your medical needs. The only difference with their protests was that instead of a hundred people demonstrating, it was three or four senior citizens, none of whom looked like they really wanted to be holding a sign in the first place. The other former protestors had grown too old to continue yelling above everyone else, or they had moved south where they worried about their new life rather than the previous, unhappy one that hadn't worked out so well for them. The few protestors devoted to displaying their discontent held up signs questioning the wisdom of providing booze to the depressed but leaving the sick to fend for themselves. They believed you were letting cancer patients suffer while handing loaded guns to the suicidal masses.

The rebuttal was that everyone knew their limits for drink. If they chose to exceed those limits, then that was each individual's personal choice. On the other hand, only doctors knew enough to prescribe the correct amount of each medication to be taken. If you caused additional health problems by overmedicating, the fault lay with the people who provided the drugs. The machine's maker would never be sued—there were no more practicing lawyers by that time, the last courthouses were hearing gavels bang for the final time—but they didn't want one final blot on their conscience.

Giving the everyman a chance to drink away his worries was a lot different from allowing them to create any type of in-house pharmaceutical they wanted. If a man in Seattle or Chicago just happened to be extremely depressed because he didn't have any kids and would never have the opportunity, well, here was a machine that could give him a beer to dull the hurt. If a woman in New York or St. Louis couldn't make the journey south with everyone else, she could pour herself a glass of Cabernet and fade away while remembering the good times. There's no telling how many people chose to stay in their houses while everybody else headed south just because they could relax in front of their fireplace with whatever sweet wine or dark beer they wanted.

The nights I sit around drinking wine by myself, I imagine what I would do in various situations. If I had the option of either packing all of my things, not knowing where exactly I was going to be living, or staying here in my own home that I'm familiar with, I would choose the latter. Getting to sip on a glass of champagne while I stay here just makes the deal that much sweeter. Not to insinuate that's why I'm here right now. Until a couple of days ago I couldn't have cared less about drinking away the pain.

I'm here for Andrew. Everything I've ever done has been for him. But still, while I'm affording myself the chance to daydream other lives, I can't help but imagine getting a chance to see Paris from the top of the Eiffel Tower, imagine riding a camel out to the pyramids, imagine seeing the lights pulsate in downtown Tokyo. So many things I never got to see or do. So many parts of the world I'll never get to know. If that's not reason enough to go back to the kitchen and have another glass of wine, I don't know what is.

February 22

These past two weeks haven't been good to me. The day after going down to the Johnsons' house I came down with another cold. Andrew has another fever as well. The infection on his forearm hasn't gotten better. My hand feels like it's going to fall off. I've spent my days sitting on the recliner with three blankets over me, going in and out of sleep like someone struggling to survive an operation. There's no way to know how much of my fever is caused from the cold and how much is from the infection in my hand. I make sure, though, that Andrew has just as many blankets covering him as I have for myself. My clothes are soaked with sweat each time I wake up.

My first thought upon opening my eyes is always about the Johnsons' house. The fact that Andrew also has a cold makes me wonder if I got him sick, he got me sick, or if there is something in the house making us both sick. Probably the mold. The times I'm not under my blankets, I'm cleaning Andrew. I change his diapers and pants whenever I feel good enough to stand and walk around. I don't feel guilty anymore when I wash him on the sofa instead of taking him to the bathroom. It's no longer a matter of being lazy or of my back aching. In my weakened state, the more I walk the greater the threat I might stumble over my own feet and hurt myself. A couple of months ago, my ego would have kept me from admitting that.

I focus on the pain in my hand to block out what happened down the street, but not even my searing, gimpy hand can shut off my mind. I will have those images stuck in my head for the rest of my life.

February 23

I looked though another of our old photo albums today. The entire book was filled with images of Andrew and me during the first ten years we lived in Camelot. Every single picture was taken somewhere within our neighborhood. There were no pictures of us at the Grand Canyon or the Statue of Liberty. Not a single picture showed us at a baseball game or at a restaurant. Even then I rarely ventured further than a few miles from home. If Andrew was with me I wouldn't travel further than the Johnsons' house. Most of the photos were from inside our home or in our backyard. Some were taken at the Johnsons' house when they hosted cookouts.

Every couple of pages, equaling a year's time in the chronology of our lives as represented in pictures, there were photographs of us from Halloween. Halloween was always my favorite holiday, and the pictures of us from that day always make me smile more than any other. I used to take issue with how some Blocks were treated by their relatives; it seemed insulting to parade a Block around the neighborhood with a new haircut or freshly painted fingernails. These things were done to demonstrate how much the Block was supposedly loved by its family, even though the Block had no idea it was being put on display. One guy down the street even got his Block brother's arms covered in tattoos so they had matching designs. The Block's brother was nice enough to wear sleeveless shirts so everyone could see their matching ink. The Block had no say in whether or not he wanted his arms permanently covered in dragons and fire. I wonder what he would have thought if he gained consciousness one day and found Asian-themed tattoos covering his arms from shoulder to wrist. Would he look down and say, "Wow, awesome!" or would he get up and walk to his brother's room, lean his head in, and say, "You stupid dick."

Halloween was the one time I didn't worry about whether or not Andrew would feel silly if he could see what I was doing or, more importantly, what he was being dressed as. One year I was Abe Lincoln and he was George Washington. Another year, I was Chewbacca and he was Han Solo. One time we even dressed as Hulk Hogan and Ric Flair. The Johnsons were one of the only other families in Camelot who bothered acknowledging Halloween once the world's population started plummeting. Most of the world was eager to forget the pseudo-holiday as soon as there were no more children around to go trick-or-treating. The six of us—Andrew and me, Mike and Mindy, and their two Block sisters—had costume parties a few years, but more often than not I would dress Andrew in a fancy costume, get into one myself, and then we would watch a movie as though it were just another night. Mr. Lee came over one time to ask if our incinerator was acting up the same way his was, but when I opened the door dressed as Captain America, with Andrew at the end of the hall dressed as Spiderman, he stuttered and walked away without saying anything else. The Johnsons told me he went down to their house for help after thinking better of asking me. He didn't fare any different there: they were all dressed as dwarves. Mr. Lee never did get his incinerator fixed. He turned back for home without getting anyone's advice on how to dispose of his trash. A week later he left the neighborhood.

As soon as our costumes were finished, I would get the camera out and take a series of pictures with us acting out our new identities. When I was Larry Bird and he was Michael Jordan, I filled our old basketball with air and took pictures of Andrew shooting over top of me. It was difficult to prop his arms against the table to keep them in a realistic position. And of course he was sitting down in his wheel chair while I was crouched on the floor to make it look like he was able to jump over me. Needless to say, that year's pictures didn't turn out very well. When I was Hulk Hogan and he was Ric Flair, however, we had pictures of him giving me a cheap eye gouge followed by a picture of me dropping a giant leg on him as he lay in the middle of the living room floor. If he had his own opinions, Andrew might think this behavior was silly, and I'm usually conscious of not pushing my appetites on him, but I prefer to think that on this one day of the year he would love dressing up with his brother and acting like we were famous movie characters or historical figures.

The thing I noticed this afternoon when looking at these pictures was that I wasn't laughing uncontrollably like I normally do when I pull this particular album off the shelf. Instead, I was doing my best not to cry. I excused myself from the sofa where Andrew was sitting, went to my bedroom, and cried for a good ten minutes. I'm not even sure why I was crying, let alone why I was crying then and not any other time in the past twenty years. Lord knows I've had plenty of reasons to do so. Every day I'm given a new excuse to cry if I ever needed one. I could have cried when the Canadian sisters left or when the Johnsons snuck away in the night. I could have broken down after the dog showed its true colors or when a rat ate holes in my birth certificate. Who would have guessed that it would be a photo album of Andrew and me wearing hilarious costumes that would finally break my spirit.

February 25

Time hasn't done anything to make my hand feel better, nor have the few medicines I still have lying around the house. The spreading purple skin convinces me I'm not just being pessimistic. The pain keeps my fingers from moving. I clank away at the keyboard like an ogre. The days of my precision typing, as taught to me by Mrs. Jenkins in high school, are long past. One hand performs with the fingers dashing around half the keyboard. The other hand makes giant lurching movements. One hand belongs to Jekyll. The other belongs to Hyde.

Compared to the energetic and capable man I used to be, I'm only a partial human being. Before, I had sore knees and a bad back, but I could still take the trash out and put my clothes on like a normal person. With a worthless hand, I struggle to do anything. I'm one-fourth the person who used to host neighborhood cookouts and take Andrew outside to watch the sun set. I'm one-eighth the person who used to carry a bag of golf clubs from one hole to another in the blazing sun. How much more of myself can I lose before I'm incapable of taking care of myself and my brother? What will I do when that day arrives?

There have been more noises than usual coming from my patio ever since the door shattered. I was crazy to think a dining room table would keep the wilderness out. A bear comes to the other side of the wooden table and growls at the smell of forbidden food. I can't tell if it's the same bear every day or different bears all sensing the same delicious treasure. Yesterday, two bears fought over the right to sit outside my broken dining room door. The loser went back into the woods to take care of his wounds. The victor remained on my deck until he eventually lost interest and sauntered off. At other times, when the bears aren't here, wolves make their approach, checking for gaps in our defenses, then let out howls. The animals have always known Andrew and I are here, but now they can smell us at night, and might even be able to hear me snore.

The table won't keep a bear out of our house. Not if it gets frustrated and rams its full weight against the barrier. It would stumble over the table before approaching Andrew. It might not recognize him as food if he doesn't move or cry out. It might get confused and look for something more entertaining. Knowing Andrew was out there, defenseless, I would have to yell and draw the bear's attention. It would see me as the moving and frightened target it wants. It would probably leave Andrew alone after it was satisfied with me in its belly, but the wolves and dogs wouldn't have the same hesitation. They wouldn't give two thoughts about whether or not he was food just because he wasn't screaming. And just like that, our house, the final occupied house in the neighborhood, the last house in Camelot, would be empty too.

February 26

What will happen to my diary once I'm gone? And how many other diaries, pages filled with thoughts and fears like mine, are scattered in abandoned neighborhoods all around the world? Are the diaries of people from Japan and Greenland filled with the same concerns I have? Does a man in rural Spain wonder if he should have taken the train to Portugal with his Block brother before it was too late, before the tracks deteriorated and no one else could join the community in Lisbon? Does a woman in Australia write about the unbearable heat, about her broken AC and how long she and her Block sister can tolerate the hundred degree days before they succumb? Surely there was another man, maybe in Russia, maybe in Peru, who wondered if he had made the right choices. Were they okay with how things ended up? Would they have done things differently if they could have seen where they were at the end, when they and their Block sibling could no longer take care of themselves?

What would they have done differently in their lives, not just in the final days or years, but when they were young and believed anything was possible in the world? What had these people thought when they were in middle school and still dreamed of being famous actors or rock stars? Would they have taken that trip abroad with their friends if they knew the opportunity would never repeat itself? Would they have told the girl down the street whatever she wanted to hear just so they could cop a feel, or would they have understood that that girl was also looking for something meaningful in the world? Would they, as little boys, have held a magnifying glass to ants walking on the sidewalk? Or would they appreciate that the ants were here before them and would be here after them, and because of that, and because they were living things, no matter how small they were, would they have been left alone?

Were there people in each corner of the world scribbling down all of their thoughts while their Block brothers or sisters sat quietly in another room? What was the point? Why not just be honest and tell their Block relatives what they were thinking? Why do I write about all the things I would never think to tell Andrew even though he can't hear what I say? Why do I protect his ears from the harsh truths of the world? Is that why I leave the room any time my hand hurts or when I can no longer resist the urge to cry and don't want him to see me break down in tears? I know, deep down, he can't hear the concerns I voice or see the tears I shed, but even as an old man I can't help but shield him from them.

Maybe that's what the other diaries around the world talk about. Maybe a man in Korea used his diary as a way to have all the conversations with his Block sister that he could never have with her in real life. Maybe a woman in South Africa used her diary to describe what it was like for a Block to grow up in a land that never stopped trying to learn how to treat everyone as they deserved to be treated. Hell, maybe one or both of the Johnsons was keeping a diary while they lived down the street. Maybe each night after their Blocks were asleep, they would head to different rooms and write down all of their thoughts from that day.

If Andrew could read what I write here, would he understand where I'm coming from? Would he tell me to buck up, or would he simply give me a hug and, like he does now, say nothing?

February 27

My hand is black. It hurts so bad I keep from doing anything with the entire arm. I type with one hand now, the other arm sitting uselessly by my side because any movement sends shooting pain to my shoulder. If Andrew could help me and if I knew how to do it, I would cut my arm off at the elbow to stop the pain. The discoloration has spread past the bandages wrapped around my wrist. The purple and black are slowly moving up my forearm. I don't need a medical book to tell me the infection is going to keep spreading until it kills me.

The dog still appears once or twice a week. I see it through the kitchen window, but I don't refill the water dish anymore and the dog doesn't come all the way up to the patio like it used to. The days I do see it, it's always at the edge of the woods, looking at my house as though wishing to explain a terrible miscommunication between the two of us. I stare at it and it stares at me, but neither of us does anything else. I want to go outside and shake my crippled hand in the air to show it what it did. I would yell at the Labrador until it felt bad and whimpered. If the dog is still around after I'm dead and Andrew's nutrient bag begins to run out, it will get to see my brother go hungry and will understand the extent of the betrayal it brought on me. It's one thing to trick me, to cause my downfall—I deserve the rotting hand if I can be fooled by a common dog—but my brother has never done anything to deserve this fate. Andrew has never lifted a hand to an animal. He has never cursed the forest animals or wished for their deaths. I watch the dog until it disappears back into the line of trees, then I take more aspirin, hoping it will numb my hand. It never does.

One of my dreams from last night was so vivid I still feel like I was actually there. It didn't involve the neighborhood, the animals in the forest, or my hand, which feels like it's going to fall off. Those things, or symbols of those things, were all covered in other dreams I've had recently. No, of all the things it could have been about, the entire dream was me sitting in my second grade class with my old classmates. The classroom was exactly how it had been when I was little: four rows of chairs perfectly arranged to face the teacher, pictures of former presidents on each wall. All of the chairs were occupied by the same students who had used them seventy years earlier. The only difference was that we were all eighty years old. Our teacher, Mrs. Peirson, wasn't in the classroom. We sat patiently on our chairs and waited for her to come through the door. If we were eighty in our dream, Mrs. Peirson would have been 130 years old, obviously much too old to be alive, but we still expected to see her walk into the classroom at any moment.

All of my fellow students had the same features as when I knew them in second grade. The eighty year-old version of Sarah Siller still had chubby cheeks and boogers at the edge of her nose, only now she was hunched over and drowning in wrinkles. Bobby Morrows was still covered in freckles and had bushy red hair, but now his teeth were mostly gone and even when he squinted he could barely see anything. I recognized all of them immediately, no matter how long ago I had last seen them. And they all knew me. Betsy Hendrickson passed me a scribbled note asking if I would be her boyfriend during recess that day. I circled YES before sliding it back across the desk.

Each of us had lived our lives the way they had actually been spent. I had worked on a road crew instead of going to college, then come home and taken care of Andrew the rest of my life. Sarah Siller grew up and volunteered at a shelter for Blocks, where she took care of hundreds of people who were abandoned or orphaned, until she had a heart attack and passed away. Bobby Morrows moved to Mexico after high school and was never heard from again. Everyone assumed he had been murdered, but no one knew for sure. Betsy married her high school sweetheart, even though that was the extent of the family they would ever be able to have. She accidently got pregnant a couple of years later. Knowing it would be a Block and not knowing what to do with it, she killed herself with a gun. And yet, there we all were, all of us elderly, all of us back in elementary school as though it was just another day of learning math and history.

Mrs. Peirson never did arrive to teach us. It didn't matter, though. Each of us was happy to sit there and wait. The bell never rang for the next class. That didn't bother us either. We sat at our desks for what felt like an entire day. I'm not sure how long dreams really last, if the entire dream was over and done with two seconds after it started, or if I spent a couple of hours of my sleep in that state. It felt like I must have started dreaming as soon as I went to sleep and didn't stop until I woke up the next morning.

The dream ended the same way it started, with us in our seats waiting for the day's lesson to begin. We passed notes and gossiped about all the other kids the same way we had when we were little. Some kids made deals as to which parts of their lunches they would trade with each other. No one talked about what it was like to grow old without any kids of our own. There was no talk of our younger siblings who couldn't attend their own classes or play catch with us after school. We were all happy just to be where we were. And that was the entire dream.

I woke up amazed at the amount of detail my mind had processed. Bobby Morrows's hiccups sounded exactly as they had seventy years earlier. His lips had tiny cracks at the corners because they were always too dry. Betsy smelled like overripe fruit. Her eyes were bright blue, and she had a small imperfection on one iris. They were details I hadn't remembered for seventy years, they may not have existed at all, but in my dream my senses were alive. I was able to see exactly how the sky transitioned from a shade of light blue to a shade of light grey as it got closer to the horizon. I heard the crickets outside in the grass.

After the dream was over I stayed in bed with my eyes closed because I knew as soon as I opened them I would be back in my bedroom in Camelot. It was still dark when I woke up, even though it was the next morning. The shades were down and the sun was only starting to come up over the trees. I stayed motionless as long as possible so the intense sights, sounds, and smells in my dream could linger without interference.

My true senses came back when I opened my eyes and looked around my bedroom. I couldn't identify the two figures in the framed picture hanging on the wall in front of me. I knew it was Andrew and me, but we no longer resembled the people in the photograph, wouldn't have been picked out of a police lineup for possibly being the men in that picture. I inhaled deeply but didn't smell anything. Our house had to be stale with mildew, probably much worse, but none of the odors registered. I heard a dog bark from off in the woods. There were probably a hundred other sounds around me that I didn't hear anymore. It made me wish I could stay in my dream where I got to experience more of the world around me and be content doing so.

It was at that moment, under the blanket in my bedroom, that I realized I've said everything in this diary that I need to say. In the dark room, with the memory still fresh in my mind of the dream that had just played out, I finally understood why I've been recording how our lives have unfolded here in Camelot.

It wasn't for me, it was for Andrew.

It was to make sure there was a record of what life was like around the sofa where he lived. It was to record how the world fell apart around him even though he never complained or seemed inconvenienced by it. It was to show that even if he couldn't talk or hear, he had someone who loved him, would do anything for him.

The dream also made me wonder if Andrew has ever had his own dreams. The doctors all agreed that Blocks didn't have significant brain activity, but I never completely believed that. And what is 'significant brain activity'? Maybe he doesn't have enough capacity to talk or move, but maybe there's enough for him to have some semblance of a dream. They might not be dreams the same way I experience them, in full color and sound, detailed and expressive, but maybe Blocks still get taken to some other world when they close their eyes.

I like to think Andrew closes his eyes for a reason, that when he goes to sleep he too is taken to a world where his senses allow him to experience the world the way I do. He could play catch with me. He could laugh with his classmates and slide a note across his desk that says he'll be a girl's lunchtime boyfriend. I like to think that for at least a portion of his life he has the opportunity to be a part of another world, a world where he can do whatever he wants: get off the sofa, remove his nutrient bag, shake his joints out, walk right out the front door and go for a jog, explore the neighborhood, or go back to the beach that my parents took us to when we were little.

And I like to think that during these moments of clarity he can understand that the decisions I've made over the years have all been with him in mind, that when other people were dropping their Blocks off at the front steps of shelters and driving away, I was planning for our future in Camelot and for how I could give him the life my parents wanted for him.

Maybe, when he closes his eyes, anything is possible.

Acknowledgements

I owe particular thanks to two people for helping me work toward my dream of being a novelist: Jodie McFadden, for her constant support and encouragement; and Win Golden, for believing in my story and my writing from early on.

I would also like to thank Andres Carlstein for mentoring me through the writing process and offering advice each time I needed it, and Derek Prior for a wonderful edit of the manuscript.

For updates on future novels or for more information about the author, please go to www.watchtheworldend.com.

CPSIA information can be obtained at www.ICGtesting.com
Printed in the USA
LVOW06s1205090913

351608LV00001BA/24/P